ABOVE ALL MEN

A Novel

MG Press
http://midwestgothic.com/mgpress

An excerpt of this book originally appeared in *Verdad Magazine* and *Sundog Lit*.

ISBN: 978-0-9882013-2-3

Cover design © 2014 Jeff Pfaller

Author photo © Sabrina Renkar

ABOVE ALL MEN

A NOVEL

ERIC SHONKWILER

For my father.

1

In the dream he was afield righting fenceposts. There was a dry wind that took the sweat from him and set the grass at his feet to sawing. The wind grew stronger and the ears of corn knocked together and when he looked past the house there was a rim to the bottom of the sky. It grew tall and black and moved like the earth scrolling closed. He dropped the sledgehammer and broke for the backdoor. Each room he flew through was empty and echoed the name of his son. When he came out the front of the house David found him watching the storm grind up the field across the road and the corn in the black turned into teeth. He reached for Samuel's hand as the storm took the other, and woke.

Honey. Helene touched his arm. He scrambled and fell to the floor beside the bed and lay there grasping for something to wield. David, are you okay?

Eyes wide in the dark. He gripped the bedpost and stood. God.

You were screaming.

I'm alright.

She reached across the bed for him.

No, I'm up.

Tell me what's wrong.

It was a dream, I'm alright.

Then come back to bed.

I need to work off this head'a steam first. He stayed still a moment, then found his pants and shirt on the cedar chest and dressed before leaving the room, shutting the door behind him. Samuel was on the stairs and Red was beside him leaning up against the wall. Samuel had turned on the hall-way light.

What're you guys doing?

I heard you scream.

It was just a nightmare. Go on back to bed.

Samuel didn't move. Red was already dressed, or had never changed out of the clothes he'd worn in from the road.

Am I gonna have to tuck you in?

Samuel turned to climb the stairs. Before he could go up a step David swooped around the banister and started nudging him on to his bedroom. Samuel lay down in his bed and pulled the covers to his chest.

What was the nightmare about?

A bad storm.

Like a tornado?

No. It was different. You want some water or anything?

No thanks.

Leave the door open?

No.

David set his hand on Samuel's head. Night.

Night.

He stepped through the door and shut it. He stood beside it for a while then turned off the light and slipped to the window at the end of the hall. It was late April, and Samuel's tenth birthday had passed a few weeks before. There had been good rains for years after he was born but the last of it had come two summers ago. The grass in the moonlight below was white-looking. Downstairs Macha walked into the kitchen, nails clicking on the hardwood. David went down and followed the old lab and the dog waited until he took a seat to perch on his toes, looking back at him. His chest was still tight and there was a pressure behind his forehead. In a few hours his wife and son would wake again and he'd have to decide whether or not Samuel would come to the funeral. He was looking at nothing, thinking of Anna Danvers in that cold upstairs bedroom, of Phil finding her. Red appeared in the kitchen doorway and David wondered if he'd heard him walking at all.

I ain't tucking you in.

Red smirked and David motioned for him to sit across the table. Did you lie to him?

About the dream?

Yeah. He pulled out a chair and sat.

No.

His head tilted up. His face was dark but the line of his mouth was still curved.

It wasn't a war dream, if that's what you're asking.

Mm. So you're havin' other kinds of dreams that scare the hell out of you.

Apparently. David glanced out the window at the black and then to the counter across the room and a half-pot of old coffee. You goin' back to sleep?

I'm not sure I was asleep to begin with, tell the truth.

Why's that?

The smile faded. I wish I hadn't of come back here. Or I guess I just wish it wasn't now.

Yeah.

Red set his arm on the table. It's weird being here, Dave. After few years out there I got to wondering why I never came back before. I thought maybe I'd just made it up, that I couldn't come home. Now I know that ain't true. He tried to laugh and only managed a sharp exhale.

There's days I still wake up thinking I'm in the hooch. David lifted a hand, brushing it over his head. And somebody's gone and blown the roof off or something.

They were quiet. Red stood. You wanna go out and stand on the porch for a minute?

I could use the air. David rose and Macha with him and they followed Red to the front door. He stood aside for David to open it and they went out. Macha circled Red, wagging her tail against his leg. It was cool but not as cold as it should have been. Ahead where the storm had risen in the dream the horizon was black and the woods were a gray band. They both leaned on the porch railing and watched the yard.

You decide whether you're coming to the service or not?

Yeah. Red nodded. I'm not. I figure I wasn't near as close as you.

Macha hobbled down the porch steps to the fenceline, sniffing. They watched her going up and down the yard and then she lifted her head and returned to their feet.

I gotta say I envy you. House, wife and kid, the whole bit.

What's stoppin' you?

Red said nothing for a moment. I think I've come to terms with never getting around to it.

Are you happy? Doin' what you're doin'?

He sucked in a long, slow breath. I'd say I'm content. Are you?

Sometimes. I dunno. He shrugged. That's everybody, right? Nobody's always happy.

Red nodded.

He started shaking in the lining of muscles over his ribs. If I thought you'd stay in it I'd build you a house next door. He paused. I remember you sayin' you might want it someday.

Maybe after a few more years.

David patted the railing with the heel of his hand, frowning. I'm gonna take the dog down the road a stretch. You be here when I get back?

I'll be here.

David stepped off the porch. While we're being confessional I guess I oughta say I envy you, too.

I am the handsomer one.

He smiled. He snapped his fingers for Macha and walked to the road. She ran off into the ditch and something came flying up out of the weeds, disappearing into the broken gray of the field. She clambered out of the ditch after it, stopped and trotted to him. They walked on a while and when they came back the moon had settled behind the house. He took his boots off on the porch and slipped inside, into the bedroom. A crack of light showed from under the bathroom door. He stripped and laid his clothes on the cedar chest and got into bed as Helene came out of the bathroom. Her face was there in the light for a moment before she shut it off, deliberate, soft. She slipped under the covers and pressed against him and her nightgown was warm and her thighs and arms cool.

I thought you might have gone to check on Phil.

Considered it.

She pressed her cheek to his shoulder. Are you alright?

Yeah.

She shifted her arm and rolled onto her back. They were still touching at the shoulders. Have you thought about letting Sam come?

Yeah. Let me sleep on it some more.

The dream had caught up with him now that he was still, and he saw it in flashes of teeth. He thought of everything he had, of Samuel and Helene, the farm. He was breathing hard, and he turned to Helene to see if she'd noticed and found her looking at him. She took his hand but her grip turned hard at the sight of his eyes and he guttered like a flame.

The covers were twisted around Helene when he woke, cold, and the light had barely changed outside. Her eyelids fluttered when he sat up and he thought she might wake but she only shifted, her hair falling across her face in tangles. He eased off the bed and dressed, making his way to the backdoor while buttoning his shirt. It creaked and creaked again when he shut it. Red was at the fence, staring out. The sun was rising milkwhite and the day would warm quickly. David

reached for the spigot and began uncoiling the hose and Red
stepped off the fence and took the hose from him. He dragged
it over the dry grass to the early shoots of tomato plants and
watered them and soaked the turned ground where Helene
had planted spinach and other vegetables. When David held
his hand out Red pinched the hose and went back to close the
spigot.

You got any plans for this morning?

Not really. Go into town and see ma. You?

I try to water the cattle every so often. The creek's pretty
well dry.

By hand? Red looked across the field over the fence.

David started for the truck beside the house and Red got
in the passenger side. They drove the short way to Danvers'
and pulled in behind the barn. David got a dozen buckets
from inside the barn door and Red took them over to the
pump and they filled them and loaded them up. Red stayed
in the bed as they drove between the two houses where David
had set a few heavy tubs inside the fence. The sun was dead in
their eyes and they worked with heads averted, Red passing
the buckets down and David setting them on the ground. The
herd lay circled in the grass a few hundred yards away and
their ears perked.

Here they come. Red hefted a bucket over the fence and
poured it, the cattle shuffling toward them. They were already drinking from the first tub when David moved on to
the second and he watched Red raise a bucket high to pour
it over the outstretched tongue of a calf. When the buckets
were empty they drove back for more water and they emptied
them into another set of tubs down the road. They finished
stacking the buckets and Red sighed against the side of the
truck. I do not miss this.

You never had to water cattle.

I mean straight up work. I haven't done any for a long
time.

David smiled. He hefted the long stack over the side of the truck and dropped the buckets in and they rattled along. You know if I had any say you wouldn't have to work again.

That don't hardly seem fair. Which one of us came back to the shit to find the other one?

You would have.

Maybe.

You would. He went around the front of the truck and got in. He shut his door and waited on Red to shut his and he started the engine.

Have I thanked you lately for it?

Have I seen you lately? David began to turn the truck in the road. There wasn't any choice. I had to do it.

I'm glad you think that way.

He pulled into Danvers' drive. So am I. They pulled up beside the barn and David shut the truck off. You want to come ridin' with me?

Nah. I think I'll head into town.

Alright. Thanks for your help.

Weren't nothin'. Give the old man my regards.

They both got out. Red lifted his hand in goodbye and went to the road and David stood by the barn. Danvers' house was quiet. He walked on to the equipment barn for the loader and threw a few bales of hay from the loft on the scoop. A couple hundred yards into the pasture he set the bales and stock panels up, the cattle already loping toward him. Wheeling the loader around he watched the pasture roll by, saw the town beyond it. On the other side of town a cell tower stood rusting. Years ago he would have seen the red light brighten and fade. The phone company had cut the power to local towers and never restored it, never sent another bill. Most everyone around switched back to landlines.

In the barn the two bay horses stuck their heads out of the stalls and David carried the tack up from the rear. He fastened his bay to an overhead beam with a hackamore and heaved the saddle on, dust and hair bellowing out into the light. He waited for the horse's breath before cinching it and he bridled the bay and led it out to pasture. The land was bright from horseback. He rode east, passing the cattle and then heading south to find the creek. Mud lined the trickle of water, so shallow it barely seemed to move. He scanned the creek going west like he might find a dam to break apart. The horse went on along the bank toward the house and when they were in sight of it he stopped the horse and watched, imagined Helene rising, the sunlight pouring in through the windows rich with dust and color. Samuel always woke on his own and would be downstairs by the time she came to get him.

He put the bay up and gave both the horses fresh water and feed and left the cleaning for later. When he came out of the barn he saw the kitchen light on in the house and he climbed the steps to the side door and knocked. There was a shuffling from inside and the door opened and Danvers stood there in his longjohns. He began to speak but only moved aside for David to come in. They went into the kitchen from the mudroom and Danvers sat with a mug of coffee clenched in his hand. David stood by the chair across from him.

You holdin' up, Phil?

Set your alarm just to ask me that?

I've been working.

Danvers shook his head. His hair was mussed and greasy and a day's beard showed silver on his cheeks. He nudged at his eyepatch with a knuckle. You want some coffee?

I'm alright.

Sit down.

They were quiet. Danvers idled his eye about the kitchen until he settled on the window. The house smelled of horses. David rested his hands on the chairback.

You decide whether you're lettin' Sam come or not?

Helene wants him to go. I don't see any reason for it.

Danvers nodded slowly. You can't exactly keep it a secret from him.

No.

Well. He pulled his mug closer.

I just don't see what good it'd do him.

Doubt it'd do any good. I sure as hell doubt it.

David flexed his hands in front of him, then pulled the chair out. I'm just trying to keep him from all that, young as he is.

A funeral ain't nearly a war, Dave. But he's gonna see bad things. He's gonna grow up. He paused and his head tilted. What kind of man would he be you keep him locked indoors his whole life?

Yeah.

I ain't tryin' to convince you. But you're as close as we come to family. Danvers peered down into his mug. His face bunched and he sucked in a breath. Well, there was a minute where I wadn't being pitiful. His shoulders shook and he dropped his fist on the table. Would you get out please?

David pushed the chair back. He went to the mudroom and stopped at the door and left. Climbing onto the porch at home he heard footsteps from inside, the resonance of old wood. Helene was midway to the kitchen when he opened the door and she turned. I just got a call from Jacob Miller. He wants you to call him back.

What for?

He didn't say.

David went to the phone. Delivery's probably gonna be late. He dialed the number and it rang twice. It's Parrish. He listened. After a moment he hung up the phone and walked highfooted to the bedroom and got his keys and billfold and checkbook. When he came out he yelled from the door, Helene in the living room. I gotta go. Miller says there's some business going on about the gas. I guess that storm we heard about was the real deal.

Of course it was.

I'll be back. He ran down the road for the truck and drove to town. Passing the corporation limits sign, the first few houses. Wide yards, driveways, thinning as he got toward the square. He slowed under the dead stoplight. The bank and post office stood at opposite corners, a brick apartment building and a laundromat at the others. Carl Brown was waiting to the north and pulled around after David. They passed the local gas station, price tickers long blank, and drove out of Dixon the ten miles to Banning. He pulled into the station with Brown behind him. There were already a few other trucks in the lot. He got out and went into the store. The other farmers were at the counter or reclining against newspaper racks and shelves and drinking coffee from styrofoam cups, Fogel and Spangler bickering in a corner. Miller stood behind the counter and at the sight of David waved them all toward a door. They filed into the disused garage, the doors shut and the room dark. Two dozen oil drums stood around the pneumatic lifts in the center of the room. Miller put up a hand.

I wanted to let you all know about this first. I got a call four o'clock this morning sayin' that freak hurricane wrecked all the refineries off the coast. He thumbed outside. What we've got in the tank is all we're getting for I don't know how long. In about half an hour there's gonna be lines of people out there wantin' what they can get. We'll be dried up before noon.

What about our deliveries?

There won't be any. I siphoned off as much diesel as I could hold in these barrels here and the ones behind the building. You're all decent folks and without you we'd probably starve, so I wanted to let you know. Seventy-five a pop. Take as many as you can load up and come back for seconds, if there's any left. That's all we got.

The farmers hushed. David came forward. Take a check?

Sure.

He stared at the barrels. He took the checkbook from his back pocket. Eight.

You sure you can haul eight?

Yeah. Hands reached into pockets behind him and he felt their nerves. David wrote out the check and gave it to Miller. He shouldered by the farmers and slipped out through the front of the store. When he'd gotten in his truck the garage door had been slung up and he backed in with the window down and heard Miller and Brown talking, Miller shaking his head. David got out and Miller hauled a metal ramp toward the truck. They rolled each barrel into the bed and when they finished David got a tow rope from the cab and looped it around the endmost barrels hanging partly over the tailgate and fixed the hooks into the eyelets on either side of the bed. He looked at the tires, at the stance of the truck. He got in and drove out of the station.

He took the curves and stops carefully, feeling the bob and slow of the fuel in the bed. At Danvers' he spun the truck around in front of the equipment barn and backed it in. There was a stack of old lumber up against the wall and he pulled a couple two by fours to the bed and rolled out the barrels. He left them on their sides and drove back. There were already cars lined up and people with gascans standing by when he pulled up to the station. He parked beside the building and worked through the line of people at the counter. A clerk was manning it and David raised his hand. Where's Jake?

The clerk leaned around the first customer. He's in the other side.

Thanks. He went through the door to the garage. The barrels were cleared out and Miller was sitting at a desk in the corner with a small lamp on. He turned from some papers as David came closer.

Dave, you're shit out of luck. Someone got word to Skillman. It's all gone.

He was paralyzed, then his jaw ground aside. You're kidding. All of it?

He got everybody. Town's dried out. Miller pivoted in his seat to better address him. You can't blame him, Dave. He's got to make money same as the rest of us.

David tried not to curse. He spun on his bootheel. Hell.

You know another few barrels wasn't gonna make any difference. He nodded to himself. We should've gone electric a long time ago, like they warned us. It's just the weather did us in early, instead of runnin' out.

Which is sort of poetic.

Miller raised his eyebrow. How do you figure?

 Screwin' ourselves. We made the weather this way.

Oh, yeah. Weather's screwing us one way or the other, for sure. Hopefully you fellas make it out of this damn drought.

David rubbed at the back of his neck. He glanced at the door.

You remember what I said, now. We gotta stick together. Times are changing.

David nodded and said goodbye. Back at the barn he righted the barrels and covered them with a tarp. When he finished he walked home and stood on the porch, leaning over, rubbing his back. The sun was coming high and there was a hot breeze starting from the southwest. The house sheltered him but he could feel the pull of the air and see it in the trees. He left the porch and stepped in, smelled something baking. Helene was taking a pan of zucchini bread from the oven. There were glass jars in boxes on the counter and a pot of water boiling on the range.

Stepping up our canning, huh?

We don't have much of a choice.

Can I do anything?

You can watch. I'm just cleaning the new jars. She checked the water, dialed the burner down. What happened with Miller?

Storm wiped out all the Gulf oil rigs.

She straightened. The radio didn't make it seem so bad.

I imagine they wouldn't want people panicking. Miller said there's nothing left. I got what I could.

What are we going to do?

He shrugged. Work, same as before. I got us a good little bit.

And once that runs out?

I don't know just yet. He thumbed toward the hall. Sam upstairs?

Reading. You're not concerned?

David reached for the refrigerator door and peeked in. Just occurred to me I've yet to eat this morning.

Have some bread to tide you over. She cut a wedge and gave it to him. You want to talk about Sam now, or are you gonna ignore all your problems this morning?

He had lifted the plate to his face to smell and looked at her, smirking and letting it drop. I guess we better.

Does Phil want him to come?

Yeah.

Well.

I don't want him to. I really don't, babe.

We could let him decide for himself.

He'll want to go.

I know he will. She turned from the counter to look at him and she was smiling softly. Her eyes were warm. I promise it won't kill him, David. It'll be alright.

He flattened his hands on the table, looking between them. I'll ask him. He pushed his plate back and forth and stood. He went upstairs. Samuel was sitting against the wall under his window, reading.

Mornin' kiddo.

Hey Dad. Samuel put his thumb between the book pages.

You know Aunt Anna's funeral is tomorrow.

Yeah.

David watched his face. Do you want to come? It's up to you. You can stay with Grandma if you like.

Samuel glanced to the floor. I'll go.

Alright. He watched while Samuel turned his book over on the floor and stood to go to his closet. He hung a long-sleeve shirt on the doorknob and set a pair of khaki pants over the arms of a small wooden rocking chair.

Is that okay?

David forced a smile. Yeah. That's fine.

2

For part of the afternoon he just stared at the combine and tractor in the equipment barn wondering if he should sell them, if anyone would take them. He'd listened to the radio after lunch and it was nothing but talk about oil, people worried about freezing come winter, waiting to hear if the government would do anything. Dixon and all the towns around it had switched to coal years ago, once the mine opened up. He hadn't thought about what would happen elsewhere.

He started disassembling part of the compact tractor's engine to fix a seized piston and it took him two hours before he gave in and hammered it with a mallet. The piston shot down the cylinder and the ring flew past his face. He picked up the rest of the loose pieces of engine and set them on the table, sliding open a drawer and dumping them in with the GPS consoles Danvers had had mounted on the tractor and combine years back. He pressed the power button on one and it booted up, a satellite dish on the screen spun and spun, the battery blinked. Walking out of the equipment barn he passed the fuel tanks blistered with rust and knocked on each to hear the hollow ring. He checked on the horses and kicked down a little hay from the loft, freshened their water. He cleaned the stalls, taking the wheelbarrow to the manure pile and emptying it, the wheel jumping over the uneven gravel. When he'd exhausted all of his chores he washed his hands at the pump beside the barn and went home.

Helene had pulled a jar of garden vegetables from the pantry to heat on the range and served them with chicken. They ate quietly, Samuel looking out the window and at Macha, standing in the doorway where they made her wait during meals. David asked how school was and he said fine, and he asked Helene and she said fine, eyes flicking to his and away. Macha took a step into the kitchen and David snapped his fingers and she turned and lay down. Samuel picked at the last piece of zucchini and Helene reached over with her fork and popped it into her mouth, smiling.

I was gonna eat that.

You were not.

I might've.

David pushed his chair out. He turned on the radio in the living room and let Macha out the front door. Samuel cleared the table and ran hot water for the dishes. The day had gone cool and David went onto the porch hoping for rainclouds and found the sky empty. Nothing rose over the town and he stayed there watching until the phone rang. Helene's footsteps through the hall, her muffled voice. She called his name and he stood in the doorway.

Something else break?

It's Red.

He opened the door and took the phone from her. Hey.

Helene was staring at him. Red asked him to come to the bar and have a drink. David started to cover the mouthpiece.

Go on. Helene stepped back, waiting.

David told him maybe and put the phone in its cradle.

He's drunk. The sun isn't even down.

I know.

You do what you want.

David lifted his hand between them. Why are you mad at me for him being drunk?

We both know what'll happen.

It's been nine years.

And neither of you have changed. I saw it in your eyes as soon as he walked in the door. Then last night?

Now you're gonna yell at me for a bad dream.

You're a million miles away, David.

He leaned against the table. So I'm supposed to tell my best friend to leave? The man saved my life I don't know how many times. Sam's named after him, for christ's sake.

Helene's eyes burned and narrowed and she glanced at the living room doorway. Samuel appeared there and without looking at them went out the front door. Helene and he were quiet for a moment and they turned back to each other. David rubbed at his brow.

He's not good for you. He wrecks you when he's around.

David nodded.

Her arms had been crossed and one dropped to her side. I don't like fighting him for you. I lost last time.

You did not.

She rolled her eyes. Whatever you say.

He watched her, stony. This shouldn't be that big a deal. I'm just meeting him in town.

Keep talking.

Why?

Because you're going to sound awfully dumb when I say what I want to, and you're going to walk out after. So keep talking. Get it all out.

This is stupid.

She began to smile. Are you done?

I'm about tapped, yeah. He put his knuckles down on the table.

You ran out on me with as much notice. She gestured at the door. This, right here? Is exactly what you did that day. And you do it every day, and some more than others I think maybe you won't come back.

How can you think I'd do that?

There's a precedent, David. You've done it before.

Don't talk about that when Sam's around. He glanced toward the porch.

God. She rolled her eyes.

You can't keep lording that over me. I came back. You can't convince me I didn't do the right thing.

There's a huge difference between what's right and what you should do. A vast difference. People may applaud what you did but I am going to remind you every time I need to that you left me a month pregnant to bring him back. I am sick of pretending I should be proud of you for that.

His vision flickered black. Had there been something between him and the door he would have tried to rip it apart. He managed to turn the doorknob and to walk down the porch steps and on the lawn he saw Samuel and Macha under a tree and his anger seethed again until there was just the road beneath him in a light blur as he staggered over it. He moved fast to keep himself from pausing at a fencepost and breaking his hand.

When he got into town he tried to be occupied with the shape of pavement and the paint lines and to not look anyone in the eye. The bar appeared before him and he went inside and ordered a beer and whiskey. Red was sitting at a corner table. There were a couple miners seated along the bar and a farmer and teenaged son by the door. He brought the beer and whiskey to the corner and sat opposite Red. Foam spilled over the neck of the beer.

Dave?

He tilted the beer up and pulled.

Dave.

He put it down and shook his head. We got in a fight.

Over what?

Me comin' out to drink.

Red's face puzzled. How?

He flung up a hand. I don't know. I can't see straight I'm so pissed.

Red sat back in his chair. He didn't say anything for a while and David stared into the table, at the polish and the rings of water. A neon sign buzzed in the window beside them, flickered and quit. Red put up his hand and circled a finger in the air at the barman. She must be angry about somethin' else. Forget about it.

Through the evening they amassed a collection of bottles and tumblers. It was dark out and his eyes were afloat in his skull. The lights left trails. The music faded, was gone, was loud. Red was talking about traveling and everything he'd seen, the places he'd been. David was beginning to sink into himself, to grow smaller, to shrink into a child and hide in his body. The world didn't exist past the reach of his hand.

Was in Lawrence about six months ago.

See the memorial?

Yeah. They got it right at ground zero. It's just the pole in bronze or whatever, the arms broke off. Just like in the picture.

David said nothing.

City's mostly empty now. He looked at his glass. I guess most of the ones got hit are. I wanted to make it up to Columbus but I didn't feel like getting caught that far north in the winter. Both of them were looking around each other, letting the conversation settle. Dog's gettin' old.

She is.

I kinda miss having one. Those base dogs were about all that kept me sane some days. Searched for 'em for about a week, in the jungle. I don't know if they got blown up or ate or what.

David's head sunk to one side. I saw Collins carry one out, before my evac.

Which one was it?

Bradford's. Daisy.

Red looked out the window. He finished the beer in his hand and David saw him scan the room. The bar was mostly empty, just the miner and another man, drinking in their corners. Red brightened. Ma told me you've been comin' by sometimes. Bringing her food and such. I appreciate that.

He swung his glass between them. That's Helene, for the most part. She cooks up a casserole or something.

Said you fixed her gutters last year.

Well. He drained the glass and reached for another with a drip of whiskey left in it. He rolled the bead around the bottom.

You ever see those guys we tuned up way back when?

David shook his head. I heard one of 'em left town.

Stampin' that guy's face with the Chevy symbol's still one of the best things I ever saw.

I get a little carried away when someone brings a gun to my door.

Red sat back. They got quiet again. The alcohol was hitting him and the room muddled. He found himself drinking water, still at the table. He was angry and seemed to come awake mid-emotion. Red was shouting at the miner. David saw them moments away from broken glass and the barman setting a gun on the counter and he stood, stumbling over his chair, and walked out. It wasn't very late but he was tired, and he hoped for a long walk to sober himself so he might go home.

Hey!

David kept walking. Red's footsteps caught up beside him.

What are you doing?

David lifted a shoulder high to shake something off. Not doing this again. I'm gonna go home, apologize to my wife. Tuck my kid in if I ain't too late.

Red fell back. David didn't turn. Pieces of his memory blew through him as if from some repository, flying like scraps of paper. Muzzle flashes, bodies. Red beside him, screaming for him to kill everyone. Soldiers mounting a fence and jumping over. The shadow of a plane overhead and then spinning and black and flame. He'd woken up a day later with the lieutenant hovering over him. Red was gone. Men were stacking the bodies up like pieces of timber along the remaining wall of the base.

He made it as far as Danvers' and slipped on nothing in the road and sat down. When he woke again he was in bed and remembered wanting to tuck Samuel in and he hoped he had. His palms hurt from the fall. Helene was beside him. Tomorrow was the funeral, and he would have no time to apologize.

3

She woke him turning on the shower. It was light in the room and there was no sound except the water running. He got up and waited on the pain in his head to start but there was little. Red was asleep in the living room, blankets piled over him on the couch. Upstairs Samuel's door was already open and the light was on. Samuel was straightening his pillows on the bed.

Hey, bud.

Hey. Is it time to get ready?

Yeah. Go on and shower. I'll make some breakfast. He put a hand on Samuel's shoulder as he passed. He took the shirt off the doorknob and laid it and the pants out on the bed and smoothed them. Macha followed him into the kitchen from the stairs and lay down on the floor, watching him crack eggs. He took a slice of ham from a thick package of butcher's paper and tossed it to her and she licked it up. Helene came in the kitchen, hair black from the shower, and put her back to him.

Would you zip me?

He hesitated a moment, hands framing her back before he lifted her hair and pulled the zipper up, her neck thin and sunless and smooth. He let her hair down.

Is Sam getting ready?

Yeah.

She passed around him and stood in front of the stove. She scooped at the pan of eggs. I'll keep a plate warm for you while you shower.

It seemed a longer walk with his dress clothes on and

he had to resist the urge to roll up his sleeves. Helene held Samuel's hand and they were all listening to the birds and the wind in the midmorning quiet. On the north side of the road a stand of hay was ready for the first cut. They passed Danvers' house with the truck still in the drive. He gazed up at the sky, dry pale blue. Coming into town Samuel pulled on David's hand and David slung him up onto his shoulders before thinking of his collar and the wrinkles. His hands smarted. He let Samuel stay until he began to sweat and stooped over in the middle of the street and he hopped off. Two boys ran from the yard of an empty house and into another. Helene stepped behind David and straightened out his shirt while they walked. They turned north at the square and David opened the wood gate to his mother's house and they went in. His mother opened the front door to meet them in a plain black dress, a sweater over her elbow.

Am I watching my grandson here or what?

No. He's coming.

Hm. Her bottom lip rose. She bent to Samuel's level. You sure? There's only the two channels on TV anymore, but we can make do.

He's alright. Helene put a hand on his shoulder and shook him gently.

David's mother shrugged. I guess we should get goin', then. She shut the door and they went together to the street. The funeral home was a few blocks on and when they arrived there were already several cars assembled out front and the hearse was at the side of the building. Danvers had driven in from a sideroad and had parked the truck on the street and he sat still in the cab.

David jerked his thumb. You think we ought to get him?

Helene shook her head. He'll come when he's ready.

He tightened his hand on Samuel's and they mounted the stairs and stood outside the doors with the others already gathered. It was warm and bright and the sky cloudless. Mostly farmers there, Carl Brown and others with shirt-sleeves rolled up to reveal dark forearms and weathered hands. Clothes oddly clean and smooth for them all, tight fitting. David looked down at himself, at his own hands. He hadn't worn longsleeves since he wore a uniform. Samuel was staring up at him and David smiled weakly. Glenn Fogel came over to them, stepping small and slowly.

How you holding up, Dave?

He gave a slight nod. Okay. Nice of you to come.

I had to. Phil's a bit of a cuss, but he was always good for advice. Abby too.

He looked to Helene and Samuel. Was Abby that convinced him to give me a job to start with. Might kick us off the property now, without her.

Fogel laughed and looked to the ground. A man approached them in a full suit of gray and Fogel gave a quick goodbye. The man removed his Stetson.

David, Mrs. Parrish. He bent to Samuel's level and stuck out his hand. Sam.

Samuel shook. Hello, Mr. Skillman.

Skillman stood up and met eyes with Helene and David. I'm sorry for your loss. How are you all?

Getting by. David looked again at Samuel, hoping to gauge him. How's the mine?

Goin' pretty well. About to start in on some new property.

Where at?

Henderson's old place, buttin' up on your southeast end. Title just came through.

David exchanged a glance with Helene. Skillman leaned toward David slightly.

How long was Anna sick for? I didn't realize she'd gotten so bad.

Helene grasped David's arm, then took Samuel and his grandmother inside. He was shocked at her touch. He turned back to Skillman, keeping his eyes measured. She was laid up with pneumonia through winter. Old as she was, sitting around like that ain't good. She got a clot in her leg that hit her lungs.

Damn. He shook his head and patted his leg with his hat. You seem kinda knowledgeable.

Passing interest.

How's that?

I was a combat medic. David saw Danvers coming and pointed to the street. Better go. He met him at the steps. Danvers stopped and sighed deeply. At his approach most of the others began to file through the doors.

Well. The spectators're all here. Let's go get my money's worth.

They went in. He found everyone in the lobby and they took their seats in the front. Through the ceremony David watched Samuel for some reaction but it seemed lost on him until it was over and they all stood to file by the body. The casket was high enough that Samuel could just see in and David wanted badly to pull him away but he watched as Samuel put his hands on the edge of the wood and rose on his toes. He dropped back and David was wasted by his son's face. His eyes were vacant but deeper in David saw it hitting him and he saw something like grace fleeing in the fall of his shoulders. Helene took him aside and the four of them went into the lobby and Samuel sat with Helene kneeling in front of him and his cheeks cupped in her hands. David stood off to the side taking single steps toward Danvers in the viewing room and back to Samuel and he could move no further. After a while Danvers came out and his lips had been pinched away and he looked at Samuel and just shook his head and left. They followed him out and Samuel and his grandmother walked to her house while David and Helene went with Danvers to the cemetery. There were a few mourners already gathered and then the hearse came and they carried the casket to the green sunshelter erected in the field. David and Helene stood by, arms around Danvers, feeling him shake. After a time Helene went to get Samuel and David sat with Danvers on the hill while two men took down the shelter and brought in a small bedless truck. They lowered the casket into the ground and lined up a concrete slab and lowered it as well. The men got in the truck and drove away over the hill. Danvers' mouth bunched. Alright. Don't leave now I might not ever.

David stood and helped him onto his feet. Danvers lifted his eyepatch and snuck a finger in and set it back and they limped down the path out of the cemetery. Waiting at the road were Helene and Samuel in the truck. When she saw them she slid to the middle of the bench seat and had Samuel climb onto her lap while David and Danvers got in either side. Danvers reached his hand around and pulled Samuel's face to his and he kissed his temple.

Hey boy. How are you? His voice was rough and broken.

Samuel said nothing. Helene put a hand on his back and patted it. David started the truck and drove into town, east at the square. A half-mile down the road they stopped at Danvers' and David idled the truck in the drive.

Why don't you come eat with us?

I got things to eat around the house. There's food spoilin' as we speak.

Bring it down. There's no reason for you to putt around that place.

Oh. Danvers made a face. Well.

That's enough of a yes for me. He drove on the short distance to their house. Macha left the porch as they climbed out and followed them back. David held the door open. They filed in and Danvers stopped at the door and looked back off the porch. The dog stood at their feet, waiting.

We're gonna keep you busy, Phil. Just stay busy for a while.

Danvers heaved up his shoulders and they went in. David motioned him to the living room and walked to the kitchen.

Helene stood at the counter dicing dried beef.

That broke my heart.

She didn't look up. It broke mine too.

He shouldn't have been there.

She laid the knife down. Do you want to blame me for that?

You wanted him to go.

I wanted him to make his own decision.

David pivoted toward her. He's ten. There's things he doesn't need to decide.

Maybe you should have said that. Maybe we could have had a rational discussion about all this last night.

Don't.

Or any time, really.

He backed off. Not today.

I'm not trying to fight you. I'm being serious. Why didn't we talk about it? Why didn't we sit down and weigh things?

I don't know.

She nodded slightly and took up the knife again. She started dicing the beef and she slid the blade along the cutting board to gather the strips. Her mouth jutted slightly askew. For a moment he was struck by her, by the black dress and her hair put up and the litheness of her arms. He found Samuel and Danvers sitting together in the living room, Samuel reading a book with his feet propped on Macha's flank. His back was straight and his shirt was still tucked in.

Sam. David pointed at the book. Uh uh.

Oh, he ain't botherin' me.

It's rude. Put it up.

Samuel stood off the couch and went upstairs.

I wouldn't discourage a reader, Dave. He's liable to wind up like you or me.

David sat in the chair across from him. His legs were tired. Not like I really know what I'm doing.

I never raised any. Seems like you're doin' okay.

I wonder sometimes.

Where's your buddy?

I don't know. Maybe with his ma. He turned his head toward town as if he'd see it through the wall. Samuel was coming downstairs. David patted the arm of the chair for him to come over. You can read later.

Okay. Samuel stood beside the chair.

Dried beef gravy for supper. You want anything else, Phil? Anything from the house?

Danvers lifted his chin. Nah.

Somethin' to drink?

I'm alright.

David held in a yawn and set his head in his hand. Why don't you go see if your mom needs anything?

Samuel left the room and after a moment their voices trailed back.

Do you need help with anything? With the plot or anything?

Danvers stared off, out the window, across the room. We had these plans set up for when one of us died. Buy cheap caskets, cheap stones. Use that parcel we kept back from you on the edge of the property.

You told me. I remember.

He tilted his head toward his lap. I just couldn't do it. I couldn't see her in a box. And now I need money for the headstone. He looked up. Are you okay with me selling the parcel? Skillman made me an offer. I don't have to.

It's fine.

I figure it's not as pretty anymore, with the mine being so close.

You don't need to explain yourself. I understand. Macha rose and turned, dropping to the floor beside David. He reached and petted the dog's back. You know we could just help you some.

Money's tight. I know it is.

We could help.

Danvers shook his head and they got quiet. There were sounds of cooking and footsteps and the sound of birds outside in the budding trees. The ticking of the mantelpiece clock. The screen door in the kitchen opened and shut and David imagined Samuel walking out into the yard. He saw the boy studying the bark on the trees or following the path of an ant. He imagined Samuel's hands, in strange symmetry with the rest of him. They were long but the fingers were not. Palms broad and square, wrists thin like his mother's. A longness, a height to everything about him that couldn't be added together, couldn't be measured to say this is where his size came from. He looked like his mother. All he had of his father were the eyes and the hands, and he thought he might have something else of his, the call, the wandering. There were times watching him play or walk or just standing at the fence that he reminded David of himself and his namesake both. When he was born David thought it was a gift to them. To Red for being who he was and to Samuel that he might have some sliver of that strength. He stood, breaking out of the thought. You want a beer?

Alright. Danvers nodded.

David went into the kitchen. He moved quietly and opened the refrigerator behind Helene.

Almost done.

Okay. He got one of the beers Red had bought and shut the door.

Tell Phil he can come and sit down.

David started for the living room. Danvers was at the door waiting.

I'm headin' home.

Now, come on. Helene's about got dinner ready. He cracked a hairline smile.

I gotta go home eventually, Dave. I may as well do it now.

He set the can on the hall table and stood still. Danvers

opened the door. David stepped toward him.

Are you gonna walk me out there?

I might.

Well I can't stop you. They went out the front door and onto the porch. Danvers paused at the railing and put a hand on it. We were always sorta solitary people. We met pretty late in life and we never got to have kids for whatever reason. He breathed in slow and turned his head aside. It was either gonna be her or me standing here. I'm sorta glad she got spared it.

He felt a hollowness in his chest. That if he spoke his heart would echo. Danvers stepped off the porch and walked to the road. David stood there a moment after he'd gone around the bend and went inside. In the kitchen David looked at Helene and he raised his shoulders.

I can't imagine. I don't want to.

What? Samuel had been bringing plates to the table and stopped.

Nothin' bud.

Me or Mom dying?

Yeah, that. He came toward Samuel and put an arm around his back. You don't need to worry about it. We're all gonna be around for a long time.

Samuel nodded. He let him go and David thought he could see in Samuel's eyes that he understood.

<hr />

David was standing with Macha on the front porch when Red came around the bend. Macha struggled down the steps and then trotted to meet him and she circled his legs and came back to the yard. Red lifted his hand and dropped it and David raised his.

How'd it go?

Pretty rough. Sam took it hard. He shrugged. Maybe it's

better this way. Maybe it would've hurt him worse to see it later. I dunno. He hung his head out past the railing to see the sky. It wasn't long after midafternoon and the sun was still far from the western horizon. You want to come riding? There's a little work to do.

Sure.

Let me go in and tell her.

Helene was at the sink and Samuel was still at the table. He stopped in the doorway and then stood beside Samuel. Helene was washing the dishes. I got to see to the herd real quick. Will you be alright?

Yeah.

He patted Samuel on the back and nodded toward the sink. Why don't you let those be, hon?

Because things need doing here, too.

Well. He turned. I'll be back. He left the kitchen and got his hat and jacket from the coat rack. At the sound of the door Red stood up from the bottom porch step and they walked down the road toward Danvers'. Macha followed them until David pointed at her. You stay.

The dog halted and turned back. They went on to the barn. Samuel's silver bay stood cribbing at the stall door. He led the horse out and they saddled it and David's in turn and Red took them out. David lifted the emasculator from its peg on the wall and wiped it clean with a rag. He poured disinfectant over it and his hands and shook them dry. Red blanched when he stepped out with it.

You didn't say you were doin' that. Isn't it a little late?

Pretty close. But you're on the hook now. He took his bay toward the gate and Red followed. He let them through the gate and stepped up into the saddle and he watched Red struggle up. When he was settled they rode southeast, cutting across the property. They rode in silence for a long while, taking in the faltering grass and the few trees. They passed the remnants of old boundaries, fallen fenceposts and the squared foundation of a long-gone shed. They leaned back as their horses stepped down a grade and righted. Topping it they saw the herd gathered at the creek in the distance. Red turned to David.

Know him by sight?

No. But it's not like there's two hundred head here. Shouldn't be hard to find.

Red smirked. They separated and cut into the animals to spread them out and they circled and he watched Red ride around the periphery from the corner of his eye. There was something in his silhouette. The rope in David's hand turned gritty from memory and he was in the trench by the dry riverbed. It was raining like it always rained and the sky was low over the trees and he could see them coming out from behind the cover of ferns and dwarf bamboo and sliding into the draw and running toward their side. Red was first over the mouth of the trench and David was there with him and they were rushing to meet the soldiers and when Red called to him and pointed he didn't know how it was not pouring.

He's right here.

David spun the horse. The calf was at the edge of the herd and David dropped the loop over its head easily and pulled it tight and he dropped from the saddle. Red was still on his horse and David passed the rope to him and he rode off until the calf dropped to its knees and David pushed it to the ground and knelt on its shoulder. Red came over and handed David the emasculator and pulled on the calf's foreleg. He patted its neck.

Docile enough thing, ain't he?

Killed his momma comin' out. David rolled to the calf's rear and pinned the tail to its back with his elbow and pulled the scrotum free of the legs. He took the knife from his pocket and lined the blade up and cut and pulled. The calf recoiled and screamed and Red lay overtop it to keep it from thrashing away.

There's the fight.

He took the calf's testes and pulled them until the muscle in the cord separated and he crimped the first with the emasculator and held it tight. The tail slipped loose from under his arm when he reached for the other testicle and the calf began whipping its tail about and it spiked on the knife lying at an angle in the grass.

Hell. Blood was painted across his chest. He crimped the second testicle with his face averted. He opened the tool and stood away to get a spraycan from the horse and he doused the scrotum with it. You can let go.

Red pushed off and the calf stood wobbling. It ran to the herd with the skin flapping red and pink at its rear. David stooped to pick up the knife and he wiped it on the seam of his jeans and put it in his back pocket. There was a spat of blood on Red's cheek and across the sleeve of his shirt and hands. David spun around to find himself in the field and he saw the horses standing aside grazing and he wiped at his brow with the back of his hand. The smell of tissue and insides were on his fingers. He closed his eyes.

Got a headache or something?

No. I'm alright. They mounted and headed for the gate. The light was just beginning to pull from the air in the east. Red was ahead of him and from his shape alone David was there again with the soil and blood slathered on him like porridge. Red was cutting the femur from a soldier in the middle of the draw. David shuddered and leaned from the horse and vomited. The horse stopped and Red sawed around and helped David into the grass.

Jesus, bud. What the hell?

Between his fingers there was a give like the rubber tube of an artery. His ears were ringing. He felt a pressure like a fist behind his forehead, not punching but pushing.

Hey, come on. Red slapped at his cheek. David rolled his eyes up. He retched once and fell onto his hands and knees and he stayed there for a while with Red sitting on his haunches beside him, holding his hat. The land was beginning to color from the sunset and it was getting cool. Eventually David sat and he wiped his eyes and mouth with a handkerchief. He sat there breathing slowly. He held the handkerchief wrinkled up and he began to fold it and cocked his head.

Do you still have that bone? That femur?

Red put his hand on the earth and he shifted his weight. I think it's in one of those holes you found me in.

David shook his head.

Do you have yours?

He closed his eyes. What?

Red leaned back. He stood slowly. Come on. Let's get you on your horse. He took David's arm and hauled him to his feet and they walked together to the bay. The horse was watching them and it pushed its muzzle to David's chest as he passed. David put his foot in the stirrup and Red boosted him and he swung his leg over. They rode close by until they reached the gate and Red opened it and put the horses up. When Red came out of the barn he put his arm around David and they walked down the drive. David kept his head low. They stopped at the bend and Red gripped David's shoulder.

Are you okay? You don't want to pile this on the family.

David nodded. I'll make it.

Nothin' to hash out?

No.

Alright. He put his arm around him again and they climbed the porch steps. Red opened the door and David went into the bathroom to wash out his mouth. It was coming on twilight through the windows when he walked into the hall and saw the three of them together listening to the radio. Helene moved over for David to sit on the couch beside her and he did, leaning over, elbows on his knees. Samuel was sitting on the ground by Red. David breathed in and sighed, covering his face with his hands and rubbing. Red's duffelbag was full and closed.

I'm gonna leave in the mornin'.

Samuel closed his book, thumb in the pages. Why?

I just don't like stayin' put much. And I think I'm wearin' your Daddy out.

Samuel glanced at David. Red smiled slowly and then looked away.

I think it's just been a long few days for all of us. Helene found David's hand. Maybe you'll feel differently about it tomorrow.

Later that night Red brought the chairs from the dinner table into the living room and set them by the couch. He spread a sheet over them and threw a blanket and pillow underneath. Red and Samuel crawled in and David watched the beams of flashlights cross the sheets. He went back to the bedroom and lay awake holding Helene long after she fell asleep, after the shuffling in the tent stopped. The dream came back to him and the whole of the day and he felt that some battle had already been lost.

There was a knock at their bedroom door while it was still dark. He didn't move though he knew what it was. Red knocked again and David rolled the covers off and stood. He opened the door. The hallway was cool and it felt like a window was open somewhere in the house. Red had his bag slung over his shoulder. Macha was standing beside him and in the living room he saw Samuel's head sticking out of the tent, on a pillow.

Well, Dave. I'm headin' out.

He nodded. He tried to delay the moment to get the fog from his head and to find something to say.

Red stuck out his thumb and scratched his neck, the bag lifting. When I talked to your woman she acted like you don't do this at all, have episodes. I figured it was me.

I don't want that to run you off. I. He looked at the door. He pointed to the porch and they stepped out. Red had taken

David's jacket from the coatrack and handed it to him. It was a little later than the first morning and the east was lined with the weak early light that stayed and stayed and then became dawn. They leaned against the railing on the porch steps. Finally David stuck his hand between them. I want Sam to get to know you.

I'll write.

You never write.

I will.

David jerked his head aside.

I was gonna leave yesterday but it seemed like a shit thing to do. I just can't hang around any longer. I feel like I'm wasting time.

You can't even say goodbye to Sam?

I already did. He's in there pretending to sleep.

David said nothing. Red shifted from the railing and stared at him.

I wanted to tell you to be careful. I don't assume I know what's eatin' you, but it looks like it's got you by the throat.

David grimaced.

Things're gonna get worse. I saw some rough shit out there, back east. He paused and looked at the yard and beyond. It was good to see the godson.

I'm glad you did. David stepped down to meet him and they shook hands tightly and hugged. You take care.

Always. Keep your head down. Red backed away from him into the yard and started walking. He headed east, away from town, toward the sun.

4

That morning he found Samuel in the living room reading. It was still dark and he'd wanted to ride out and dig the new fenceline. The lamp was on and when David came into the doorway Samuel looked up. Macha was at his feet.

Morning.

What're you up so early for?

I couldn't sleep.

Did you have a bad dream?

No. I just couldn't sleep. Samuel looked at his book.

Can I get you anything?

I'm okay.

Alright. He sat beside him. The window in the room faced west and the sky through it was lightening as a whole, slowly pulling out of the sable dark. Eventually Samuel's head began to bob toward the book and David settled him against the arm of the couch and pulled the afghan from its back over him. He set the book on the endtable and stood slowly, bending to shut off the light. The sky seemed bright now in the dark and he went to the kitchen to brew a pot of coffee, Macha clicking behind him. He sat at the table while the coffee perked and he remembered the years before. He thought of throwing up in the field and a pang hit him, that he was sick. Red had exiled himself and he should have done the same. Made better use of himself some way. Now there was no opportunity.

He drank the coffee when it was finished brewing and grabbed his hat off the inside of the door in the bedroom and shut it without waking Helene. Macha slipped through the door behind him and he patted her head and told her to stay.

The lights were on all through the bottom of Danvers' house. At the door he stopped his hand from knocking and waited for any sounds inside. There were none and after a minute he left the steps to saddle his horse, setting a postholer by the barn door. He went to the house again and knocked and there were lumbering footsteps and Danvers opened the door, his eyepatch off and left eye staring wild.

They sat in the kitchen. The table was full of dishes, a crockpot. Danvers was still in his undershirt from the funeral. The shirt was thin and his belly stretched it but he was gaunt.

Early, even for you.

Yeah. Wanted to get started moving that fence.

You need some help?

I'll just be digging some holes.

Danvers grimaced, putting his hands on the table like he'd push it away. Suit yourself, then.

Do you want to come out with me?

No.

Come on. Let's ride.

No. I'll stick around here and eat some of this potato salad or somethin'.

David stood. Just come out.

Danvers' head tilted and he fixed David with a cross-eyed stare. Get.

David left. He grabbed the postholer and mounted up and rode. It was getting light but there was a thin haze over the sky and everything was subdued. It felt like fall. There was a soft wind going from the west that cooled him and the horse twisted its head and sneezed and went on. The grass rippled. It was over a half hour to the parcel. When he reached it he turned the horse toward town and could see how it would have been when Danvers had planned everything, the land still wide and natural. He passed on heading southeast, under high tension wires. It took him a little while after to register that he should have hit the fence a few hundred yards back, that the grass was laying flat, and then the horse came on the wire and it balked and stopped. The wire pinned the grass down and the posts had been pulled with it and someone had dragged the whole fence from where it had been.

Fuck. He spun the horse, scoping the empty field. The cattle were back on the eastern side, he thought, but wasn't sure. A panic rose up in him and the horse felt it and began to prance. He pushed it onward and they started at a clip over the wire and he felt angry, and bold for trespassing. The stretch of land ahead had been pasture and field and was now fallow, overgrown, and he wondered if soon most of the land around the town would be the same.

Not long after he crossed the wire he could smell the damp earth and shale, the bitten powder of rock that reminded him of explosions. On his right stood two houses, bought out, that they'd yet to tear down. A shed and a garage to plow over. Along the road a few split-shifters were walking home. He rode on and the ground rose up slowly and cut to a level gravel plain that the horse trotted down. Below them the ground fell steeply away and swinging around on the pit were trailers and a mess hall, a cabin near the road. Heavy engines and the pouring of rock. He pushed the horse further toward the pit and it sidestepped and he stopped to take in the gray hole, to see the trucks moving, the few men walking. He rode around toward the cabin and two men came out of the hall as he slipped from the horse to tie it up. He still had the postholer clutched in his hand.

What do you want, cowboy?

I'm here to see Skillman.

He's out.

I think I'll try knocking on his door.

The two miners squared off to him and the younger one took a step closer. You're Parrish, aren't you?

Yeah.

You got my brother fired.

David shrugged. It's about to run in the family if you don't get out of my face.

Hey, fuck you.

He glanced at the other miner and then stood a few inches from the younger. David was a little taller and his hatbrim hit the boy's forehead. You tore out my fence. My cattle could get loose.

Skillman property now.

Quit acting like some tough son of a bitch and get your boss.

They were silent for a moment and the young one narrowed his eyes. The other one reached between them and pushed David and before he had his arm back David grabbed the man's hand and wrenched it so that the miner came forward and nearly flipped over himself. David raised the postholer to strike and stopped, looking at the young miner.

Get Skillman.

The young man skipped backwards and ran to the cabin. David shoved the other miner away and he fell and kicked David's shin. David drove the postholer against the man's chest, pushing him flat on the ground.

I will take your goddamn head off.

The miner's eyes were wide, hands in the gravel to scrabble back. You're crazy, man.

Remember that. David glanced at the cabin and set the postholer in the ground. Skillman came out in front of the young man and he stopped several feet away from David.

Did you break one of my men, Parrish?

You tore down my fence.

I what?

The fence is tore down where we're splitting property. Just layin' on the ground. Posts pulled and everything.

Skillman held up a hand like he was attesting to something. I didn't authorize that, Dave. The paperwork ain't through yet.

Someone did. There sure as hell's a lot of open range back the way I came. You gonna do something about it? And tell me you fire that prick behind you for starters.

Skillman glanced at the young miner. Did you do this?

It wadn't me.

Skillman nodded and looked at the ground. His face bunched for a moment and he raised his head and came forward. What can I do to set us straight?

You can replace that fence.

Done.

David breathed in. He glanced from the miner still on the ground to the young one. He looked at Skillman. If I get any more shit from this mine, Skillman.

What?

I been nothin' but hassled by you jackasses coming and going out of here. I'm tired of it.

Skillman pointed at him with two fingers. You asked for every bit of trouble you got. I like you, Dave, but apparently I'm the only man in town who knows you're a hard case.

He turned. He'd never tied the horse and it had wandered toward one of the trailers. He grabbed the reins and got up into the saddle, boosting himself with the postholer. I can name a few who know. He rode out.

The haze had been burned through by the rising sun and left the morning warm. The mine kept its own temperature and humidity and riding out was like coming into a new land. The wind that had been cool was now warm. The heat and pressure in him blew away with the breeze. He thought of Samuel asleep on the couch as he crossed the fence and Danvers in the kitchen and Helene. He rode over the dry creek and saw the cattle settled around the watertubs, and beyond them the flat plain of his cornfields. There were only now the thinnest shoots rising from the dirt, pale.

At home he found Helene waiting for him. She had poured cups of coffee and put the mugs in their places on the kitchen table. David sat across from her and pulled the mug toward him but let it sit.

Are you okay?

His head cocked. Yeah. I'm fine.

You don't seem it. You haven't been.

David opened his mouth like he might chew on something. It was funny having Red around. It messed with me a little.

He said you broke down. If something's wrong we need to talk about it. We can't let it fester.

He raised and dropped his hand. He said nothing. Helene tapped two fingers on the table and looked at her coffee.

When we had that fight. And I said I worry you won't come home one day?

David nodded.

Sometimes I don't think you ever did.

That's not true. I'm always here. It was seeing Red again, being around him. I love you too much to be gone. I love Sam too much.

She winced a smile. I wish I thought that was enough. I wish I could be as idealistic as you.

5

Early June. It was hot and there had been only one brief rain in weeks. The grass was all blond and thinning to the cracked ground below. There was no green save their garden and the corn. Cicadas ground loud in the trees. David rode in from checking the cattle and fences and staring for a long while at his fields. After putting the horse up he checked the fuel tanks and went to sit at Danvers' kitchen table, working at diesel figures. How much they had, how much they needed. Danvers sat in the living room through the wide doorway, fans arrayed around him. David set the pencil eraser-down on the table and tapped.

You think we can do without the glyphosate?

What? Danvers blinked heavily, stretching his head up to hear.

I said you think we can make do without the herbicide for a season? He stood and came into the living room.

For a season?

David raised an eyebrow.

You don't have enough fuel, right? What makes you think you're gonna come across more later? Did they feed you some bull about getting the rigs back online?

David said nothing. One of the fans had flipped a book open on the sidetable and the pages lifted and fell back.

Come next year you're gonna be plantin' and pickin' by hand. I don't know if you've thought about that or not.

I have. I thought maybe you'd have some advice.

There ain't any secrets. Get some mules. Hire hands.

David glanced away. The fireplace was shut up and the

floor before it ashen, black from ground coals. The doors on it clacked together from the wind and clacked again when it cut out. We don't have the money to hire anyone.

I know you don't. You don't have the money to buy all the animals you'll need. Or the stables to put 'em in. You're gonna have to cut way down.

Did you ever farm that way?

No. My pappy did. Him and half a dozen other men that lived in your house.

He hung his head. You don't think we'll get any more gas?

I don't know why you keep on asking questions you know the answer to. Danvers leaned toward him. Name me one thing that's broke down since the war that got fixed. You can't do it. Can't hardly get mail. Highways are all broke up, government won't repair 'em. Eighty's been more pothole than road for years. They say they're getting things done but if you told me all the politicians was in some mansion laughin' it up I wouldn't be surprised. He sat back again and gestured toward the window. It's all illusions, is what it is. You might as well wind the clock back a hundred years and call it 1930. Airplanes and spaceships. Your boy probably don't know we had men on the moon. Might not believe you if you told him.

David turned away again.

It ain't a bad thing, son. Where did all that get us? All that achievement, all that technology. Right here. Got us to right here. And that's the only place we was ever gonna go. He mopped at his face with his shirtcollar.

I don't know if I can believe that. David went to the kitchen table and picked up his hat.

People farmed a lot longer without gas than with. Don't get too down.

David nodded. He picked up the pad of paper and started home. It was cooler on the road and he could hear a wind high overhead. He climbed the porch steps and they creaked and shifted under him. A boy and girl younger than Samuel were standing in the hall with Helene tying their shoes.

You find a couple strays?

Babysitting. They're Corinna Brown's.

Taking them home?

As soon as Sam's done sulking, yeah. She stood. David went past her to the kitchen and she followed.

What's wrong with him?

He wanted to buy a book from the library. I wouldn't give him the money.

Well. He sat at the table with the pencil and paper.

What're you working on? She stood beside him, bending over. He saw down her blouse briefly and she caught him and smacked his arm. You.

He smiled. Can't help it. He reached for her waist and pulled her next to him and he turned back to the paper. Wasting time, mostly. We need to put down herbicide but don't have the fuel. Danvers sorta yelled at me for not thinkin' ahead.

What do you mean?

We're gonna be planting by hand next season. No way around it. He pushed the paper away. What's with the kids?

Corinna needed them out of the house for a while. She called me earlier. I guess things are a little dire.

I believe it.

They could hear Samuel coming down the stairs. Helene went toward the hall and looked back. We'll be home soon.

He nodded and sat forward over the table. The children filed out and for a moment the house was filled with footsteps. When they were gone he shook his head and stood up to go out the backdoor. Hotter still. He waited on Macha to find him but she never came, and he crossed the yard to the fence and leaned on a post, feeling the wind. Dry and constant like it was blown from a machine. He circled around the house and called for Macha and when he got to the front door he stopped. The shadow of the porch fell slanted and between the slats of shadow and light he saw a form. Aw hell.

He left the door wide and stepped down from the porch. He peered through the trellis at the side and saw it as just a mass, a stripe of gold along a ribcage. It was her. He paced to the other side and saw the trellis was scratched at and dug under. He pulled at the thin wood bars and they warped but didn't budge. He pulled again and stood and wrenched at the wood until it began to crack and he let go and kicked and kicked again. A hole broke in the center and he began snapping the pieces and he kept on until he'd ripped the trellis apart branch by branch. He threw the pieces scattered behind him and knelt looking at the body of his dog. Then he crawled under the porch with his chin barely above ground, eyes adjusting and he could see her tongue between her teeth, eyes closed. He reached out to touch her. A bead of sweat rolled down his forehead to his nose, dripped off. The porch was too low for him to carry her so he crawled out back into the daylight and went inside for a sheet and spread it out beside her. He lifted her up and slid it underneath and began pulling her backward. He hit his head on a beam and cursed and stood when he was clear, rubbing at the egg. His eyes were burning. He pulled the sheet from under the porch and wrapped Macha in it, then he sat down again and uncovered her head and stroked her ear. He patted her neck and sat there a little while. Helene appeared beside him and he looked up at her expressionless.

Where's Sam?

He's at the library. Skillman saw him and gave him some book money.

I don't know what to say to that.

Neither do I. She shifted. Do you want help, babe?

He wiped at his forehead with the back of his hand. Eventually he rose to carry her into the backyard. He laid her down under a tree by the fence and went to the shed for a shovel and started digging. The dirt he broke up was light and powdery. Samuel came walking out the backdoor and got a small shovel from the shed and stood at the grave. He looked at David before he pulled the sheet from Macha's body and David nodded. He petted the dog's flank and put the sheet in place. David stopped for a moment and met Samuel's eyes.

You don't have to help, bud.

I want to.

He almost reached out to Samuel but the dirt was between them. Samuel started digging. When they were finished David put the body into the grave and he stood over it and told Samuel to go inside. He waited until he heard the door and knelt in the hole. He wiped at his eyes with his shirtsleeve and stood to dig again. He cast shovelfuls of dirt onto the sheet until he had no more dirt to replace and he stood leaning against the shovel and he was sick with dread. He was sweating and shaking and deep beneath him he felt something move.

6

After dinner David told Samuel to get Macha's things so he could take them to the attic. Samuel finished the dishes and took her bowls from beside the refrigerator and carried them into the hall. Helene lined up beside David, arms pressing. She was looking at him and he was staring out the window.

David.

Yeah.

She put her head on his shoulder.

One helluva day.

They heard Samuel overhead and David stepped back. He walked upstairs, Samuel standing by the drop steps with a box. David reached for the rope and pulled the door down and set out the loose wooden ladder. He took the box and climbed up into the attic with Samuel following. The room was nearly dark and he felt in the air for the string of the bulb. There was a plywood path down the middle of the attic and alongside it boxes were stacked over the supports, ancient insulation between. He set the box down at the end of the walkway and saw Samuel pointing. He hadn't come up off the steps.

What's in there?

David leaned over to see the writing on the box: Army. He cast about for something to distract Samuel, for something to let him explain the box away. There was nothing, and he wasn't sure how long he'd been silent. Stepping over to the box he set his hand on the seam and turned to him. You want to find out?

Yeah.

Come up here. He pointed at the box of Macha's things. Put that up in the corner there and I'll show you. David waited on him to pass and opened one side and for a fumbling moment thought the femur was there. There was only his uniform, a shoebox, the old things. He set the box down on the walkway and Samuel came over. They sat together and he let Samuel pull out the contents. First the dress uniform thick and musty, the combat medic badge still fastened. When Samuel laid it down across his knees he looked at David with his forehead knit close and something pulling at his lip. He took out a knife, the blade rough with nicks and chips. Next were the boots, the shoebox of letters and trinkets which he opened and flipped through. There were pictures of David's mother and a few of Helene. A few paperbacks and faded magazines. The box was empty but for a small glass vial. Samuel picked it up and held it to the light. Various metal slivers that rang when he shook it. There was a larger piece the shape of a heavy button. He set the vial down on the floor.

That scar on your stomach.

You know what those are?

Yeah. He began to put the things back. He paused at the shoebox. Could I read these?

When you're older.

He put the shoebox back and then the boots and folded the dress greens. They stood and David carried the box to its place and they went down the steps. He pushed the door up and they went downstairs. Helene stopped them in the hall.

What took you?

We got caught looking at stuff.

She nodded. They passed her and Samuel followed David to the kitchen and out the back door. David got the hose out and watered the garden. He checked the hanging plants on the porch around front, Samuel following along. When they'd finished the sun was long set and in the east the sky was already transparent, dark, full of stars. David sent Samuel to shut off the water and came around coiling the hose over his arm. They met at the backdoor and stood together.

Why did you hide those things?

I didn't really hide 'em. The Christmas lights are up there too. You think I hid those?

Samuel gave him a look and David smiled slightly.

It's something I don't like thinking of. And something I never wanted you to have to know about.

Why were you fighting?

You mean me or us, America?

America.

They didn't teach you that in school?

He tilted his head dully. We're learning about presidents.

David smiled. He looked across the yard, out over town. It was a big war. People were fighting all over the place. But it started when some people bombed some cities, then we bombed 'em back. Red and me fought in Costa Rica. That's way down south.

I know.

We were fighting these guys that didn't like America much. A bunch of countries got together and said they didn't like how we treated them.

How did we treat them?

He rubbed at his face. It's complicated. We needed oil for gas and—you'll learn all about it someday, I imagine.

Okay. Samuel's eyes were distant, thinking. It makes me proud of you.

Why's that? He gestured to the small concrete stoop at the backdoor and they sat.

I dunno. You fought. You were brave. You must have saved people because you were a medic.

How'd you know that?

The medal with the snakes.

David smiled. Listen. I fought when I was just a kid. Red and me, we dropped out of school thinking we were gonna save everyone, be big heroes. But we weren't. We just caused your grandma and Red's ma a lot of grief. I don't regret it. But whoever I saved or helped, it wasn't worth it. The only thing that makes it worth it is that now there's peace to raise you up in. I hope that because I fought you won't ever have to.

Why not?

David's face bunched. It is a terrible thing, bud. You're too young to even know. You just have to trust me. It ain't exciting, or fun. I don't want you to ever have to go through it.

But what if I want to be like you?

David felt like he was sent rolling in the air. He tried to focus on a point in the yard. Don't ever be like me. The things I saw, Sam. Things I did. His fingers extended like he might gesture at the horizon. I want this world to stay beautiful for you. I want what I did to have meant something.

Okay.

Yeah? You believe me?

Maybe.

Well the whole point is that you never find out if I'm right. He put his hand on Samuel's head. Come on. They rose and went into the house and found Helene in the living room. We watered everything.

I noticed. Her voice echoed. They both stood in the doorway to the living room looking in at her. The radio was on low. It's time for bed.

Samuel and David exchanged small frowns. Alright. Samuel walked over and hugged her and she kissed his cheek. He started up the steps. David watched him go.

He found my box of Army stuff.

She raised an eyebrow and he went up to Samuel's room. He was sitting on the bed tugging off his socks. David watched him get under the sheets and pull them up to his chest.

Thanks for helping me today.

You're welcome. I'm sorry about Macha.

Me too. He watched Samuel's eyes and saw the void come

into them, saw that he was looking at nothing. He came forward and leaned down to kiss Samuel's forehead. Goodnight, Sam.

Night.

David turned off the lamp and shut the door and went downstairs. He sat beside Helene on the couch and slumped against an armrest.

You should talk to Skillman.

He lifted his head from the couch back. What am I supposed to talk to him about?

Selling some property, David.

Phil gave that land to us. I ain't about to sell it.

He wouldn't blame you.

The hell he wouldn't.

We can't live off the good years much longer. If the weather gets any worse we won't turn any profit at all.

This ain't the first drought people have lived through. We need that land or we sure as hell won't turn a profit. We're farmers. You need land to farm.

We're people. People need food to eat.

He made a face at her. What's that we grow out there?

I'm serious.

So am I. We sell that land and it'll only last so long. It won't do Sam any good when he's our age.

You know how far away that is? You know how many meals I have to cook between then and now, how many bills we have to pay? She put up her hand. Let's not fight about this tonight.

Alright. I'm okay with that. They sat quiet for a while. He tried not to think about Macha, about her not being in reach to pet with his foot. There was a matting of fur in the rug where she would lay. He closed his eyes. A country music program came on a couple nights a week, and he turned up the radio as it started. There were occasional commercials for local businesses. The last president used to address the public every so often, on the radio or television. Through computers when the networks were up. Now they heard little from anyone outside of the state.

Near the end of the program he eased and saw Helene had relaxed and he scooted closer and put his arm over her shoulder. She kicked at his foot.

So what'd he think about your big secret?

About what I expected. David stretched. Said he was proud. I tried to discourage that as best I could.

She said nothing for a minute, listening to the music. I'm going to start hand-washing the laundry.

Why?

Reuse the water. We should start watching how we shower, too.

It may come to that. But I'd just as soon we keep a few luxuries while we can.

Mm. She rose and took his hand. Come.

David leaned over to shut off the radio and followed her to the bedroom. He took his boots off at the door and they both stripped down. She pulled him close. He settled over her and kissed her neck, pushing her hair clear with his lips. She nudged him aside and rolled on top of him. When she began to sit up he pulled her back.

He walked into Dixon in the morning while it was still dark. A horse hitched to a street sign balked and stamped when he rounded the corner and he gave it berth. The diner was lit up and heads of farmers bobbed out of the window to coffee or plates below. On one side was a doctor's office that had long been closed, the other an empty shop, mostly vacant apartments above them all. He went into the diner and scooped up the local handmade newspaper from a rack beside the door. A woman behind the counter acknowledged him and shifted her apron.

Coffee?

Yes'm. He opened the paper and skimmed it. The headline was about the storm, the gas running out. He flipped the page. An article on the drought, a few lines of local interest: Tully's Lumber to close in Banning, relocating to Dixon. A sheet of local ads. He looked out the window at the dark streets, the orange lamplights, nobody awake save those in the diner. Behind him two farmers were talking about the drought. He felt the same as he had the morning Red and he first left home, walking to Banning to catch a ride to a recruitment office the next town over. Talking themselves up at the door. Inside with the others he went numb when they began calling units. It never occurred to him they could be separated. By luck they were all grouped together to replace heavy casualties. He remembered Red's expression, unfazed.

He finished his coffee. He paid at the counter and walked down the road in the dark. A train was coming into town from the east, the dry air shuddering. Already Samuel had seen death, had felt it. He wondered if that was the first step, making acquaintances. And then how many steps were between Samuel and himself. Himself and Red. Helene opened the bedroom door as he was taking off his boots. He looked up at her.

Give me some time. Give me a few years.

Then what?

He set his boots by the front door. He said nothing.

7

A morning later in the summer. He'd made breakfast for everyone and gone to shower when he heard footsteps on the porch and saw the postman walking to the road. There was a letter from the post office that said they were to have no more deliveries. After he'd washed and dressed he found Helene in the living room reading, feet on the couch and a cup of chicory coffee and the letter by her head. The shower was running overhead and he climbed upstairs. He pressed himself against the door and pounded on it. Hey in there!

What? The water stopped.

How's it take you twice as long to shower as me and you're less'n half my size?

There was a pause. I have smaller hands.

David laughed. He stood at the window a moment to look out at the morning and came back downstairs. Helene poked his side with her foot and he rubbed at her legs absently.

Gotta go into town for some liniment. Sam's horse is acting up.

She hummed and smiled. You told me. The bathroom door opened and floorboards creaked from Samuel walking to his room. David let go of her legs and leaned on the doorway while Samuel came down. You ready finally?

Yeah.

Let's go. Samuel fell in behind him and they both waved as they went out the door. David rolled up his sleeves and he watched as Samuel did the same. Samuel's eyes were on the ground and David's on the corn, drying already and the ears small. They both glanced into the yard as they passed Danvers' house. You ready to go back to school? You only got a couple weeks left.

Yeah.

Been a good break?

Mhm. He was quiet for a moment and looked up at David. Do you think Red might visit again soon?

No idea, bud. He likes to wander.

Samuel began to say more when a truck came down the road behind them. David pulled Samuel toward the grass and they stopped to watch it come on. When the truck got close he saw it was from the mine and it slowed and stopped beside them. Skillman was driving and he rolled down the window.

How dee, Dave. You got a minute?

I do if you do. He pointed at the truck.

Skillman seemed puzzled for a moment then killed the engine. He leaned against the door, arm crooked out. I would give you just a heap of money for some of that land.

He tipped his head to Samuel. Go on.

Samuel walked a few steps away and stopped.

Dave, I don't know where you get the idea that I'm a bad guy.

We could start with your men tearing out my fence.

I already told you I had nothin' to do with that.

Alright.

We got it put up the next day, didn't we? Skillman held his hand out, offering his words.

Look.

Don't worry about it. You're entitled to your opinion. I do good work and you know that. I helped a fella the other day got his leg caught in an auger. Brought down the cutting torches myself. He seemed to stare at Samuel for a moment and David wanted to step in between. I just want you to know that my offer for that land is still as good as when I asked Phil for it.

I don't know how many times we gotta tell you.

I'm not asking for all of it. I did the research. I'd be giving you more than five years' worth of what you make out of what I'm asking for, on top of the property value. That's five good years. You might not see that much out of it for twenty.

David's face was stiffening. Who knows, maybe longer.

God forbid. Skillman turned to look the way he'd come. You know I gave Phil a more than fair price for that little plot. I knew why he was selling it.

That's sweet of you.

At least consider the offer.

He smiled. No thank you.

Skillman drew his hand back in the window. You're sure.

Yeah.

Well, keep me in mind. Skillman rolled the window up and the truck started forward. David caught Skillman's eye in the mirror and watched him go before he and Samuel went on.

What was he saying, Dad?

He wants to buy some land off us.

Why don't you do it?

Well, a couple reasons. Whatever he pays me, it won't last longer than the land would. That land will always be there, for me and you, even your kids. The money would only be good for a little while. Things are tough now, but they'll turn around.

Is he a bad person?

Not really. It's just hard to trust folks with that much money. I guess generally we're all after something. I got no reason to pick on Skillman for that.

What are you after?

They neared the first houses of town. He breathed in deep. Food on the table. For you to grow up happy.

What about you and mom?

We're happy if you are. Are you?

Mm.

Mm, the boy says.

The phone rang. Samuel rose from where they all sat reading in the living room. He went into the hall and answered and he brought the phone in and handed it to David. It's Mr. Fogel.

David took the phone and he gave the book to Samuel. He stood and listened and hung the phone up in the hall. He looked in on the living room while stepping into a boot. He's outta diesel. I'm gonna head down to the old man's and roll out a barrel for him.

You're giving it to him? Helene peered at him from over her book.

We'll see if he brings his billfold.

She glared and he weathered it.

So what if we gotta pick a couple acres? Be good for us.

A corner of her mouth lifted and she closed the book in her hand. I don't want to hear you complain when you do.

I won't.

You need to make sure you keep some at home for us.

The diesel, or me?

Both.

It all comes around. Just watch.

She glanced at Samuel and came over to David. You believe that?

For the moment.

I bet you do.

He tried to smile and it came out seeking. You'll be getting some flowers out've the deal, I imagine. That count for anything?

You might break even.

He grimaced and went out. It was getting dark already. He listened to himself walk along the gravel road between the fields and the bulks of cows and the corn. There were head-lights coming down the road as he reached Danvers' and they stopped, the truck sputtering. The lights dimmed. A figure came toward him and when Fogel got near, David raised a hand. Cut it a little too close I see.

I don't suppose you got a little gascan, do ya?

He smiled in the near dark. Crickets had begun to chirrup. We've got somethin'. He motioned for Fogel to follow and they went to the equipment barn.

Appreciate you helpin' me out. You sure you can spare the gas?

David looked aside at him. Wouldn't be out here if we couldn't. He hit a lightswitch. On the table sat a gallon gascan, tools. A once-translucent plastic siphon hung on the wall behind it. He picked them up and pried the lid from a barrel. When the can was full they went to Fogel's truck and Fogel emptied the fuel into the tank. He put the can into the bed and David sat on the tailgate while they drove to the garage. Fogel backed the truck to the barrels and David set the two by fours up against the tailgate and they rolled a barrel to the ramp. They pushed it up onto the bed and leapt after it to stand it up. David jumped over the side and Fogel closed the tailgate.

Heard something from a railroad buddy this morning. Said they've been kicking droves of folks off cars. Whole families. Apparently everyone's leaving the cities.

Where're they going?

Who knows. California? You always hear California's doin' okay.

Maybe we oughta give it a shot. David ground his hands together, wiping at the gritty feel of the diesel.

Don't know if I could deal with the hippies.

You think there are still hippies?

Maybe not. Fogel looked off, setting his hands on his hips and arching his back. Well, thank you. He walked around to the front of the truck. You ever need help with something you let me know. He stuck an arm out as he drove off.

8

It was just after harvest and the fields were full of stover. The wind never stopped and against any windbreak leaves and cornhusks built up and were covered in a thin layer of dust. Whirls of it before him in the street. The post office was only open once a week now, and he found a line of people waiting in the lobby. Carl Brown was filling out a card and David came up to him.

Haven't seen you in a while. I miss your haul?

Didn't have one. Replanted and nothing ever came above ground.

Shit, Carl. I'm sorry to hear that.

Here to give a forwarding address.

What?

Brown nodded. We got a buyer already. I feel kinda bad for 'em honestly. Nice little colored family, don't know what they're getting into.

David shook his head. I'm sorry to see you go.

She's got some family's gonna put us up. It's just what we need to do.

Well, good luck to you. David shook hands with him.

I appreciate it. He grimaced and fanned the card toward his face. I need to get this in.

David watched him slide the card to the clerk and when he went to leave David dipped his head to him. You take care.

You too.

He tightened his lips. He waited his turn and the woman got his mail. It was a single letter, from Red. He thanked her and put the letter in his back pocket and went out. At the square a gust of wind blew past him. It was after noon and the sky was beginning to cloud over in the west. It was getting cooler. He took the letter from his pocket and opened it and read it walking in the middle of the road.

Dave,

Told you I'd write. I'm gonna keep this short so I don't shock your system. There's a letter in here for the godson, too.

I wanted to let you know I traveled down to the Gulf just for shits and it ain't there anymore. The storm was worse than they said, or I guess people were too caught up in losing their oil. A lot of folks died and there's been looting, gangs running around. You wouldn't think this was America. You'd think we were still fighting Jimenez in the shit. The place is a wasteland. People are pouring in from Mexico. Apparently they got their own drought.

This isn't much of a letter. As promised, I guess. I just want to make sure you've got your shit together. Give everyone my best. I come by this address every so often, so you can write back. I'm doing fine. Hope you are too.

Keep your head down,
Red

He read the letter over again and put it back in the envelope. The address was somewhere in Utah. At home he set the letter on the counter and started in on the pile of books he'd gotten from the library and from Danvers. Old schematic books with thin yellow paper, full of drawings and diagrams of plows and yokes and seed drills. He studied them for a while, then got a notepad and began listing supplies. Beside some entries he put asterisks to mark what he might scavenge from abandoned farmhouses and his own equipment. When he finished the list he heard footsteps on the porch and for a moment he waited for the skitter of Macha's paws on the wood floor. Helene and Samuel came in and David stood to meet them.

Hey.

Hi Dad. Samuel began taking off his shoes.

You got a letter from Red. It's in the kitchen.

Really? Samuel lit up, running past him. David smiled and Helene met his eye.

How was school?

She shook her head. I'm just wondering why there isn't any dinner waiting for me.

Guess I could make some eggs. Eggs work?

She started for the kitchen and he followed her. Samuel was reading the letter, rapt. It was a full page long. When David stood by him Samuel began to drift into the hall and went upstairs.

Helene stood over the table for a moment. What are all these books?

Schematics. Gonna have to build some new equipment for next year. Between this and no-till it's about all I got for ideas.

You'll figure it out. She opened a cabinet and pulled out a skillet.

Somehow that doesn't make me any less tired.

Red wrote?

Yeah. Mostly bad news. The phone rang and he looked toward the hallway.

You can tell me later.

David sighed to himself and stood to answer. It was Glenn Fogel. They talked about their harvest and Carl Brown briefly, what their plans were for next season.

What I really called for was to tell you I got a present for you. Sort of.

Oh yeah?

I picked up a couple draft horses. Figure if I let you use one it'll about pay back the diesel you gave me.

Hell. That wadn't anything.

Yeah, it was. It got me through the season, believe it or not. We had to pick some of the corn by hand but that's what I got a son for. I'd of broke my back without that barrel.

Well, I'm glad to give it. They talked for several more minutes, David trying to get off the phone. Finally he thanked him and hung up. David came back into the kitchen, smiling to himself.

Helene spoke from over her shoulder. Talking to your girlfriend?

Fogel. Man can talk a leg off a wooden chair, sometimes.

She turned at the stove to look at him. Imagine being married to him. Becky's a saint.

After dinner they sat on the porch. Helene put Samuel to bed and when she came to their room they stood together, undressing in the dark. She was quiet and when they lay down he put his arms around her and felt her tense.

What's the matter?

We had a meeting today. The school was waiting on money from the state and we just got word that it isn't coming. The state's bankrupt. There's not enough money for next year. For anything. We would have shut down earlier like the other schools if the mine hadn't been doing so well.

He frowned against her shoulder. I'm sorry, mother. He leaned to see her face and the side of her mouth tugged. I saw that. Go on and smile.

She smiled. She rolled over to face him. I'd better do it now, huh?

He would have spoken about the letter but her face was so sad and what light there was showed in her eyes all liquid. He kissed her. Her chest sank.

Sam will be eleven in six months.

I know.

Did you ever imagine yourself getting so old?

We're not old.

I know. But did you?

No. He pulled her closer so that he didn't have to look at her. I think I skipped from the church steps to the hospital to us sittin' in rocking chairs on the front porch.

She laughed against him. They were quiet a while. What if we left?

He let a slow breath through his nose. Fogel mentioned folks are leaving all over.

Oh?

Trains full of people running out of cities.

Maybe they have the right idea.

She had said it lightly and he said nothing else but the idea stayed with him.

9

He built the equipment through the winter with Danvers overseeing. He was thankful for the work and to be as busy as he was. Every morning he let the cattle into the cornfields and he and Samuel drove them in every night and he watched the little snow that fell stick in the ditches along the roadside and turn red from dust. Whenever he held his hammer or sat his bay he heard the wind and nearly saw it, the dust it carried. Saw it in currents plying around him like a stone in a creek. Watching Samuel swoop and flank the herd one evening he stopped and Helene's words came to him. He thought that now was the chance to leave, to take what they could and get away. For a moment he could feel the horse under him tense and the adrenaline pumped into him but he didn't move. It deadened in his limbs and weighted them and slowly he held up the reins and rode toward the cattle.

The days got longer. There seemed to be a new season between winter and spring which was timeless. The trees in the yard began to bud and stopped, the red in them fading until they were the same color as the bark. He watered the trees occasionally but it did nothing. The morning of Samuel's eleventh birthday David read an article in the paper that said a farmer across the state line had been robbed and beaten to death, his corpse eaten by his dogs.

David had made a seed drill from the diagram and tried it with his bay on the northern field, working for several days before he called Fogel and had him bring down the draft. It was hard work and tedious, following the draft to check the row units, stooping. To the south a tail of dust rose thin, someone plowing. When the sun swung over to the west he had Danvers call Fogel for the horse and they met outside the barn. David twisted at his hips, stretching, and he looked at the pasture between the buildings. The draft was tied to the side of the barn.

Thanks for the animal.

My pleasure. Same time tomorrow?

Much as I'd like to sleep in.

Fogel smiled. David looked again toward the pasture and he saw something dark red come burning up out of the ground to the south. The blood drained away from his face and pooled in his stomach. He reached for Fogel and caught him by the arm.

What in God's name? Is it a fire?

The scrim of red rose higher as they watched and it seemed to undulate and twist. It grew taller still before David moved. Jesus. He started running for the house. He heard Fogel behind him. He was already on the gravel and pounding up onto the porch. He opened the door and shouted in. Sam?

Helene started to the hallway from the kitchen. He's at the library. What's wrong?

Shut the windows tight. There's some kind of storm coming. David ran out as Fogel reached the porch and he tossed an arm at the truck and he'd already started backing when Fogel dove into the bed. He tore out of the short drive and onto the road. He was still staring at the storm as they pulled into town and he slowed the truck by the flower shop long enough for Fogel to leap out. David drove south down the middle of the street as the red came on over the town, the creek consumed, sun blotted. It knuckled across the ground like an enormous fist, its bottom black and the top rearing far overhead. He pulled over short of the library and when he killed the engine the first wave of dust hit the windshield. There was a bundle on the sidewalk and in the thickening haze he made out the shoes at the bottom. He opened the truck door and was stung and blinded, the door slamming behind him. The grit stuck in his teeth as he called to Samuel and the bundle moved. David pulled his shirt off and looped his free arm under the boy and put the collar of the shirt up against his mouth. He scooped Samuel under his arm and spun, the truck gone in the rust, and ran into the bed. He opened the door and dropped Samuel on the bench seat and climbed in after him. He lifted Samuel's face to his and saw his eyes raw and colorless in the twilight. Samuel said nothing but clung to David and buried his face in his chest. David put his arms around him and peered out the windshield. The front of the truck had disappeared.

Are you alright? He heard nothing back. He leaned to the glovebox with Samuel in his lap and took out a bottle of water. The light inside popped. Look at me. He tilted Samuel's face up again. Keep your eyes open. He cradled the back of his head and poured the water just above his brow. Samuel blinked. The water ran streaks down his face and David stopped to let him breathe. He took a drink and offered the bottle and Samuel drank. He shuddered and pushed away to sit next to David. They both looked out at the void around them. The sidewalk was visible beside the truck and nothing beyond it. The dust hissed along and it collected and swirled on the windshield. The truck tilted. He watched Samuel wipe his face with the shirt. Are you okay?

Samuel picked at his eye. Yeah. He was about to say more when a bluish arc of light crossed the hood of the truck. The mirrors grew horns like gas torches. Dad.

It's okay. We're safe in here. He reached to start the truck and static shot his hand out and lit the cab. He swore and grabbed the key again but nothing happened. He rubbed at his numb fingers. The air outside was dark, the only light coming from the flamelike projections on the side mirrors. He could barely make out the shape of Samuel's face and hands. We'll just have to wait a while. It'll die down soon. He thought he saw him nod. The dust had built halfway up the windshield.

I was trying to run home.

I know.

I left my book.

We'll get it. He listened to the wind. There was a watch in the change tray and he picked it up and examined it but couldn't read the time. They sat. He guessed twenty minutes had passed when it seemed to get lighter, slowly so that he had to close his eyes and judge the change by memory. It wasn't long after that they could see past the hood of the truck and then the curb and down the street. The head of the storm was moving over the tops of the houses and stores. It tumbled like smoke, like a twister fallen over. He waited a moment and opened the truck door and stepped out. Dust fell from the cab and was carried off by the dying wind. Samuel got out on the other side and walked around to him and they stood in the street. He'd stopped the truck half on the sidewalk. The walls of the bank and the other stores were drifted up with dust. The gutters were filled, the dust flowed up onto the curb and the streets and alleys and any standing place where there was purchase was covered. David took his shirt from inside the truck and slung it out and slipped it on. The sky was scoured white. The sun itself seemed raw. They both stood in the street a few minutes longer, joined by the few storekeepers and townfolk who came out blinking and some of them leaning against each other or the dirty walls of their homes. Fogel and his wife stepped out of the flower shop. David got back in the truck to start it, the engine misfiring once and turning over. Through the open door he saw Samuel dig through the sand and shake his library book out before climbing in. They drove toward home. A woman was already sweeping dust out her front door. They sped up outside of town and David saw the color of the soil had turned to what had fallen. The storm, umber now, was crawling over the northeast like a plague of insects. They pulled into the drive and David called out at the front door.

Helene?

There was a noise from the bedroom. In here.

He opened the door. Helene came out of the bathroom dragging bunched-up blankets and pillows from the tub. Are you alright?

She dropped the bedclothes. Yeah.

You just set in the tub and waited?

I couldn't budge the mattress. She shrugged. What was that?

I dunno. He looked at Samuel. Just dust, a dust storm.

Helene sat on the bed. I watched out the backdoor after you left and you would have thought—I don't even know. She shook her head and brushed a hand across the bare bed. Her palm came away red. I guess we'd better start cleaning.

I need to check on the animals. And the old man, for that matter.

She sighed and nodded.

I'll be back to help in a bit. David leaned across the bed to kiss her and he gripped Samuel's shoulder. The wooden floors were coated finely with dust, their tracks from the front door brushed through. He went down the road to Danvers' and knocked at the side door but there was no answer. The latch on one of the stalls clacked to. Danvers came out of the barn and put a hand up.

I put Fogel's horse inside. Boys got a little spooked, nearly busted out the sidewall.

They okay?

Peachy.

Are you?

Oh yeah. Little duster never bothered me.

Is that what they call those?

What I used to hear 'em called.

David rubbed his forehead. Think it's screwed me over?

Hard tellin'. Danvers turned to look at the field to the north. You haven't plowed so you ought to be okay. Everybody who did just lost all their topsoil.

He nodded. Have you seen any of the cattle?

No. I imagine you're okay. Take more than that to suffocate a cow.

David went by and Danvers watched him tack up the bay. He led the horse out of the barn and put his foot in the stirrup and stood up onto the horse. He grimaced at Danvers. Worried about all this.

I would be. I am.

David clicked his tongue and Danvers walked beside him and opened the gate. The grass and the bare trees were dusted and along the fenceposts were small piles of sand. David rode to the creek and he sighted the herd around a locust. They were all aground and he appraised and counted them. He dropped from the horse and walked over to the nearest heifer. Her eyes gummed and her coat matted and coarse but aside from that nothing. He wandered afoot, watching the dust rise and stopping once to pinch the dry grass and eye the grains on his fingers, to blow them clean. He rode clear to the edge of his property and he put his hand atop a fencepost and stayed that way staring south. He felt the slight warmth of the sun on his face and he felt it fade. He'd closed his eyes without realizing and found he was praying. His breathing tight and heavy through his nostrils with his head bowed and the sensation of his chest expanding beyond its bounds, something white and hot reaching out from it.

10

He gave himself the morning to rest and in the dull early light saw the dust everywhere, on everything, even though they'd cleaned. It was on the blinds and curtains and tabletops. Samuel came downstairs and Helene was drinking chicory coffee at the table and both of them were bland from light and dust. The only color he seemed to see was from Samuel's eyes, cold and electric, like the sky through frosted glass. Like his own. He felt tired, restless. Alien to the house and to Helene and Samuel. He passed a hand through his hair and felt the sand caught there. When they finished eating breakfast he showered and dressed. He found Helene in the backyard, bringing in the laundry from the clothesline and they said nothing about the dust that shook out of the sheets or that rose from their footsteps on the lawn when they went to tne backdoor. David held it open for her.

I'm gonna go into town for a bit.

Why?

There's that family that moved into Brown's old house. I've been meaning to go out and introduce myself for a while.

And you think today's a good day to do it?

As good as any. I don't want to work the horses so soon, so I can't do any planting.

She stood on the step, laundry basket on her knee. Her eyes sharpened and she went inside. The door slapped shut behind her.

All the houses in town were open to sweep out the dust. David raised a hand to the people he passed and they nodded gravely and returned to their work. At the square the intersection had been swept to one corner and the dust there reached almost mid-calf. He went on out of town toward Brown's farmhouse, the land in the distance hazed with a dry fog, the cell tower a mile off a thin spike dividing the sky. There were tracks going through the yard and he followed them to the porch, swept clean. He knocked on the front door and stepped back. Someone walked up and a girl a year or so older than Samuel opened the door and stood there with her hand on the frame.

Yeah?

David smiled. Hi. I'm just here to introduce myself. Are your parents home?

Are you sellin' somethin'?

No. I'm a farmer.

She raised her head and disappeared into the house with the door wide. A few moments later she returned behind her mother. The woman put her hand on the frame above her daughter's.

Can I help you?

I'm David Parrish. I wanted to welcome you to town, see if there was anything I could do for you.

You're a little late for the committee.

I'm sorry I didn't get out here earlier. We've been switching out equipment and planting. Between that and everything else, well.

The mother held her mouth tight and finally she put her hand out. I'm Delia. That's Melanie, behind me.

David shook her hand. Pleased to meet you. Melanie stayed where she was.

My husband is out back workin' on the windmill if you'd like to see him.

Thank you. He stepped off the porch and went around the house to the backyard. The windmill was set deep into the property where Brown had grown hay. Last season's crop stood wilted and beat low. There was a path trod in the hay and at the end of it a man bent over the pump of the windmill. David waved when the man rose up. The man wiped his hands on his jeans and took a step forward.

What can I do for you?

I'm David Parrish. I farm on the east side of town. About five months late introducing myself.

The man smiled wide and put his hand out. O H Reckard.

David shook. That stand for anything?

He shrugged. The story goes my Daddy didn't trust the hospital. Thought they'd charge him for the ink to print my name.

No foolin'?

No foolin'. Though some would say the O stands for ornery.

They were quiet for a moment, both with dimming grins. David turned aside. How're you doing out here?

Well, we're fine so far. But we haven't had to do any real work yet, either.

You farm before you came here?

Nope. From Atlanta. Born in South Georgia. I was a country boy for a while, moved into town when I was about ten. Did a two-year stint in the desert, moved to the big city when I got back.

What branch?

Marines.

Army.

Oh yeah? O H leaned against a leg of the windmill.

Talamanca Mountains.

Oh, man. I heard that was it.

David nodded, quiet for a moment. What brought you all the way out here?

Had a good job working for Coca-Cola until the factory closed down. After about four months this man on the street-corner stands up on a box and starts yellin' about how the government was tanking. Said there wasn't any way they could run the city anymore. Month after that the hurricane came through. Then there was nothin'. No water, no power. He paused. So I loaded up the car and we drove as far as we could. Around East St. Louis, and I swear to you, that same soapbox guy showed up a little bit dirtier-lookin' and said 'Farmland for the taking. Farm, best chance they is.'

David kept back a laugh and O H smiled.

Gave us a flyer with a phone number on it and that's about how it went. We lived outta the car for a couple weeks. Worked a shit bank security job in Banning until they went under. One day I called the number and they showed me the place, I bought it. He spread his arms at the hayfield and everything around them. And here we are. Farmers.

Well, you probably couldn'a picked a better town. I hear it's worse just about everywhere else. Have you started planting yet?

Huh uh.

You know how you're gonna plant?

Huh uh.

David raised an eyebrow at him. You got anything to plant?

It's already in the ground, ain't it? The bank said—

Oh, bud. No. David smiled. He watched O H look at the field. The hay's up just because there was nobody here to cut it down. Everybody around here just started planting.

O H grinned crookedly. Shit. He braced his hands on the crosspiece behind him.

What have you bought besides the house?

You're lookin' at it. We got a pig in the side pen, came with the place.

Well. That's a good thing then. Means you haven't sunk any money. He scanned along the ground like he might find a solution there. David put his hand to his mouth. He took it away. You got a couple options. You can try to stick it out to next year on what money you've got, buy up to be ready then.

Or you can stand in front of me when I tell my wife I'm gonna help you plant when I finish my own fields.

O H tapped the strut under his arm. I tell you what. Here's a third option. He lifted his hand in the air and trotted two fingers along. You walk backwards out of here and I keep workin' on this pump and time'll just go in reverse right up until I forget the bad news.

I can try that if you like.

Son of a bitch. He shook his head. First that sandstorm, then this. I mean I ain't afraid of a day's work.

You want to talk it over with your wife?

I'd better. She'll probably throw me out either way.

David pivoted on his heel to see the house. I oughta tell you too. No water comin' up?

Dry as a bone.

It ain't because it broke. There's no water to be had.

Man, you are just a black cloud. He shook his head. He pushed off the windmill and they started for the house. I wonder how long it would'a took me to figure it out.

Couple months?

Longer, probably. Probably not until someone was eatin' a ear of corn in front of me.

David laughed. I'll swing by tomorrow morning, get your answer?

Sure. If I'm hangin' from a tree you don't need to call the police. It was Delia, justifiable homicide.

He winced. They came to the patio door and O H opened it, Melanie at the kitchen table playing solitaire.

Wife?

What did you call me? They heard Delia from the front room.

I called you wife. Did you go and change that? I gotta sign those papers too, you know.

You keep callin' me wife and you'll be seein' those papers. She came into the kitchen from around a corner.

We got things to talk about.

Like your failin' memory? She put a hand on her hip.

Like that, yeah.

David began to sidle away. It was nice meeting you all.

You too.

He nodded to O H and walked to the front door. From the road he scanned the southwest for signs of a storm and found the fields and horizon vacant.

The weeks were long. He took the last of the diesel and ruined the irrigators with it, let them run and water the crop a final time. He watched them roll, water fanning down onto the earth. Standing in the dry grass and kicking up the smell of summer months early. When the irrigators hit new dust it lifted like a red fog, settled, melted. O H and he split the cost of a pair of mules from an old farmer outside Banning and finished the fields. The farmer told them he couldn't hack the work. When David asked him what he was going to do he said he didn't know.

11

It was a quiet day weeks from harvest. There was a moment to himself in the kitchen when he saw the letter from Red on a stack of old mail and he wrote a reply, telling him of all the recent events and asking him to write back. It had rained long enough to turn the dust to a sludge that dried smooth and Samuel and Melanie were in the yard breaking plates of it from the ground and throwing them against the trees and fenceposts. David scooped up two shards and rapped them both over the back of their heads and ran, boots punching through the molded dust, plates thrown after him and shattering on the road, both of them shouting after him and laughing.

Riding into town the dust had run thick in the gutters and coated the siding of houses in a shell. It had been trod through in the middle of the street and dried and turned the sides of boots the color of clay. He slid the letter in the outgoing slot at the post office and walked on up the street. O H was eating in the diner and David went in and sat at the counter with him. He ordered coffee. The waitress brought it to him and he sat over it.

Ready to start shuckin'?

Not really. How long you think it'll take?

Long as Fogel and some other folks help, couple weeks. Go through all the other farms, our fields. We still havin' a party?

Course we are. Roastin' up the pig, too.

How'd Mel take that?

Hell, she don't care. Never gave it a name. She's a city

girl. Should'a heard her the first time I sent her out there to clean the pen.

He drank and looked out the diner window. Speaking of.

A group of children crossed the street, Samuel and Melanie with them. A boy shoved Samuel and David stood from his seat but Samuel spun around and pushed back with a smile. The other boy ran a circle and they stopped. Skillman had met the group. He doffed his hat to them and he bent down and pulled out a handful of change, smiling at a woman passing by as he did.

Huh. David breathed over the rim of his cup. Every time I try to hate that man he goes and does something like that.

Never met him.

Well I guarantee he'll come in if he sees me. Just you wait.

The children passed around Skillman and he was grinning. He walked by the diner peeking in and stopped. The bell rang when he opened the door and came to the counter.

Howdy folks. He leaned over the counter, removed his hat and looked at O H. I haven't had the pleasure.

O H Reckard.

He put out his hand. Charles Skillman. You can call me Chuck or Charlie or whatever suits you. I answered to Chubs once upon a time.

O H smiled and shook. Mr. Skillman works.

Works for me, too. You own that land 'bout a quarter mile west of town.

That's me. O H stuck a toothpick into a pickle slice and ate it. He cut his eyes toward David. Well, I got to get back. Delia's liable to put me on a spit if I don't do some work today. Probably gonna anyways, going out to eat.

David smiled. I'll see you.

He turned to Skillman. Good to meet you.

Likewise.

O H paid and left. Skillman stood off from the counter and turned to David.

How's business?

Not the best.

I'm sorry to hear it.

David studied the last of his coffee, the flat prism of oil on its surface. I have a hard time believing you got to where you are by taking whatever name people want to call you. Knockin' your forehead against the ground.

Skillman faced the counter again and raised his eyebrows. You never know. Maybe that's exactly how I got here. He breathed in. I hired Jacob Miller on a while ago.

Yeah?

Mhm. We've got a position or two still. Got some new seams. He waited for a reply and none came. Jake sang your praises. And you know I like you anyway.

Are you offerin' me a job?

Part time. Work around your needs.

He finished his coffee and pushed the cup forward. I'm tryin' to decide whether or not I ought to be offended.

It's not charity. I'm not softening you up.

You say that.

Skillman paused a moment then smacked the heel of his hand on the counter. You are god damned hard to deal with, you know that? He glanced up at the waitress and frowned. Sorry ma'am. He took up his hat and left.

———

At the beginning of harvest some of the local farmers and their families gathered, going from field to field to pick the corn. They brought mules for carts and buckets, chairs to sit in when shucking. The men and older children went along the rows pitching the ears into carts. Melanie drove a wagon. When David called Fogel to see when he wanted help he said there wasn't any need. He'd plowed his fields with the draft and the duster carried everything away.

The day after the last field O H made a bonfire at the house and roasted the hog. He and David stayed near the fire, rotating the spit and watching Melanie and Samuel run in and out of a remaining stand of corn, hiding from each other.

Hey, you got this?

David nodded. Sure.

O H smiled and ran to the rows, disappearing.

David turned to the table, and Helene met his eyes.

Where's he get his energy?

Wish I knew. I could use some. David let the spit swing back and put his hands in his pockets, sighing. Delia came out the back door with a pitcher of lemonade and circled the table, pouring glasses full. David took up his glass and drank.

It's just Kool-Aid. We don't have any lemons.

I ain't picky.

Shame we couldn't get Phil out here.

Yeah. He doesn't leave the house much anymore.

Helene looked at David and nodded toward the corn. You want to bring the children in for dinner?

Delia flicked her hand at the field. Leave O H out there. If he don't wear himself out he won't sleep tonight.

David laughed and started for the corn. The stalks were brittle dry and he could hear them shifting all around them, the footsteps of one of the children. He walked between the rows and saw the flash of Melanie and then of Samuel.

Time to eat, kids. He heard them running deeper into the stand. O H was standing still and straight the next row over. He came to life grinning.

Smell that pig, man. I'm dyin'.

Well let's get at it. He yelled for the kids to come out and they waited at the edge of the field, Melanie and Samuel staggering through to the open air, breathless. David batted Samuel on the back as he passed and they sat at the table to eat. David banked the fire enough to get at the hog and O H began cutting portions. They came to the table and everyone sat and passed the food around. The sun began to set and when they finished eating they set up tents of sheets near the fire. When the sun was down David fed the fire and it grew high and they all sat watching the flames.

⊩━━━━━━━━━━➤

At the end of October O H came to the house and they stood on the porch with the air cool and dry and the trees bare, shriveled leaves sticking up out of mounds of dust. O H took a letter out of his pocket and set it on the railing.

Bank jacked our rates up.

What for?

Hell, I dunno. Cuz it's Monday?

David sighed.

Apparently they're doing it to everyone. Delia said she heard on the radio a deputy got shot tryin' to serve an eviction notice.

Sounds like old times.

Yeah. You wanna start selling bathtub gin? Just for authenticity's sake.

You'd do better making whiskey around here.

O H nodded. I can do that. He took up the letter and glanced around like he might throw it away. What should I do?

Oh hell, bud. Like I know. I'd be in your shoes if Phil hadn't just given us everything. This place was his. Land was all his. Signed it over to me when he got too old to hack it.

Well, what do you think farmwise? You think we can make it work?

He shook his head. I do not know. They quieted. Feel like I don't know a damn thing, sometimes. With these storms I'm half-tempted to pull stakes, go someplace where the dirt ain't trying to eat us.

O H gave a stiff smile.

Unless the weather turns there won't be a profit for a while. You greenhorns flooded the market, margins are thinner.

Hey, I'm just doin' what the man with the cardboard sign told me.

Yeah, they always steer you right. He rubbed at his cheek and looked at the field beside the house. The doubling of fence where the grazing land stopped and the broken cornstalks began. He watched O H picking at his nails. What if we moved you out here?

What do you mean?

He thumbed to their right. Take an acre and put up a little house. Work with me.

You serious?

He nodded to himself. Yeah, I'm serious. We bust our asses helping each other and it's just driving corn prices to the ground. This way we solve a little of both problems. He'd leaned and set his forearms on the porch railing. Have you told Delia?

No. I'm hidin'.

What I thought. Go tell her.

O H looked at him. He shook his head slightly. You're some kind a saint or somethin'.

David soured his face. I'm gainin' just as much as you.

Whatever you say. They shook hands and he stepped off the porch. You think your wife'll go for it?

I imagine. Be more worried about yours.

You sure?

David waved him off. Good luck. He watched O H go, and had his hand on the door when he heard the snap of cloth from the clothesline. He stepped off the porch to go around the house and found Helene shaking out sheets. Her hair was over her face.

I am more than fed up with this dust.

He helped her take another sheet off the line and they flung their arms up and down and rattled the sheet between them. So, mother. He let the sheet settle. You talk to Delia about how they're doin'?

How do you mean?

Moneywise.

They're not well off, if that's what you're asking. She began to fold the sheet and joined her hands. He mirrored her movements and they stepped together.

I guess. They met hands and she took the sheet from him. I told O H I'd help him build a little house.

She'd bent to put the sheet in the clothesbasket. You what? Where?

Here. He pointed across the yard to the field beside the house.

She straightened up. She seemed taller than she ought.

I couldn't think of anything else to do for them.

How exactly are we gonna help them when we're going to have a time feeding ourselves this winter?

He shook his head. I won't be buyin' anything. Just let a acre go and donate some time. He watched her walk back to the line to take a pair of jeans down. I can't farm all this land by myself. With O H helping out we can get it done. It's probably the only way we can.

She folded the jeans and set them in the basket.

What do you think?

She stared at him and put a hand on her side, waving the other toward the field. I don't know, David. I trust you.

It'll be nice. Having them right next door. We've never really had neighbors. Just Phil.

Mhm. She thinned her lips. You can't work for free, you know.

I don't.

If I didn't pay attention you'd give the shirt off your back to any man on the street. Then you'd ask if they needed mine.

He smiled and tried not to laugh. It's a prettier sight, at least.

I'm serious, David. What if you got hurt? If you broke your leg putting their roof on we'd be done. I don't think you realize how close we are. We can't afford you getting laid up.

He sobered. Well. I dunno. I don't know that we can afford not to try, sometimes. We wouldn't have got through this season without that horse Fogel lent us. And that was payback for the diesel. Everything you're looking at right now was given to us by Phil.

I suppose. She took another pair of jeans down.

It can't ever be the wrong thing to do.

I know your views on right and wrong. Helene folded the jeans and looked at him. She paused and set the jeans down and came forward. Tell me what you'll do when it comes down to feeding us or doing the right thing.

Don't start this again.

She shook her head a little ruefully.

Haven't you noticed how much happier Sam seems? When he's around Mel it's like he's actually a kid. Having her right next door'll be good for him.

Of course I've noticed. But I know that's incidental to bringing them here. You just saw another opportunity to help someone and you had to take it. For whatever reason.

He stopped from grating his teeth.

I'm not letting you out of this. Tell me what would happen if you had to choose, one day. Would you let us go hungry?

He tried not to back away from her or turn his head. He tried to match her gaze, intense and dark, hooded by lack of sleep. No.

No? You haven't said no to anyone yet, David. Except Skillman, and he's the only man around who could help us. You've said yes to everyone who's asked. Helene shifted her feet. You're so hellbent on protecting Sam from life and death and all these things in the future and you don't see that we're one step away from having nothing. She stopped. We have to come first. Sam has to come first.

He does.

He doesn't. Sam in twenty years does. You want him to have this perfect life you never had and it's already too late for it. He was never you to begin with, and this— She lifted her arms to the land around them. This land isn't even yours. You're not a farmer. It's not in your blood.

It could be in Sam's. That's just what I'm working for.

She shook her head.

It starts somewhere. It could start with him.

But this is all we have. This is what we have, right now. And we might not even have that for long. We might not get the time you asked for. That's what I'm trying to tell you. We have to feed Sam to adulthood before you can bequeath him anything.

But if we're not trying for that.

She waved him off. Go ahead and build the house, David. If it makes you feel better. She went to the clothesline. She looked as spent as he felt, and thinner. What are you making up for?

He'd moved to the back door, and didn't turn to answer. He waited a moment and opened the door.

12

Materials for the shack were scrounged wherever they could find them. Wood and shingles from abandoned barns, a torn-down shed. For insulation they used cornhusks and old newspaper. They found an antique outhouse in a backyard a few miles out of town and hauled it intact to the rear of the shack. The roof was put on in mid-November. The weather was dry and the southerly wind was strong again. There were two storms before they finished and David knew dust would fall endlessly inside. All through building he watched his cattle roam about the field behind the house and he could hear them snorting. The soil was being covered over with the dust and the empty yard of the new house and the fields and the road were much alike, redbrown and smooth. Broken cornstalks sticking up out of the sand. Through the construction Samuel dragged Melanie back and forth to the library and when he came home one day David found him reading a novel about a soldier. He had to stop himself from taking it away.

It was early afternoon and they were nearly finished painting the shack. They were at the rear wall with the bucket of whitewash and a pail of milky water. A film of dirt was on the surfaces of both and the paint on the walls gritty, the brushes heavy with dust. They had been painting for a few hours. O H dropped his paintbrush into the water and wiped at his hands, stretching.

I'm goin' into town for beer.

David dipped his brush into the water and shook it out. Okay. He watched O H round the corner. The southern sky was white and it cleared as he drew his eyes north. He took the brush out and started painting again. He'd finished the wall himself and was thinking about giving the whole house another coat when O H appeared holding two six-packs, a few beers missing already, and waved him in. They sat at the table picking at the flecks of paint on their skin and looking around the interior, the dirt floor and bare walls. The windows from a collapsed barn with hazy glass. The house was dark. They were quiet for a while, crowded, pressed in.

O H raised his beer. A toast.

To what?

To havin' no further to fall.

David took his beer and held it up slowly. They touched bottoms and drank.

I saw somethin' different in my mind when you said 'build a house.' Dirt floors. Dirt fuckin' floors.

It could be worse. We'll get some floorboards in soon.

O H looked at him. You tell my family that. Tell them it could be worse than walkin' on a dirt floor in they own home. We had a house back in Atlanta. Bigger than yours.

We'll build you a better one when there's money.

Yeah. He craned his head up and put his arm over the back of the chair. Jesus.

What?

You can't know what this feels like.

David said nothing. He finished his beer and got another.

I guess I thought it sounded good. Sounded good on paper. But lookit this place. It's bad enough for me but puttin' Mel in here. I don't know, Dave. I don't know if I can take it. Livin' on your property and workin' for you.

You're not working for me. You're working with me.

O H ignored him.

Call it yours.

He brought his gaze to level.

Call the place yours. It's yours.

He began to laugh. I love you man, but you are fuckin'

clueless.

David stared at him, his beer halfway to his lips.

Don't even. Don't even worry about it. You mean well. Just shut up.

David held the beer still, then raised it and drank. He twisted the ends of the can in his hands and crushed it between them. He drank another. They were quiet again for a long while and David could feel the alcohol working on his empty stomach. Dust began dripping and flowing down from the ceiling as if it were suspended in oil, falling in seams before them. The windows had gone opaque, brown and nearly lightless. David stood up and the chair skidded in the dirt and he lurched and caught himself on the table.

It's another storm.

O H smiled. More floor. He wiped the mouth of his beer with his shirt and drank. G'won home.

David went to the door and stood by it for a moment. He opened it and a window creaked and a draft sucked through. O H brushed his hand over the table to send him on and David ducked out. Everything was rust-colored and turning darker. He raised his shirt up over his nose and held it and went out of the lee of the house and nearly fell over from the wind and the sting of the sand. He pressed his shirt to his mouth and began to walk with his eyes closed. A few steps out he stumbled over a cornstalk and fell, another stalk jagging across the inside of his arm. The shirt was ripped from his face and he choked and turned away. It was as though he were rushing through a black tunnel. To the north there was a weak light, the shapes of trees and fenceposts in silhouette. He got to his knees and stumbled forward with his hand shielding his eyes. The ground was almost visible and by the vague shape of his boots he followed his steps and found his way to the porch. He stepped inside and closed the door and slumped against it, picking the dust from his eyelids.

David?

Yeah. He heard Helene coming from the kitchen. A flashlight blinded him.

Are you okay? You're bleeding.

I fell. Is the power out?

On and off. She knelt in front of him and lifted his arm. Let me get some water.

I'm okay. He took her hand and she stopped mid-rise. The house creaked.

You smell like beer.

O H wanted to drink.

She stood. Go shower. She handed him the flashlight. Here. Don't come out until you're sober.

She left. There was a dim brown light coming through the back window and candlelight flitting off the kitchen walls. He rolled onto his hands and stood and went into the bathroom. His face was ghoulish in the mirror, eyes ringed with dust and swollen red, hashmark abrasion on his cheekbone. He undressed and turned on the shower. The water ran cold and he sat down, a stripe of brown flowing to the drain, swirling. The lights went out and the pipes choked and stopped. He made sure the shower was off and waited with his arms on his knees, his head down and eyes closed, dripping. Eventually he stood and dried in the dark. The flashlight was in the sink and he clicked it on. He damped a cloth with alcohol and swabbed his arm. It stung sharp and cold and he took the cloth away and dropped it on the pile of his clothes and dressed in the bedroom. When he finished he stepped into the hall with the flashlight in hand. All the windows were dark and the wind was still high and moaning against the house. The children were on the floor in the kitchen, Samuel and Melanie at the window, staring out over their breath on the glass. Helene was sitting at the table with Delia. They looked at him as he crept by, stepping past the children to get to the basement. With the door open he could just see the stairs. He went carefully and opened the breaker door by feel and switched on the flashlight. He reset the breaker and the kitchen lights came on. As he mounted the wooden staircase the breaker popped and the lights blacked. Helene came to the door.

We tried. It just keeps shorting out.

Yeah.

We've got dinner ready.

He climbed the steps. The children had started eating and their spoons clacked against the soup bowls. He hadn't heard them nor smelled the beef stew simmering. He ladled a bowl for himself at the stove and leaned against the backdoor. Helene was back at the table with Delia, Helene without a bowl. You gonna eat?

I've been picking at it since I started cooking.

He said nothing. He tried to see out the window but there was only the reflection of them all, candlelit. Delia was looking at him.

Where's Ornery?

He stayed. David stared into his bowl. I think he wanted to see if he could patch any holes the dust was comin' through.

The duster didn't let up until late in the evening, and it was after midnight before all of the children were picked up. The night was black enough it seemed the storm hadn't passed. He came out onto the porch with the flashlight and started backwards when he swept the beam over the yard. Everything the light touched was dust, covered over, feet high. It was as if the house had fallen upon Mars. High drifts across the road rose at fenceposts and troughed between like a stone wave, and where it was able the dust rolled evenly across the field and yard. Shadowed undulations in it like the paths of snakes. He switched off the light and stood in the dark listening to the soft breeze and there was an attic warmth to the air. It felt like he was still inside, in some other room. Through the gloom floated a single square of light from the shack and then the light was cut as O H stepped between.

The wind kept steady the next morning. He and Samuel

went out with woodworking masks and goggles tight on their faces. The back of the house was sloped up with sand as high as the kitchen windows and they dug out the backdoor and made a path to the shed. While Samuel finished, David strung a length of rope from the porch to the side of the shack to lead them between by feel. He met Samuel and they walked to the barn and got their horses and David hitched his to the cart for hay. It was slow going through the dust and David had to dismount to push the cart on, past the halfmoon of a calf fallen and nearly covered over. The wheel tracks and footprints filled in and were swept away. Two old cows and four yearlings had dropped and two were partly eaten. The living wandered across the new desert with strings of brown mucus hanging from their jowls. Samuel dug trenches to the ground and David tried to lead the cattle to the hay he'd brought but they were dumbstruck and even when roped to the bales, would not eat. He loosed a heifer and dropped against a dustpile. He sat there working the rope and glossing over the land when the wind shifted and the horses began to stamp.

Dad. Dad. Samuel was pointing past the herd at a thicket of dry brush grown around an old line of fencing, nearly buried in the drift. A ragged and mangy coyote had appeared from out of the cover and was trotting toward them. Samuel dropped his hand and the coyote broke into a sprint and leapt and was on him before David could move.

Dad! Samuel fell into the dust, the coyote atop him raking at his chest. Samuel tried to roll but the coyote shifted and ripped at the collar of Samuel's coat. David grabbed the shovel beside them and the coyote leapt too late, the blow ringing off its skull. It thrashed its head and David hit it again and it bared its teeth, stunned, and David flung the shovel away to lift the coyote by the throat, its legs swimming. He drove it into the piled sand until it began frothing and was dead. David let go of the coyote and stood. He breathed out and looked around himself and saw Samuel there staring with his coat ripped open and eyes wet and red. Motionless.

Oh, Sam. God, you okay bud?

He nodded. David trod over to him and pulled him close. He was stiff and turned his head from David's chest. He started to cough.

Alright. He stepped away. Let's go home. He tied a length of rope around the legs of one of the fallen yearlings and hauled it to the cart. Taking the reins he led the bay and they headed back. They put the cart and horses up and David rigged a pulley from the rafters to hang the yearling to butcher. Samuel started getting water for the animals and David watched him. He wasn't shaking that David could see. When Samuel finished David walked him to the road. I'm gonna talk to the old man real quick. Be okay going home?

Yeah.

David waited until he'd gone around the bend, then went back and knocked on Danvers' side door. It opened and Danvers peered down and stepped aside. I see you've been out in it.

Lost six head. He lifted the goggles from his eyes and blinked and rubbed at the seams pressed into his face. He followed Danvers in and shut the door. We've got a coyote problem.

Oh, do ya?

One went right for Sam. Jumped on him out of nowhere.

You take care of it?

Yeah.

Well, I can make you some traps if you like, show you how.

Whatever'll work. I just want to kill the damn things.

Find some cables and some stakes, tall ones. You don't need any fancy cages or anything. Danvers was by the counter and he was reaching down a glass from the cupboard. He set the glass on the countertop and cocked his head slightly. You look like hell, you know.

I believe it.

Danvers blew into the glass and filled it from the tap. He handed it out to David.

Thanks. He drank and breathed heavy through his nose. He drained the glass and put it on the kitchen table. The dust was thick over its surface.

You haven't been by lately. He waited on David to speak. Helene says you aren't at the house much, either. Said so when she dropped off one of them loaves of bread. Cleaned meanwhile. He gestured at the room, now dust-coated.

I've been busy. Money's tight.

You lookin' for some work?

Avoiding it. He looked off. Skillman offered.

Well, money can't be that tight then, if you can turn down a job.

David grimaced. He stretched the goggles over his forehead. Danvers stood there and when David turned he leaned forward as if to stop him. David had already slipped the goggles down and was out the door.

Outside the wind had picked up and a low red haze held over the land. Once out of Danvers' yard David stood in the road beside it and spun in place until he'd taken in the desert in panorama. The world seemed shortened. The fenceposts and trees all had their bottoms cut out from them and they stood now like children's versions of themselves. He imagined how the dunes must have built up against the shops in the center of town and how porches might be swallowed. The school playground with a dwarfed metal slide, swing-set chains sunk into the ground and the seats eaten up. He opened the front door and stepped inside. It was a Saturday but there were children in the house, along with Melanie, eating leftover stew in the living room. David smiled at them and went on to the kitchen. A pot was on the stove and there were rags hung up to dry on the curtain rods above the windows. He got a bowl of stew and sat eating when Helene came down the stairs. She was carrying dirty rags and when she looked at him she stopped.

Where've you been?

What do you mean? I was talking to Phil.

Samuel came home half-crying. He said a coyote attacked him?

Yeah.

He's scared to death, David.

I got it.

I know you did. I think that's what scared him.

David breathed in. His hands withdrew from the table.

Are you okay?

As good as I can be.

She stared at him.

Was I supposed to do something different?

I don't know. Maybe not choke the thing to death in front of your son and let him walk home alone?

He lifted a hand. It would have killed him. I killed it.

David. She closed her eyes. Can't you see this place is falling apart? How much more is it gonna take?

I don't know what to tell you, Helene. Things get tough. He stood.

In the shed he found a spool of cable and old railspikes and he got the shotgun from the ceiling and carried them down the road. Danvers showed him how to make the noose of the snare and to tie it to the stake. They took wire hangers and cut them to hold up the nooses. David took the snares into the pasture and planted them at the old fenceline where the coyote had emerged, digging through the sand until he hit solid ground. He could hear the sand grains tapping at the lens of his goggles. The freshest kill from his herd was nearby and he took out his pocketknife. There was a moment flickering in his head before he knelt and cut under the calf's ribs and dug out the heart from the chest. He cut the heartmeat like an apple and lay thick wedges of it on either side of the snares and he drove his forearm into the dust to scrub it, abrading the fluid and blood. He rose, patted his arm free of dirt. The wind snapped around him and he figured there was an hour of rusty daylight before he needed to return. The image of Samuel falling with the coyote atop him played and replayed in his mind. There was nothing to tend, no animals to husband. He waited out the daylight lying over a dune with the shotgun.

13

The next morning the sky above him was the same color as the sand below. After Samuel woke up, David gave him a shovel and told him to dig the fences around the house, always in sight, and rode out himself to dig the border fences and check the traps. They were empty and the hunks of heart buried and he dug them up and wiped them against his coat and laid them back. There was no way to tell if anything had been there. None of the animals had been taken down. He set to the fences and when the sun was fat and the land around him tepid with bronze light he watered the animals and went to the road. Helene came down the path and he forced a smile to meet hers.

Gonna butcher that calf?

Try to. She huffed. I see us sick of beef in the near future.

Well, I figured we'd give most of it away. Between the kids and Red's ma and mine. Cut down on leftovers.

She showed a little smile. It's not like I can turn them away.

I'm not complaining. Just sayin'. David looked down the road. I gotta go into town. He moved to go on and stopped, kissed her and felt the grit between their lips. He took his bay from the stall and rode, looking over his shoulder. Dixon lay buried under the sand, drifts reaching toward mailboxes and over porch steps. The streets were dug out a lane wide, the dust furrowed as high as the horse's belly. Ahead sat a nearly consumed car, the sand sinking in through an open window. He passed a few miners at the square headed toward the restaurant or the bar and their uniforms were a bland palette

of coal and red dust and worn blue cloth, Miller at the end
of the group. They ignored David as he rode by and Miller
split off to go in a door for the apartments above the diner.
David hitched the horse to the top of his mother's fence and
got down. The walkway was swept, the dust already sliding
back. His mother opened the door before he came in the yard.

Where's Sam at?

Home.

Well, get on in here before I have to sweep again.

He went inside with her, and she pushed him toward the
living room. He sat on the couch and she sat in a chair looking at him.

So what's the matter?

David pinched his mouth to one side. He brushed his
knuckles across his jaw. What was it like, raisin' me?

She studied him for a moment. It was a walk in the park
and I always knew just what to do. What do you think?

I don't know. I feel like I'm screwing up.

It's hard. Even when your father was around. She paused.
You've been a dad longer than him, you know. You're much
better at it.

He gave a thin smile. Skillman offered me a job. I didn't
take it 'cause I didn't want to owe him anything.

How is taking a job owing him?

It just seems like it. You know he's hassled me about buy-
ing land, and then he offers me a job.

Mhm.

I wonder if I was just making excuses, it was just pride.
Or stubbornness. And now things are lookin' bad enough I
feel like I don't have any other option. He had been looking
between them or away and when he turned to his mother she
was smirking.

You're just now getting desperate. When you're really
down you won't have anything to say about pride. She shifted and lifted a finger. Do you remember when we had that

apartment on Race Street?

Kinda.

I slept in the closet. There was only the one bedroom, and I let you have it. I wasn't ashamed. I did what I had to. No single mother in this town would bat her eyes at that. And nobody'd blame you for taking a job.

Alright.

I've worked at the office for I don't even know how long, now. I've gotten three raises. Just three. She held up her fingers. Pride's for rich folk.

Okay. He smiled. He stood and hugged her and she kissed his cheek.

You better have my grandson out here before long.

I will. He left and got on his horse. He rode south, past the square and the granary and the dry red wash of the creek. It had been a long while since he'd been by the mine and it had grown wider. The dirt was gray with red drippings and everywhere machinery stood half-erect or idle. Far below him a dumptruck rolled by a mineshaft. He rode on until he'd reached the line of trailers and Skillman's cabin. He tied his horse to a post and knocked on the door. A whistle blew. The door opened and Skillman stood there like a gray wall.

Dave. Kindly surprised to see you here.

He took a step back. I am too.

Skillman looked at him for a moment. I've just got a minute, if you want to have a seat.

Okay. He followed Skillman into the cabin. It was a single room, the wood stained dark. There was a desk with two plush chairs in front of it and a couch to the side. A polished cavalry revolver hung on the wall behind the desk, the head of a buck mounted on a rafter in the middle of the room. Skillman pointed David to one of the chairs and went over to a small sidetable and poured a cup of real coffee.

So I imagine you've come to ask me for that job.

That's right.

I can't give it to you. His back was toward David, bent to stir something into his coffee. He straightened and brought the cup over to David. You like it black?

It took David a moment to unfix his jaw. Yeah.

Like I said, I can't give it to you. Skillman handed him the cup. It appears we've hit a boundary. The newest seams are tapped already. He stood against his desk. Fact is I have to lay off the people I brought on.

David stared at the carpet. He sat, beginning to slouch in the chair. He felt paralyzed. The cabin grew and shrank.

I'm due to head up north. Oversee a new mine. If there's anything else you want to tell me you need to do it now. I'll be gone for a while. He leaned back and crossed a heavy forearm over the other. David felt him watching and he felt and heard him shift to his feet. I wouldn't take that land from you now. You're backed into a corner. You'd end up regretting it.

He nodded. Skillman took the coffee from him and put it on his desk and stood beside him. David got up and rubbed at the side of his face and looked Skillman in the eye for the first time since he'd come to the door. He didn't mean to but he squared against him and Skillman only stared back. Then he put a hand on David's shoulder to guide him and they walked out together and Skillman shut the door behind them.

Best of luck, Dave. I don't know what it'd take to turn things around, but whatever that is I hope it happens.

Thank you. David loosed his horse and got on. He gripped the reins and rode away. In the barn he stabled the horse and put up the tack and he stood in the spare stall breathing, holding his breath, eyes shut. He pushed a foot forward and lambasted the stall door, shoulder behind his fist. The door shuddered and a nail bent, pulled half-free. Samuel's bay kicked in response and he heard wood splinter. His middle knuckle felt wide and rubbery immediately, and when he opened his eyes Samuel was there.

What's the matter?

David shoved his hand in his pocket. Just frustrated, bud.

About what?

Oh, money stuff.

Can I help?

He smiled. No, buddy. You do enough for me already.

Samuel didn't move.

You finish digging?

Yeah.

Go on home and get somethin' to eat. I'll be up soon.

Samuel cornered his lips. Okay.

Two days later he came home from running traps and Samuel found him standing on the porch and handed him a thin roll of money. David looked at it and at Samuel.

What's this?

Money.

Where'd you get it?

Mel and I've been shoveling people's walks in town. Mom said we could. We shoveled Red's mom's sidewalk for free.

David smiled and warmed. Oh bud. That's awful nice of you. Here. He handed the money back. Go on and buy some books or something.

Samuel didn't move.

I tell you what. They're closing down that flower shop in town. Why don't you get your mom and Delia something?

Samuel nodded, hesitant. Okay.

Good. He put a hand on Samuel's shoulder and pulled him close and shook him. You're a good kid, Sammy. Mostly when you're sleepin'. But you're a good kid.

Samuel swatted at David's stomach. David held him there, looking at the field.

14

It was January and truly cold. When the snow fell it was white only briefly before the dust covered it, and the snow was always thin and gave little water. David was putting a shovel away in his shed after cleaning Danvers' steps and the front porch. The snow was old and had melted down and iced and the clouds gone on, the sky clear and stars hard and bright. He had opened the shed door when he heard a thud, set the shovel inside and shut the door again when he heard another. Helene was in the back window and she left and there was another thud. After a moment she came to the backdoor and opened it, leaning out.

Someone's breaking into O H's.

He already had the shovel back in his hand. Stay inside.

She began to close the door and stopped. Don't hurt him.

He waved her off and snuck along the side of the house. The thudding was loud, and as he closed the distance between himself and the shack he could hear wood splintering. He trotted low the rest of the way, carrying the shovel motionless in his hand, and braced up against the side of the shack. The wood vibrated. His pulse was high in his head. When he cleared the side he saw a thin man dressed in shirtsleeves throwing his shoulder against the door. David spun the shovel around, holding the head against his forearm, and he stepped lightly forward as the man backed for another charge. David swung across the man's thigh and he fell, eyes wide. He made no sound. The handle cracked and the moment stretched wide, the wood dropping into the dust and snow. David fell to him, swatting him across the face with the shovel and again on the backswing and he threw the shovel away and gripped the man's collar in one hand, throat in the other and threw him up against the shack.

The fuck are you doing?

The man sputtered, face welted and bloody. His eyes were watering and his pupils wide as dimes. He groped at David's shirt, trying to shove him.

You tryin' to break in here?

I thought it was empty.

It's not.

Okay. He seemed to nod. Okay.

David breathed through his teeth. Helene was calling to him from the front porch. The heaviness fell away from behind his forehead and he dropped the man to the ground. He looked at the shack, the door busted in, the wood bright where the hinges had been ripped off. Helene was on the front steps and Samuel was at the door. He stepped away from the man. Call the sheriff.

Helene went inside. Samuel took her place at the steps and pointed past David at the man, struggling to his feet. His leg collapsed underneath him and he fell again. David leaned and gripped him by the shirtcollar and began to drag him toward the house, waving for Samuel to go back in. The man grabbed David's arms and started rambling and David stopped halfway between houses to twist the man's arm around and pull him by the wrist. He hauled the man to the porch steps and he set him up against a post. Samuel was at the door.

Go on in, Sam.

What happened?

Nothing. Go inside.

Is he drunk?

Go inside.

Samuel left the porch, reappearing in the window.

You're lucky I don't kill you. You tried my door you'd be

dead.

Where am I?

Hell if I know.

What?

David glanced aside. I know where I am. I got no idea where you are.

The man said nothing. He scratched at his arm, pale and scabbed. His eyes scanned around and his head followed almost as if it were floating, bobbing slightly. Helene looked out at him from the door and nodded.

Did you break my leg?

No.

I can't feel it.

Consider that a mercy.

The man went quiet, and David heard O H and his family round the bend, Melanie driving the mule with the cart behind loaded down with pallets and dirty sleds of fiberglass insulation. O H hopped off the cart and started toward David.

What's goin' on?

He jerked his thumb toward the shack. Caught him trying to break into your house.

The hell? O H came toward them, handing the bags back to Delia and Melanie, and they moved on to the shack.

I dunno. He's out of his gourd. Dudn't know where he's at.

O H stood by David and tilted his head to look at the man. You clock him?

Yeah.

If I leave you with him will he come up dead?

Depends.

Well. Try not to kill him. O H walked across the yard to the shack. He came out with a thin jacket and pushed the man from the post and slipped the jacket over him.

What're you doing?

The guy's about blue, Dave. O H zipped the jacket up and

left the man's arms out of the sleeves, tying them around the post and knotting them.

David stepped away and looked around himself. The sky had gone completely dark and the snow was gray. Squares of light fell from the windows of the house and in the beams he could see dust settling. Delia and Melanie came out of the shack and Delia stopped at the side of the house.

Can I use your tools?

David nodded.

She ducked the rope and disappeared around the back. The man blinked hard, shaking his head. Melanie was still standing there and the man looked up and she sneered. The backdoor opened and shut after a minute and Helene came from the back with Delia, holding a drill. Delia called for Melanie and they strode across the yard to the shack. She lined the door up on its hinges while Helene knelt to fit a screw into an eyelet.

Someone gonna help me with this or not?

O H jogged over. David stared at the man, his head hanging down, body slack against the jacket. The side of his face was swollen and there was a line of white matching the seam of the shovel. Helene passed behind David to get to the porch and went inside and he heard her padding around in the hall. The wind was blowing through something on the house and whistling and when it faded he could hear a horse and it came into view with Miller atop it.

Howdy Dave. He dismounted.

Evening. David took the reins and tied them to the porch railing. The horse was heaving and there was a pattern of sweat below the saddle blanket. When'd you get deputized?

Not too long ago. Got let go at the mine. They were quiet for a moment. Miller was looking at David and finally he nodded toward the man on the porch steps. What happened?

Heard thumping next door, found this guy knocking the door down. You want me to get O H?

Who's that?

Neighbor. He put a thumb to the shack. It's his house.

Miller lifted his head. Yeah, get him.

David jogged across the yard toward the shack. He knocked softly and glanced down where the door was cracked. O H opened it, swinging the door back and forth.

Yeah?

The deputy's here.

He stepped out. They walked to the porch and David left them at the steps and went inside. Helene was standing against the doorway to the living room with a cup of coffee and she held it out to him.

Is that Jake?

Yeah. He took the cup by the top and drank. Thanks. He paused, drank more.

How will he take him to jail?

I dunno. Never seen a guy get carried off on horseback. They turned to watch. O H and Miller were standing together in front of the man. After a few minutes Miller glanced at the window and beckoned. David set the coffee down. I imagine I'll have to ride into town with them. She pursed her lips and he kept on looking at her. She said nothing and finally he dropped his hand to the doorknob.

Sam was watching you the whole time.

He stared at the floor. There was a tightness in his throat that he heard in hers. Neither of them moved until he opened the door. Miller was putting the man in handcuffs and O H was crossing toward the shack. Delia and Melanie had begun to unload the cart and haul in the insulation. Miller glanced away from the man, lifting his chin.

Like it if you came into town with me. Get your statement.

He loosened the reins from the porch railing and got on the horse. David walked beside him as they followed the man into town. In the open the grit was blowing hard and David tucked his face into the front of his coat for shelter. A sand drift had broken and slumped across the road and the man stumbled over it, rolling and righting himself. The man's head drifted about when they reached the outskirts of town and Miller directed him north. There was a half foot of sand in front of the door to the old police station and Miller and the man stood aside while David kicked at it until he was able to swing the door open. The lobby was dark. He found a light-switch and they walked down a hall.

Wait in there. Miller pointed at an open office and shuffled the man down to a holding cell at the end of the hall. David stepped into the office and sat in front of the desk and waited. After a few minutes Miller walked back in, tossing the jacket over.

You really put the boots to him. Years gone by you might've been hauled in, too.

What's he high on?

Miller sighed, rounding the desk, and slumped into the chair. In the good light he seemed haggard. Meth, most likely. Though he's a bit placid for it. He cocked his head back and his Stetson fell to the floor with a flat smack. He made no move to collect it. Second shift is killin' me, Dave.

I can imagine.

Third is okay. Least you're able to sleep half the time. Miller raised his head and leaned forward in the chair. He put his elbows on the desk. I heard you tried to sign on at the mine. How'd that go?

Worse than I expected.

Miller smiled. Everybody's gettin' pinched these days. He gazed up at the ceiling. Yeah, it's about as bad as I thought things'd be.

What do you mean?

You remember how I said times were changing. He looked at David and reached for a pen on the desk. He began to click it by his ear. I just sorta saw it all fallin' to pieces.

Didn't quite see these dust storms coming, but I guess you can chalk it up to the same shit. His eyes wandered off to a corner of the office. You remember what I said, yeah?

About what?

About everyone havin' to stick together.

Yeah. David sat up. He had his hands braced on the wooden arms of the chair.

You know how good the mine's been for this town.

I know how good people say it is.

Miller's eyelids drooped for a moment. He flipped the pen around in his hand. If you sold that property you'd be givin' me and about a dozen other guys a job.

You're a deputy.

You want to know how much I get paid for stayin' up all hours and hauling in junkies? It ain't a lot. And not all of them are as spacey as your friend there. He tilted his head toward the cell. Mining's not the best job there is but it pays better than the county. And it ain't just me, Dave. A bunch of other guys got laid off. We'd get put back on, you'd get a fat check. And I can't imagine Skillman wouldn't offer you some cush spot for makin' him richer.

David stared at him for a moment. He breathed deep and sighed and he opened his hand and lifted it from the chair. I been over this with him a hundred times. I'm not interested in employing the town. I can't worry about that.

I helped you and all the farmers around here when the time came. I'm just askin' you to return the favor.

Because selling us diesel was doing us a favor.

What have you got to lose? However many acres of desert?

I'm not selling.

It's the right thing, Dave. You got the means to put food on the table for a bunch of people in this town.

I'm the father of one kid, Jake. Just one. There was Helene in him and a rising anger at Miller and only a little doubt at his hypocrisy.

Miller clenched his jaw. You've got the opportunity to help your fellow man and you won't do it.

That's right.

Miller was motionless save for his thumb slipping over the pen plunger.

You still want my statement?

Miller waved him away. I don't need it. His voice was thick. You took in that nigger without complaining.

David spun back around, eyes narrow. You know what'll burn you worse? He didn't have to ask.

Go to hell, Parrish.

David grinned smugly and went out. It was still long dark and the wind was blowing and the night had the feel of restlessness that came in the later hours and he felt righteous walking back until his eyes found the house.

15

There was a storm a week later that reburied the fences and drove the cattle off the property. When David and Samuel rode up on them the entire herd was rangy and wheezing. Their muzzles were chapped, the rims of their nostrils cracking. A few more had fallen. They chased the herd in and O H joined them to dig the fences. David called around to see if he could sell some off and by the end of the week he'd made an arrangement with a butcher halfway across the county.

Before they left the next morning Helene made them stand still while she daubed petroleum jelly under their nostrils and she tied wet handkerchiefs to their faces. She told them a few of the kids that came around had begun to cough and turn ill. They rode out with O H afoot and they cut a dozen head from the herd, leaving O H at the gate, and drove the cattle onto the road. The day passed for clear as they came through town, the sky white and the wind low. Many houses now had dust over the porches and it was clear the owners had stopped cleaning, the dust pushed away only in a semicircle at the front door. A few farmers at the diner saw the cattle coming and stood at the intersection to hie them on. By the afternoon they had opened their coats. They broke for lunch in the road and Samuel raked the ditch to see if the animals would graze. The weeds uncovered were burned by static and below them the dirt was cracked.

Don't worry about it.

Samuel looked back at David.

They're going off to get slaughtered. They're not getting any fatter.

As they rode southwest the dust got deeper and everything around them came to level almost perfectly. There were whole lengths of fence covered so that the top wire could be cleared with a step. They passed a barn half underground, the roof caved and reaching to the dust. Ahead in the distance was a copse of gray trees and after half an hour they passed them and saw a few small houses on the other side. The dust had blown up to the sloped roofs and had come through the window of the second house. Samuel rode by to see inside and caught up. A small black line took form far down the road. The sun was swinging low and it was a while before the line thickened and became a man, a dirty paper mask hanging at his throat. He kept his head locked forward as they came near and he stepped out of the road and trod over the flattened ditch and into the field to let the herd pass. David watched him from the corner of his eye and the vagrant never turned, never looked aside.

They reached the butcher's property by early evening. He came out of the front and swung his arm for them to go around. They followed him to a pen and herded the animals through. When the gate was shut David leaned down to shake the butcher's hand.

Much obliged.

It's business. I needed it same as you.

He looked toward the house. The pens ran clean to it and he guessed the whole back was a meat locker. There was a trough on either side of the pen. You mind if we rest our horses?

Not a bit. Come on in and sit for a while if you like.

They let the horses water and followed the butcher into his house, slipping their masks down to their necks. There was a glass counter full of meat in the front room and two doors. The butcher took them through one into his living room and the three of them sat in front of a television, an old computer set beside it on the stand. The room was dim and there was a low hum from the freezer at the rear of the house. The butcher went into the kitchen and called out.

I've got some beer, if you want a drink.

David looked at Samuel. Sure. They heard the refrigerator open and the two of them stared at their reflections in the television screen.

You can turn that thing on if you want. Nothin' but the snow races and bad news, anymore.

Samuel stood. He switched it on and the screen popped white and the picture appeared. It was local access, text about a free dinner at a church, a reminder to leave outside lights on at night. The butcher came back in with two bottles of beer necked in his fingers. He twisted the caps off with his free hand and passed a bottle on. David watched him bend the caps in his palm and set them on a side table. He gestured toward the television with the bottle.

I heard we haven't seen looters like the rest of the country has cuz of these storms.

What's that?

Folks're afraid to come here, all around the dustbowl states. Think they'll die of thirst or something. He drank. What I hear anyway.

David mused. The screen changed its text, a prayer meeting for rain. They drank and Samuel sat looking at the television. He changed the channel and a show came on, black and white. The butcher laughed.

That show there's about fifty years older'n your daddy, boy. They must put on whatever they find in the basement.

Does the computer work?

The butcher glanced from Samuel to the table. Oh, yeah. Old hobby of mine.

Is it connected to anything?

No. If times were better me and a couple boys were gonna see if we could get something set up, least to Banning. But. He raised his hands to nothing.

David finished his beer and set the empty bottle on the floor between his feet. He looked at Samuel and shifted in his seat to see if it was getting dark but there were no windows. He stood and stretched his back. I appreciate the drink. We oughta get goin'.

The butcher nodded. Let me get you your money.

David and Samuel filed behind him. He led them to the front and walked around the counter to pull out a ledger. He scrawled something down and tore out a check and handed it across to David. Let me know if you want to thin your herd some more.

I will. They went to the door. He nodded in goodbye before opening it and they walked out. The sun was halved on the horizon and it lay in a quavering molten pool. The light cut suddenly from the ground and they watched a duster pull up from the southwest like a black sheet. They quickened the horses and David watched Samuel's eyes, his grip on the reins. They passed the houses and David led them toward the trees and they dismounted. He took the packs from the horses and Samuel followed him through the treeline. It was dark as night by the time they had gathered enough wood and he had to search for the matches by feel. He started the fire and it grew fast and the shadows of the trees fenced and backed. They sat next to each other on their sleeping bags, eating sandwiches and passing a canteen between them, staring at the fire, straining their ears. The wind picked up and the fire leaned with it. They looked at each other as the wind slowed and stopped and then snapped the fire out and they were in thick dark with the dust pelting them in volleys.

Dad?

Here, I'm here. David reached out for Samuel's voice and pulled him to his bag. He unzipped it and threw it over his back and wrapped it around them. You okay?

Samuel nodded, clutching at the edges of the bag. David shifted his legs and felt the sand fill the rim of his pants where his shirt was lifted. The branches rattled overhead. He realized his eyes were open and shut them. Samuel's back rose and fell and he could feel his heartbeat. They were still and silent and he had no idea how long they'd been so but felt the sand heavier and heavier at his back and going higher until it was nearly at his shoulders, pushing.

Late in the night the wind slowed and he woke Samuel and wrapped him in the sleeping bag. He dug through the waste for the other bag and pulled it free from the sand. The night was pitch dark and the fire had been buried. He kicked until he found embers floating in the black and dug through the sand for fistfuls of grass. The blades caught and he blew at the coals and they brightened and the grass flickered and curled. He blew again and coughed on the air and made a small flame. He pulled wood from the dust and laid it on the fire and he could see himself and the nearest trees and Samuel behind him. The horses came toward the light, shivering. David led them ahead, patting their necks and talking to them. When they'd calmed he sat beside Samuel on the sleeping bag and they watched the fire. David shifted and a spark leapt between their shoulders. They said nothing for a while.

How's school going?

Samuel laughed once. It's not really school. I just go to the library and Mom makes sure I bring home a new book. He had the canteen between his hands and he drank.

You don't do those little classes she has?

No. She makes me stay for the math, but I'm too far ahead for the rest. She said she's working on new stuff for me. He reached for a twig in the sand and snapped it. I'm worried about her.

Why's that?

I never see her eat.

David looked away.

What are we gonna do if the storms don't stop?

They will.

But what if they don't? Could we find Red?

David glanced at him. I suppose we could. I don't know how that'd feed us.

He helps raise sheep. That's what he told me.

David said nothing, and they were quiet.

I worry about you, too.

Why?

Samuel shrugged.

You don't have to worry about us. You worry about you.

What's there to worry about with me?

He opened his mouth. He reached his arm out and pulled Samuel to his chest and leaned over to kiss his hair. There's plenty. I worry about you every waking moment. He held Samuel until he felt him stretch and he let him go. They both slid deep into their sleeping bags and waited for morning.

16

Months passed. He got a call from Glenn saying a railroad friend had come by, talking of a few half-starved horses by the state line. He said he thought David would want to know. David thanked him and talked to Helene and O H. The next morning he went across the yard to the shack with a bag of food and water and a change of clothes. He knocked on the door and waited. Delia opened it and stood aside for him to come in.

He's getting dressed.

Okay. David stood inside the door and set the bag down. Delia shut the door and went to the sink. Melanie was at the table eating breakfast, the rest of the dishes set upside down, bowls and cups turned over and the pitcher of milk covered with cloth. He smiled at her. How're you?

She shrugged and put down her fork. Fine.

David scanned the rough wood walls. He had been inside only once since building it. They'd put up pictures and there was a painting along the back wall where they'd put the couch. Melanie saw he was looking.

I painted that.

No kidding? He raised his eyebrows. He stepped closer to it, a creek in watercolor, bluegreen grass, a woman in front of a weeping willow. He smiled at Melanie. It's really good.

I painted it before we moved here.

Wow. He stepped away. He tried not to see the walls and the floor and to think of what she could have been, what Samuel could have been. What they could be. One of the two doors opened to the small corner rooms and O H stood there

115

threading a belt through his jeans.

We ready?

Yep.

Alright then. Let's go be cowboys. He went to Melanie and kissed her head and he kissed Delia and took a small duffel bag from her. They stood at the door. See ya'll soon.

They walked together to Danvers'. The sun wasn't long up and the sky was overcast. They readied the horses and David pointed to Samuel's silver bay.

Well, bud. Get up there.

O H smirked. I'm gonna surprise you. Be a natural. He put his foot in the stirrup and grabbed the saddlehorn and pulled himself up onto the horse. You'll want to give me your hat.

David mounted up and started forward and O H followed him out. Passing the granary a breeze hit their backs and it was cool. He thought it might snow if it got colder, if there was any water in the clouds.

So how far we goin'?

Depends. If we find a horse right off looks like it hasn't eaten for a month we might go another couple hundred yards.

Seein' as how we won't?

Be about a full day's ride one way, bit more. Probably across the state line. Glenn said he found his just inside Colorado.

Never been to Colorado.

It's nothing special. Everything looks the same until it's different.

O H grinned. I'll remember that little gem.

It's true. Especially now with these dusters.

After a while they reached the interstate and stopped their horses. There was half a foot of dust covering it, the median and ditches graded smooth. Down the length of the highway were lines of dead trees, some toppled onto the road, the dust built up against them. David dismounted and brushed away the sand with his boot until he could see the pavement, cracked and worn paintless.

The breeze died in the afternoon and the air warmed. David hadn't been far south of Dixon in years and he thought whenever they crested the soft rises that passed for hills they might see before them a desert of high red dunes or a place where the land and sky were one blur of crumbled brick. By now he knew that O H was sore but there were no complaints. It was several hours past the highway that they smelled smoke and David wished he had brought a gun. There was no source for the smoke anywhere. The plain was broken by gray trees in the distance and fenceposts and telephone poles. The fencewires were cut.

If I didn't see this every day I'd think we landed in hell.

Yeah.

You were never in the desert, right? Overseas?

I never went overseas. They sent me straight to Rica.

O H looked around them. It ain't quite like this. But it's got some of the ingredients.

David halted his horse. Let's break for a bit. He held up the reins, circling. They were in the middle of an empty field, keeping track of the road they followed by telephone poles. He dismounted and watched as O H hefted his leg over the horse and dropped down. They squatted in the dust and ate their lunches. O H lay on his back and sighed.

My ass is gonna be sore, boy.

Should have brought a pillow along for you.

Uh huh. He sat up and picked a leg under himself to stretch it. How did Glenn know to come down here?

There was a guy raised horses he heard about. Lost everything and just turned 'em loose. Killed himself.

O H stood and patted at his pants. This country, man. Goin' to shit.

Been shit.

They mounted their horses and started along the road

again. Toward nightfall they reached a crossroads and in the southwest corner sat a farmhouse. A worn picket fence ran across the yard with the dust eating up the posts and behind the house was a small barn. As they crossed the street the front door opened and a man came out onto the wraparound porch. David nodded to the man. The man's chin dipped and he put his hands on the porch railing. They passed by and passed the barn and O H leaned over.

He doesn't live there, does he.

No.

He was starin' pretty hard.

He's just a squatter. Worried we'd come to throw him out or something.

O H sat straight. If you say so.

The sun was deep behind the clouds and there was no setting, only the slow draining of color from the land and it seemed as though the ground were bleeding out, turning gray and cold. The road ahead and behind them was empty and with the going of the light the sounds they made came clearer.

I wish we hadn't passed him so close to dark.

David squinted into the dusk. Ahead was a line of trees on the horizon. We'll lay up in there for the night.

We gonna make a fire?

Not if we can help it.

I thought you said he was just a squatter?

Yeah, well. Squatter ain't an occupation.

They made it to the trees and dismounted. They led the horses in and tied them and David watered them from a small pot while O H cleared the ground. He took the blankets from the horses and spread them out and when they were done they sat in the dark listening to Samuel's horse cribbing at a tree.

Tell him to quit gnawin'. I can't hear anything else.

There's nothing to hear.

Eventually the horse stopped chewing. They'd both gotten into their sleeping bags and thrown their blankets over them.

What's the worst thing you ever did?

David sat up. You mean in the war?

I sure hope it was in the war, yeah.

What brought this on?

Just my mind wanderin'. Making conversation.

He nodded in the dark. There's a lot. I got a list of worst things long as my arm.

You don't have to say.

He thought of something near the end of his tour, innocuous. Real enough to believe. The night around him had gone darker somehow, or he had. He breathed in, pretending to hesitate. Couple days before they retook Talamanca we were holding them off at the foot of the mountain. Low on ammo, low on food. This guy named Bradford, a real shit, gets hit with a pete round, burned all to hell. David put his hands behind his head. He was staring blindly at the sky. So we get one of theirs, shoot him in the leg. I put a tourniquet on him. We trade potshots for a while. We were all short timers, nobody wantin' to miss their wake-up. Then Bradford up and died. Just sputtered and quit like he was an old car. I never liked that son of a bitch, never, but I'd been in country with him from day one. So I went back away from the line, where we had the prisoner tied up against a tree. Snuck back there and looked him in the eye while I cut his tourniquet. Watched him bleed out. Just sat there staring him down.

Damn. O H shuffled around in the dark. David could hear he was facing him. Why'd you ask if I meant in the war?

I dunno. I guess some people put all that away, right? Soldiers do bad things.

What would you say was your worst thing outside it?

He made a sound between a laugh and groan.

What?

Couple years after the war I ran out on Helene to bring

Red back.

Who?

Sam's godfather. My best friend since forever. I got wounded just a few days after killin' that prisoner, sent back to the States. Waited on him to roll in at the end of his tour and he never did. I tried hunting him up, wrote letters and called some folks. Nothing. So I made a go of it with Helene, Danvers gave me a job and the house for a little bit of nothin'. And then one day I get these letters. Whole bundle. Him talking crazy. Bad, bad shit. So I went and got him. Helene was pregnant.

Does that come in at number two? Number two worst thing?

He paused. It's the one thing I did that I did on my own, in all my life, that I know was right. All the other stuff, I dunno. Even enlisting. But getting Red was batshit stupid so I know I did it just because it was right.

I like that. Don't know if I agree with you, but I like it.

David shifted. What's yours?

Mine? O H laughed. Man, I never even fired my rifle in combat.

You son of a bitch.

Shot at a goat once.

David rolled over and threw a handful of sand in O H's direction. Jarhead motherfucker. David went quiet, thinking about Red and about Samuel. About the femur. Why'd you enlist?

Money for school. O H laughed briefly. I didn't have any future playin' ball. Knew that much.

Helene had me try a class, fresh from my tour. It never took for me.

You know, I can see that about you.

You're bein' a real shit.

Yeah, yeah. So you? Why'd you join up? Be a hero?

David sighed. Pretty much. Red and I tried soon as the

bombs started goin' off all over the place. Got shot down, too young. Tried again once things were lookin' a little worse and they turned a blind eye and let us in. We thought we were gonna save our mommas and our suzies, you know?

We had plenty of those. Surprised you didn't go Marine.

He shook his head in the dark. I guess straight Army sounded better. More patriotic. They both laughed a little and were quiet. I saw that painting Mel did.

Pretty good, right?

Real good.

Yeah, she's a regular artist. By his voice David could tell he was grinning. We were hoping back when, you know, we could fast-track her, get her in a art school. Delia wanted to see her go someplace private up in Decatur. She was good enough. Now, I don't even know what good school's doing her. Maybe she'd be better off watchin' us.

It'll do her good.

I dunno, man. What good?

World can't stay this way forever. Give it time.

How much time? More'n ten years already and it's only gotten worse. I don't think that's gonna change. Who'd change it?

He wanted to argue, to convince O H he was right, so at least one of them would believe it. He wanted to keep them both talking.

What about Sam?

Helene wants to make sure I don't pressure him into farming, let him do what he wants. But I'm kinda like you. It's hard not to worry.

He's about as smart a kid as I've ever seen.

Smart idn't the trouble. He's got this, I don't know. We had a dog before you got here, and when she died Sam came right up beside me and helped me dig her grave. I didn't ask, didn't tell him to. Just came right up. Didn't cry that I ever saw.

There's nothing wrong with that.

No, I know. It just worries me. Helene says I'm real dis-tant all the time, blames it on the war. I never notice it when she says it about me, but I see it in Sam. He can be right in front of you but really he's off in space. That scares the hell out of me.

Just sounds like he's mature for his age. I wouldn't worry too much.

That'll happen.

They were up at first light. David made a fire to warm their breakfast and O H watered the horses and untied them. The clouds had broken up overnight and in the east the light came pale and uncolored still. O H circled about their camp looking for tracks and he shook his head when he sat by the fire. They ate bacon and beans and kicked dust over the re-maining flames. They packed and saddled their horses and rode out of the trees as a weak duster blew in from the south. It rolled toward them and they turned their heads in tandem when it hit. The wind faded fast and the sun rose onto their shoulders after, their shadows slanting long across the dust.

They came to a two-lane and a sign nearby for a Colorado state route. They rode east along the highway and came on an overpass. The horses shied but they went under it and David pointed out the smokestains where travelers had made fires at the joints of beam and ramp. Beyond the overpass was an-other sign listing nearby cities.

We're in the right place. I guess just cruise around until we see somethin'.

Sounds good.

The nearest town was almost five miles ahead. Halfway there a dense line of trees grew up from the dust. The road and treeline converged a mile on and they stopped the horses before a suspension bridge that crossed the water. It flowed red, thick and smooth, riffling through a section of wire fence stretching over the creek. There were weeds and grass growing near the edge where the dust had fallen away. David started the bay onward and they crossed over the bridge and rode down into the field along the creek. The horses began to prance sideways and O H pointed out a carcass twenty yards ahead, not far from the creek. It was a horse, the jawbone open and the ribs tarped over by the shrunken hide. They pressed on. In the distance he could make out the hazy frame of a water tower.

What do we do once we find a live one?

David shrugged. See how feral it is. I dunno how much breaking a horse needs after a year or however long it's been loose. We'll just rope it and hope it follows us.

They were coming to the edge of town when a set of horsetracks curved in from the field and they rode alongside, passing the first houses. The tracks faded and split on the thinner dust in town. There were signs of feeding on the early buds of bushes and the remains of hanging plants and flowerbeds. The houses around them were decrepit and the dust trackless except for animals. The pavement widened as they came downtown and there was a long stretch of brick buildings and storefronts, the dust mounded up on the sidewalks in soft waves. At the main intersection a broad-boned sorrel draft stepped by them calmly, its shoulders and ribs working under its red hide. Another horse followed. David smiled and let out a quick laugh.

That first one. Bigger. They followed the horses, going slow. As they closed on them the stores fell behind and the houses became smaller and tighter packed than at the edge of town. O H pointed to their left and down a sidestreet was a row of empty lots, the houses burned, blackened posts sticking up out of the dust. Then he pointed up and David saw all the powerpoles had been stripped of their lines. The sky was oppressive for its unwiring.

What'd I tell you about shit getting bad?

I thought I agreed with you?

The horses had stopped in the street and were watching them. His bay came forward swishing its tail and he let it lean its head to the sorrel. He patted the blaze on the draft and it didn't shy. He slipped the rope from his saddle and tied a lead as the bay and draft circled and he slid the lead over its head. The draft shivered as he cinched the rope up and he leaned over and rubbed along its neck and withers. He payed some rope as the slack lessened and the draft tossed its head. It settled and he drew in and the draft didn't fight and he looked at O H and grinned. He gathered the rope and reins in one hand and put the bay down the street a few yards and the draft was slow to follow but came along. It sidled to them and he petted it while he looped the lead around the saddlehorn. He swept his finger in the air for O H to turn and David brought the horses to the intersection and they started the way they came. The other draft was staring at them, unmoving. They rode out of town with O H in the lead and he pointed out fresh wheel-tracks in the dust.

They broke for lunch at the creek and they let the horses drink. They ate sandwiches wrapped in wax paper and David balled his wrapper and threw it toward the creek. It fell short of the water and rolled, leaving odd wobbling marks in the dust like the tracks of a limping bird. The draft eyed the ball. David stood and went to the creek for his bay.

You think we scared off another squatter?

He shrugged. Couldn't say.

They're all pretty flighty, seems like.

Not sure why. They got as much a right to be there as anyone, now.

As much the folks who used to live there?

He stopped beside O H with the reins in his hand. They're gone. I guess if they weren't they'd have a say.

O H stood and David helped saddle his horse. They mounted up and David tied the draft to his saddle and they left the creek for the road headed west. It was a while riding before O H looked aside at him.

You really believe that?

I try to. I don't know that I do. We did take a dead man's horse.

They rode on until they reached the road north and took it. The cart tracks continued westward. It was nearly evening when they passed the camp from the night before. It got cold and colder as the sun sank below the red edge of the land. David set his hands on the saddlehorn.

You want to go wide of the house up ahead?

Seems like a good idea.

They angled their path off the road and into the field alongside it, the horses sinking into the dust in the ditches and climbing out. There was a fence ahead and they rode down it for several yards before finding a low wire to step the horses over. In the distance and dark they could see the house by the white fence and barn. Smoke was lifting almost invisibly from the chimney and the sky above was clear and populated with stars and the horn of the setting moon. O H evened with David and thumbed toward the house.

What say would the old owners have if they came back?

David shook his head. Kick the guy out, if they want.

What about him?

He looked toward O H. They halted. What are you getting at?

I'm just wonderin'. I like to know what people think. He paused a moment. Say they didn't abandon it. Say they left a note sayin' they'd be back, went out looking for work?

And the squatter moved in?

Right.

I dunno. My gut reaction is he'd better check out quick, but, really? Nowadays? He was quiet for a moment. Seems like everything is up for grabs.

But what would be right?

David shook his head, laughing a little harshly. You're rakin' me over the coals, man.

Okay. This fellow in particular. Say him. What do you do with him?

I've been thinking about it, and I can't decide. Is he hurtin' anything?

I doubt it. But there's the principle, right? If that's what we're talking about.

Is there? Is there anymore?

I'm the one askin'.

David closed his eyes in the dark. If he shouldn't break into someone's house, if that's wrong, why don't we do something?

He's not bothering anyone.

But he broke the principle.

Yeah.

I feel like I'm just as bad as him. Ever since I got out of the war I see people breaking laws and rules, being evil. And I don't do anything about it. That same principle says I ought to do something. He felt himself begin to start the horse and hated the movement.

All the right you do oughta count for somethin'.

It isn't enough. If I don't even know what to think? That might be worse than anything.

Hours later they rode past the mine, silent now and with few lights opening the pits to them. The town was asleep. When they reached the square O H was slumped in the saddle and his hands were limp around the reins. The draft horse had been falling behind every few hundred yards and he pulled it close as they came out of town and both horses followed him to the barn. He woke O H by shaking his saddle.

We back?

Yeah. Thanks for your help.

Uh. He leaned over the horse to glance at the ground. I don't recall doin' anything.

Well you kept me company. That's something.

I guess. He slipped his leg over the horse slow and awkward and stepped down. Oh, Jesus. I am sore.

David smiled. Walk it off. I'll see you tomorrow. O H cast a hand back in goodbye and David put up the horses and tack. He was wide awake and wanted to raise the house and talk with his family.

They had a small party in the library for Samuel's twelfth birthday and let him pick out several books. The old volunteer librarian was there when he blew out his candles and he gave Samuel a book himself. Two boys from Helene's classes came, brothers named Moore, and Melanie and Delia. When the party was through David offered to see the brothers home but they ran on down the street. The rest of them walked home together, David splitting off at the barn. He let the horses and mules out and looked them over. He put feed in the stalls and fresh water and found O H in the barn checking the equipment. A flash of a smile crossed his face.

Old man told me to expect rain.

David inhaled. He caught the breath and held it swollen in his chest. He set about wordlessly and they greased axles and sharpened blades. They taped cracking wood and hammered wedges into loosened mortises. When they finished their work for the day they walked to the road together and neither of them spoke of the dark blue sky overhead or the chill in the air. David went up to Danvers' door and turned back to O H.

Come in for a minute?

Sure.

David rapped on the door and stood by. Danvers shouted from inside and as he came walking to the mudroom David opened the door.

Just start coming in already. You ain't about to catch me

at somethin' shameful. He pointed to O H as they came in. I imagine your man told you the news.

Yeah. We just finished working on some of the equipment.

Don't get too far ahead of yourselves. A little rain dudn't mean much.

I know.

I don't want you to be disappointed when it peters out. He looked over his shoulder. Come on and sit down. I was napping, foot's half asleep.

David and O H followed him into the living room. Danvers sat in a recliner and they sat across from him, watching him rock.

You need to think about the farmers who ain't as smart as you. Or don't have me at their ears. You get a little rain you're gonna see every fool came out here from the east plowin' to hell and back, burying your work. No offense, O H.

None taken.

If the rain stops after that everybody's at square one.

Will things turn around if it keeps rainin'?

I don't see why not. It ain't like it was poison falling from the sky. It's just dirt. Danvers pinched at his nostrils. Once you get some rain you'll see weeds coming straight through the red stuff. Next day, guaranteed. Come to think of it you'll probably have a hard time keepin' up.

Mm. Well. David put his hands on his knees to rise. Wanna have supper with us?

Nah.

You need anything?

Nope.

I'll see ya later then. He and O H stood and they walked to the door. David called back. Thanks for the good news.

Glad to give it.

They walked home, quiet and smiling as they parted. David went to the kitchen sink for water and saw Helene through the window, standing where the garden would be. He tapped on the glass until she turned around and he met her at the door. Suppose to rain.

Finally. How much?

Dunno. Danvers wants us to wait and see. They both looked at the dirt at their feet. What's he wantin' for supper?

Grilled cheese and tomato soup.

David put his hands on his hips. That's a little plain.

It's what he asked for.

David said nothing. He stepped down into the yard and knelt and picked up a handful of dust to sift through his fingers. Then he dug to the topsoil and broke a hardened piece of earth off and cracked it in his hands and crumbled it between them.

17

It rained three times, each a full day. The rain washed the dust into a slurry of mud that ran into the creeks and melted the piles in the fields. The trees budded and the grass livened, weeds flourished with the smaller plants and sprang up all along the roadsides. Helene started work on the garden, enlarging it to take advantage and when the land had dried David and O H hoed out the weeds and planted soybeans over a span of weeks and the three of them waited for the first green of their work. Pacing the road going into town David saw the ivy winding and milkweed and the red buds on the tree branches. He walked the trails he'd used for the tractors and took his horse down other roads to the fields of other farmers and talked with them. Coming home from riding one evening and the sunlight was just golden on the land around him. Samuel was walking far ahead and David called for him but he didn't turn. When David got home he found Helene in the living room reading.

Hey, father.

Hey. Sam come through here?

I haven't seen him. What's wrong?

Nothing. I just saw him walking ahead of me. David came into the room and sat on a footstool to take off his boots. He heaved a sigh, content. Rain's takin' real well.

Helene closed the book and smiled. Oh yeah?

Mhm.

Hopefully it sticks around.

Yeah. I'ma go wash my hands. He carried his boots to the door and walked to the kitchen. He washed his hands and rubbed them over his face and he saw the silhouette of a tree move, Samuel's shoulder. The sun was orange sinking toward the southwest. He dried with a rag from the stove. Hey, you want me to make dinner tonight?

There was a shuffling from the living room. Knock yourself out.

He started rifling through the cupboards. He set a pot of water to boil and found a box of spaghetti. He got a jar of tomatoes from the pantry and he sorted through the spices they had and tried to make sauce. There was a knock at the door and David went into the hall. He glanced at Helene in passing. You may regret lettin' me cook after all.

I'm not surprised by that.

He grinned and opened the door. O H stood with a hand in his pocket.

Hey. Mel in there by chance?

David shook his head. Huh uh.

O H pinched up the side of his mouth. She knows to be back before dinner.

He peeked into the living room. You seen Melanie lately, mother?

This morning.

David turned back around. Sam's readin' behind the house. We could ask him.

Nah, that's alright. She's probably just late comin' in.

I'll send her down the line if she drops by.

Appreciate it. O H put up his hand.

He shut the door. The phone started ringing. Well dang. He was on the phone for seconds before he hung up and ran to the door. Helene looked up at him as he was halfway out.

What's the matter?

Get Sam inside. He was out and bounding off the porch and running to O H's shack. He knocked once and opened the door and stuck his head in. O H was sitting at the little table eating, Delia on the other side with her back to the door. Hey

Ornery, come on.

O H wiped his lips and rose, bumping the table across the dirt floor. What for?

Come on. He nodded back slightly. Delia looked at him and he let his eyes flick to hers and away.

What's the deal, boys club?

David said nothing. O H rounded the table and David cleared from the door and once it was shut he began to run. He heard O H behind him and David slung himself up into the truck and struggled to start it. The front end shook. O H climbed in.

What's goin' on, man?

Christ. David tried the key again. Delia had come out of the shack and she was coming toward them when the engine caught and they backed out into the road. O H was staring at him but David just shifted the truck into gear and sped down the road. It fishtailed briefly and David brought it back and dust floated in the rearview. The new flora streaked by and the dark red dirt and O H was yelling at him until finally David looked at him on the straightaway. Somebody shot Mel. Rich Spangler called, said he saw her layin' under a tree on Storm Creek Road. Heard the shots.

O H rocked back. His head tilted like he was agreeing with something. They came into town and drove north at the square. Past Spangler's property, taking the side road. O H hadn't moved. His hands were on his knees and he was staring at the visor in front of him. The woods came tight to the road and the vegetation was lush along the ditches.

He said she was by the creek.

The guardrails and culvert came into view. He stopped the truck in front of the rails and O H sprang out and started running along the berm. David scanned the trees for sign of clothes or blood and then O H jumped the ditch and screamed and stooped at the base of a tree with Melanie in his arms, her head lolled and eyes closed. She wore a purple blouse that was soaked through with blood up to her shoulders. David came and knelt beside them and he felt at her neck and her skin was cool and she had no pulse, no flutter of a pulse. O H lifted her to his chest and he stood with her legs and arms long and waving. Her feet reached past his knees and a thin-soled shoe caught against his leg and her foot twisted as he stepped forward. When David stood to follow his strength was sapped and he stuck a hand out to catch himself.

O H.

He didn't turn.

We have to keep her here. The sheriff might find something. He was still walking, clutching her body to him. They became smaller and the land slowly darker. David found himself walking to the truck, O H's shadow down the road. The sun seemed farther down than it ought. He started the truck and turned it around and pulled alongside him. The sight of her limp in his arms. He could not see himself stop the truck and help pull her into the cab but moments later she was seated in the middle leaning against O H and David was driving into town. They passed Spangler, running the way they'd come, and David saw him slow and stop in the mirror. The sun was blotted by the stores at the square as they turned toward the house. A block on Delia came riding David's horse bareback, both wild. He slowed the truck and she jerked the horse around and followed them. Helene was standing at the edge of the yard and she raised her hands to her mouth as the truck passed and stopped in the drive. He put it in park and O H opened the door and slid her out and carried her across the yard toward the shack. Delia jumped off the bay and stopped him and they fell to the ground together where the fence used to lie. Delia began to wail. Standing in the window upstairs was Samuel. David got out of the truck and leaned against the door for a moment after shutting it, and when he came toward the house Samuel vanished. The last of the light leached into the west. It was cold very suddenly and Helene rose from where the three were huddled around the body and she came up to David.

Rich called back.

He lifted his head slightly.

Should I get the sheriff to come out here? I need to get them a blanket. They won't move.

When he spoke to her she was already inside. Then she was back and walking toward them on the lawn. He climbed the porch steps and when he opened the door he saw the dried blood on his fingers and the web of his thumb, flaking. His vision warped like he'd pushed on a wide pane of glass. Samuel's door held fast. He pushed and it budged and he threw his shoulder against the door and the chair scudded along the carpet. He slipped in. Samuel was sitting on his bed facing away and his head was down. David went around the end of the bed and sat beside him. Samuel ducked himself into David's chest. He felt the boy shudder in his arms and felt his ribs and spine and his shoulder blades. A deep shame spread and seemed to dim the room. He rubbed Samuel's arm and took hold of his shoulders and held him tight. Helene was in the doorway waiting and he knew the sheriff had come. He eased and dropped his arms and Samuel sat up. David stood and she held him briefly and their cheeks met and were damp.

The sheriff is here.

Yeah.

There are deputies out looking.

Okay. He'd been staring at the floor. She took his hands and he glanced up at her. She let go and he went downstairs and out into the yard. The sheriff and a deputy were standing with O H. David came toward them and stood by. A lamp was lit in the shack and he could see Delia move about through the open doorway. The blanket Helene had brought lay tangled by O H's feet. David stopped and picked it up.

Come inside.

The sheriff motioned for David and O H to go on and he followed them up the porch steps. David told them to sit at the kitchen table and began to make coffee. The sheriff took off his hat and set it upside down on the table. He leaned forward and ran a hand over his head. Is there anybody you can think of that'd have reason to do this? Anybody thinks of you as an enemy?

O H shook his head. 'Less you count someone who don't like black folk. He looked aside, out the window. His face was blank but for a moment when it contorted, and then it passed.

If someone's threatened you at all, that counts. Did someone?

No. We got stares coming into town but it wadn't anything but people wonderin' where the hell we come from. And that was a while ago.

Okay. Would she of kept anything from you, if she'd seen somethin', or if someone'd come at her?

You'd know if someone came at her. You would've had to arrest her.

The sheriff gave a thin smile and wrote something down. David took two mugs from the cupboard and set them on the counter.

How many people you got out lookin'?

The sheriff flipped a page in his notes. Everybody.

O H brought his thumb and finger together across his lips. He turned his head aside again. Could you raise up a posse or somethin'?

I will at first light.

The coffee was done. David poured the mugs full and set them on the table. They steamed and neither of the men touched them. David remembered the deputy outside and he poured a third cup and brought it out. The phone rang when he came in and he spoke to his mother briefly. Back in the kitchen the pot of spaghetti still stood on the range, the water boiled away.

O H stood. I'm gonna go be with my wife. We done?

Sure. The sheriff stood and his head tilted slightly. I'm real sorry, Mr. Reckard. I'm gonna do everything I can.

O H looked at him. Alright. Alright. He left.

The sheriff rubbed his eyes. He took up his hat. I'm goin' back to the scene.

David followed him to the door. Helene was at the top of the stairs. He walked out onto the porch with the sheriff and as they watched, a pair of headlights cut through the dark in the field and the coroner's car came around the bend. It parked in front of the shack and the coroner got out and spoke to the deputy. The sheriff put his hands on the porch railing.

I've never had anything like this. Five holes in that girl. The sheriff shook his head. Never in thirty-three years. He breathed deep. But I imagine you've seen worse.

It's different.

How's that?

I've never seen hell and home at the same time.

The sheriff glanced at him. O H walked out of the shack and the coroner met him in the yard. One of the deputies wheeled a gurney past them. They went in and minutes later all followed behind the body in a procession and O H and Delia stood by while she was loaded into the back of the car. David wanted to go to them but he stayed fixed to the porch, watching the brakelights come on in the car and O H and Delia get in the front with the coroner. He choked on a breath and he pivoted like he'd punch the railing but stopped himself. He unclenched his hand and stood beside the sheriff.

I'm awful sorry, Dave.

He nodded.

The sheriff stepped off the porch and got onto his horse. I'll be back around.

David saw that he wanted to say more but he just lowered his head and left. David went in and locked the door and he climbed the stairs and found the two of them in Samuel's bed. Helene rose up to reach her hand out for him. He took it and sat against the bed frame facing the open door.

18

It was still dark when he woke. His back was stiff from sitting upright all night and he got up slowly. He seemed to rise into the murder, everything fitting in place as he stood. He slipped out of the room and went downstairs. Through the bedroom window the sky was just beginning to lighten. The shack was empty. When the sun rose he showered and Helene walked in as he was dressing and she lay down. He followed and put his arm around her. They slept. He dreamt and when he woke there was the same moment that he was part of neither world and that the day before had not passed. He stayed in bed with her still asleep until there was a knock at the door and he slipped away and passed a hand through his hair. He stepped outside and met the sheriff on the porch, unshaven, heavy bags under his eyes and his face twisted into something of a smile.

We was up all night with every light we could find. The sheriff rubbed at his chin to excuse it. How's your family?

Sleeping.

Wish I could do that. He sighed and looked away toward the shack. Have you seen them up and around yet?

If they ever came home I didn't see.

There wudn't anything to find out there. Grass flat from where she was layin'. He pushed a balled-up hand against his mouth to stop a yawn. God. We talked to Spangler. Guy's about a mess, seein' the body and all. Where was your boy when it happened?

Either at the library or on his way back. I saw him walkin' home around six.

You think I could talk to him?

I don't see why you'd need to.

I just want to get all sides.

He doesn't have a side. He wasn't there.

Could I just talk to him?

I don't want him wrapped up in this any more than he already is. They were best friends.

The sheriff nodded. Okay, Dave. He says something that sounds pertinent, you let me know.

I will. He glanced out to the yard and rested his arms on the porch railing. He didn't see who did it?

Nope. Probably long gone by the time he saw her. His eyes went empty and they both stared down into the flower-bed below. I can't remember anything like this. Not that there was ever that many murders around here. He thumbed toward the shack and paused. I'm gonna see if they're in. Want me to give you a call when we ride out?

Yeah, please. David stepped toward the door and waited for the sheriff to cross the yard before going inside. He could hear something frying in the kitchen and he walked down the hall. Helene was at the stove. She cracked two eggs against a pan and dropped them in. David sat at the table and watched her go about the kitchen while behind his eyes there was nothing but the new green of the trees and weeds and the ditch along the road. There was Melanie exploring or just walking and before he could find Samuel with her he grasped his temples between his thumb and middle finger and snuffed the thought.

Helene slipped a pan of bacon and eggs onto a plate and walked it to the table. Is Sam awake?

Don't think so.

She got two glasses from the cupboard. She filled them with milk from the refrigerator and set them down.

Aren't you gonna eat?

She looked at him. I already did, while you were talking

to the sheriff. She cut more bacon from the slab on the counter and began to fry it.

That for next door?

Yes. She didn't look up.

He's gonna let me know when they're goin' out.

I don't want you leaving. She was staring into the pan. Drawn cheeks. The thinness of her wrists.

He swallowed and put his fork down. How can I not go?

She shook her head. I don't want you to.

I'll talk to the old man, have him come up.

She turned to face him and she was glaring.

He tightened his lips. Get as mad as you want. The phone rang and he waited for the lull. I can't just sit here.

You can't stay here, you mean.

He met her stare and went into the hall to answer the phone. After he hung up he stepped out the backdoor and brought in the shotgun and set it up beside the table. He called Danvers and told him to bring the thirty-aught-six. From the hallway he watched Helene putting the food into a container, her back to him. He went upstairs to check in on Samuel. The curtains were pulled and the room was half dark and he lay in bed looking up at the ceiling. David stayed in the doorway for a moment and he came in and stood by the bed. You okay?

Samuel blinked, then rubbed his eyes. He breathed deeply.

I need to go out with the sheriff and everybody. I won't be gone too long. David waited for a reply. Phil's coming up to visit. He sat on the edge of the bed. Sam. Sam, do you know anything? Did you see anything?

Samuel closed his eyes and shook his head. His chest trembled.

Bud. He put a hand on Samuel's head. After a while he rose. I'll be back. He went downstairs and got the shotgun and stepped out onto the porch. He stepped off when Danvers rounded the bend riding David's bay. He had the rifle up against his shoulder.

You want to trade me?

David nodded. Yeah. He met Danvers in the yard and helped him off the horse and they swapped guns.

Found him wandering the yard. What's goin' on?

David told him. As he did he switched the rifle from hand to hand. He stepped around and Danvers turned with him.

That's, that's just—I heard the car come and go. Danvers frowned heavily and his nostrils flared with breath.

I got to get goin'. He stepped up into the saddle.

I'll take care of things here.

David joined another rider carrying a gun at the square and they rode grimly toward Storm Creek Road. They found the sheriff and deputies and a few other citizens on horseback gathered there at the intersection. Richard Spangler and Fogel among them. The sheriff hailed David when he saw him and he broke his Morgan from the crowd.

You see the Reckards yet?

No.

The Morgan took a step and the sheriff scanned the people gathered. Coroner said they left sometime early this morning, before light.

David shook his head.

Well. Maybe we'll find them, too. We're just gonna spread out, is all we're gonna do. He took the road one way or the other. He raised his arm to address everyone. Now I'm not deputizing anybody. I see a lot of guns but I don't want to hear any. This ain't the Old West. Just pick a direction, find a deputy if you see anything. Let's get movin'.

They broke into clusters and started down the four ways. David and the sheriff rode east. David had slid the rifle into the saddle scabbard and he touched the stock every so often. They stopped near the scene.

Go on that way if you want. There idn't anything to see.

We combed it about as close as humanly possible.

I think I will. David pushed his horse forward. He turned back once to watch the sheriff go on. It was several minutes coming up to the creek and culvert. He imagined Melanie bloodsoaked and lying in the grass and he was gritting his teeth and clenching the reins in his hand and he blinked the blur out of his eyes. The pressure began behind his forehead and the light took on the metal gloss it had on the mountain. He felt the heat and the rain and cut of foliage and the cool blue-white feeling of the nerves along his palms and fingers as he did at the sound of gunfire. David was already pulling the rifle free when O H came out of the treeline and he let go. He rode up beside him.

Hey.

O H lifted his head. His eyes were bloodshot.

You alright?

He looked away. No.

Where's Delia?

She not at the house? She left before I did.

David dropped from the horse to stand beside him. We haven't seen her.

O H said nothing. He started walking down the road, scratching his neck.

There's nothin' to find, bud. They've been up and down this way.

There's him to find.

David took the reins and led the horse. The road ran deeper into the country. They watched the gravel and the grass along the roadside hoping something would appear. A long-abandoned shed stood off the road a hundred yards and O H began to veer toward it. David slipped the rifle from the scabbard and followed, leaving the horse at the road and they went along the old dirt path.

Sheriff doesn't know anything new, does he?

No. I don't think so. David glanced aside at him. Did the

coroner find anything?

We got the caliber. That don't help any, though. His voice was hollow, the sound coming from just the edges of his throat. They quieted as they neared the shed. David regripped the rifle and O H lifted the latch on the door and swung it open. The tail of a garter snake disappeared under an empty burlap sack in the corner of the room. There was little to see. A patch of soot, sunlit, where the stovepipe used to be, a small table. There was a row of mason jars affixed to the bottom of a shelf above the table by nails through the lids. The jars were full of old screws and bolts and washers. O H turned to face David and he turned again and kicked the desk so it flew up and smashed the jars and the metal and glass fell and scattered upon the desktop and a handful of washers rolled off the table to the ground. He kicked it again and stepped forward and kicked the side of the shed and the wood splintered and dust drifted down from the roof.

God, dammit. Fuck this place. I come a thousand miles just to get everything took away from me. Leave the fucking city of Atlanta, come out here and my baby is killed. His hands were lifted. Jesus, Dave.

David put the rifle aside. I'm so sorry, bud.

He pushed by, picking up the rifle as he walked out the shed door. David spun with his hand out but O H only walked on, holding the gun by the stock. David followed him back to the road. He grabbed the reins on the bay and they kept going. The sun had risen well into the sky and had begun to fall again when they passed a road that led south past his property. They went on for another half hour and they passed the county sign and O H slowed and faced him. David held the reins out.

We should turn around. You're staggerin'.

You think he's back the other way?

I don't know.

I guess I'll keep goin', then.

David let his hand fall. I need to get home. I'll take that road back a ways, check it. O H cocked his chin. He scratched at it and David saw the rash. He stared at O H and then stepped up into the saddle. The horse stamped.

Tell me somethin'. O H cocked his head. What is it makes this happen? What goes wrong in a man's head that makes him do that, kill people, kill my little girl?

I don't know. I don't know, O H.

What kind of place is this anymore? He turned down the road.

David could say nothing for a minute. I'll tell Delia where you are.

He laughed sharply. His shoulders shook. Okay, man. For a moment he was still as if held by something in the air, arms and head limp. Who's this Spangler guy.

You know him. He's a farmer.

I don't know him.

David watched as he started away. He spun the horse around and took the intersection. It would be time to eat when he got back. The road split a thick strip of woods that formed the northern border of his fields and the shadows of the trees stretched cool and patchwork across the divide, the pieces of light hitting the brim of his hat and passing on. He searched the grass for sign of a gun, anything. His eyes glazed quickly and he wasn't really seeing. If Red had stayed they may have found the murderer already. He would have ridden out at once and found him and exacted with a purity the sort of vengeance David could no longer summon. He felt low for not being capable of it, not having lived that way. For ever having said he was foolish. A beer bottle glinted in the light and he jumped at the sight and cursed himself.

The road met with his own a few miles to the south. He slowed his bay as the house came into view. He stopped altogether and stared at it for a while, at O H's shack. He rode the horse through the yard and peered in the windows, rode around it to see if Delia was home. There was a mattress and sheet in the middle of the kitchen floor and what he thought was blood staining it. The breakfast Helene made was set on the table, untouched, and he sank at the thought of her opening the door. He went across the yard to the house and tossed the reins over the porch railing. He knocked on the front door and Danvers came from the living room and let him in.

No luck, I'm guessin'.

No.

He stood aside and David walked into the hall. Where's your gun?

O H has it. He's still out looking.

He holdin' up?

David shook his head. He's just about had it, Phil. I don't know what to do for him.

Danvers grimaced and held his chin between his fingers. I wish I did.

He glanced toward the stairs.

They're up there. Helene came down for a moment to see if I wanted fed and she went back up. Are you sticking around the house now?

Yeah.

I figure I'll head on out. Shotgun's behind the davenport. I'll leave it here for you just in case.

Thanks for comin'.

No problem. I kept myself in coffee. Danvers waited until David looked at him. You alright?

He took off his hat and rubbed at his head. I just don't know what to do.

There idn't anything to do. You can't fight this any more than you could a duster.

Red would've done something.

You mean the crazy sumbitch that nearly killed a man and skipped town? Oh, he'd of done a lot of good.

That ain't the point.

There ain't a point. Danvers put his hand on David's shoulder. There's no point to any of it, Dave. You just do the best you can. And you do. Nobody ever said you had to be everywhere at once or feed the masses or any such bull. He shook him and patted him. Mourn the girl. Be with your family. That's all anyone can ask.

David was still. Okay.

He dropped his hand. I'm just down the road if you need me.

Thank you. David walked him to the porch steps. Back inside he shut and locked the door. He stood at the bottom of the stairs. He went inside the bedroom to see the shack, empty still, and climbed the stairs to Samuel's room. Helene stood from the chair by the bed. The room was low-lit and Samuel was covered in blankets. They stepped into the hall.

He hasn't spoken a word. She leaned against the wall. Have they found anything?

No. I don't think they expect to.

Her bottom lip rose and she dropped her head. I don't know what to do. Delia and O H haven't come home. Your mom keeps calling. She let her hands fall against her legs and stared at him. Is this why you're always out the door at the first sign of trouble?

What?

You left here this morning so you didn't have to be in that room with us. It took me a while but I figured that out.

I go out there and help. I try to.

Her eyes closed for a long moment. It's hard being the one that has to stay, you know that? It's tiring. It's all I've ever done.

I'm sorry.

She was reading his face and finally she opened the door. They went in together and David sat on the edge of the bed. Samuel's back was to them. Helene took a book from the bedside table and began to read aloud for to him before going to start dinner. David put his hand on Samuel's shoulder. You want to come into town with me tomorrow? Go see Grandma or something?

Samuel shook his head.

I think you might feel better if you got up and moved around some.

I don't want to feel better.

David paused at his words. I know. I know it hurts. David took his hand away. Could I get you to eat with us at least? You need to eat.

He shook his head again. David put his hand back and sat with him until Helene returned with a tray of grilled cheese sandwiches. David moved to the foot of the bed and they set the tray in the middle and picked at the food. They watched for Samuel to turn around but he never did, and when they finished eating David took the tray down. He wanted to throw the sandwiches out but instead put them on a plate and slid them in the refrigerator. The sun had fallen behind the town and there were a few clouds still lit though the sky was going dark. He crossed the yard and knocked on the door to the shack. There was no answer. Back in the house he checked the locks on the doors and windows and when he came upstairs found Helene reading from where she left off in the book, lying beside Samuel. David sat in the chair and listened until he saw Samuel's chest rising regularly. He touched her arm. She switched the lamp off on the bedside table and set the book down and she and David went downstairs. He watched her go into the bedroom and he rechecked the locks on the doors and stood looking out at the dark yard and the field of beans through the living room window. Then he took the shotgun from behind the couch and went into their bedroom and Helene stepped out of the light of the bathroom. He undressed as she got into bed and he slid in under the covers. He held her cool against his chest and her hair on his lips. She nestled against him and took his hand in hers.

We'll get Sam up tomorrow.

Yeah. I want to get some lotion from ma. Looks like O H got poison ivy from the woods.

Tomorrow.

He brought her hand up and kissed it. He kept it near to his lips and he moved to kiss it again but only held it to his lips. Smelled her skin.

19

It felt like late summer, it was so warm. He sat up slowly and got out of bed. He stretched and scratched his arm and looked out the window at O H's shack. The door was hanging open. David dressed and put on his hat and he went outside. O H was dragging the bloody mattress and sheet from the kitchen and he let it go just beyond the doorway and turned and saw David. His eyes were sunk far into his head and his skin showed pale in places like it was translucent to the bone below. He nodded at David and took up the mattress again and David hurried around to help him with it, careful of where he placed his hands, and when they'd lifted it up O H stopped and stared at it.

Where're we takin' it, bud?

O H looked at him. I dunno. I dunno what I'm doin'. Burn it, or somethin'.

David gauged him. We can do that if you want. He hefted the mattress higher and started backing around to the rear of the shack. O H followed and they dropped the mattress. Do you have matches?

No.

Okay. I'll be right back. He trotted around front and stopped at the door. The place seemed darker than it ever had and there were thin ruts in the dirt floor where the mattress dragged. He couldn't make himself go in and so he ran to the house. Helene was gone from the bed and he heard stirring upstairs as he searched the kitchen. He found them and brought a small lamp of coal oil outside and poured the oil over the sheet. O H took the box of matches and struck one across the back and dropped it. The flame spread in a blue wave over the mattress and stopped and was almost invisible in the light. David backed away. At the border of the poured oil the sheet began to blacken and send up smoke. O H was rocking on his heels and his hands were out before him. David backed another step and scratched his arm. He lifted it and looked and saw the red swath and welts where he'd itched. The work of his brain froze for a moment and he seemed unable to swallow or to breathe, and then he did.

You got this, bud? You okay?

Yeah.

I gotta go back to the house.

He nodded. David ran across the yard into the house and doubled up the stairs. Helene was sitting against the wall with Samuel under her arm and the blanket was still wrapped around him. She looked up at David and she was crying.

It's all over him. He's got a rash all over him.

David set his hand on the bedpost, holding himself up. He nodded, then sat beside Samuel. After a short while he rose and went to the empty room across the hall to check on O H. The shack was afire and O H was standing beside it. The mattress springs were against the wall and the smoke rose thick and gray to join a bank of clouds sweeping across the sky. Whitewash peeled and blackened, the frame of the shack sagging until the southeast corner gave and the roof fell in, a bellow of fire and ash sent up. David came back to Samuel's room and grouped Samuel and Helene around and they sat in the dark and he waited for the next thing to come for them.

The rifle was set against the porch railing when he went out late in the afternoon. The sky was covered over with clouds and O H was squatting by the ashes of the shack. David stood beside him.

Why'd you burn it?

Figure I don't need a place to lay down anymore.

Why not?

O H had yet to turn his head. This's the first time I sat since it happened. All I did is just walk around. Up and down the road.

Did you find Delia?

He didn't answer.

O H?

Last I saw her the sheriff come in the coroner's and she smacked him for not bein' out there. He stared up at David. She didn't say nothin' to me, just left after that. I stood in the hall for I don't know how long. I thought maybe I was goin' crazy. But you ain't crazy if you think that, right?

David shook his head. You're not crazy.

I left, stood out there on the road for most of the day, thinkin' he might come back. After you left. Either he'd have a bullet for me or I'd just beat his face clear until there wadn't nothin' left. He smiled. I don't know what to do, Dave. I thought about just goin' inside to burn up but I didn't want to die in there. He put a hand out beside him and stood slowly. David reached to help but O H moved his arm and straightened on his own.

Why don't you come in and eat some dinner with us?

Naw.

We can get on the horses and start looking for Delia.

She's gone. If she ain't come yet, she's gone. I don't blame her. He stopped. He shifted slightly toward David. I feel bad for leavin' Mel to be buried here.

We'll make sure it's done right. We'll honor her.

O H shook his head. He breathed in deep. She never belonged here. He tilted his head. That's east, idn't it?

Let me at least feed you, bud.

He hadn't taken his eyes from the horizon. You heard about all that end-of-the-world shit.

Been hearing that for years now. Hasn't happened yet.

Yeah, no. It is. They're right. But I been thinkin', ever since we went to get that horse. It ain't so much that the world's ending all at once as little bits of it are. Before I come out here you'd see people down the block walk out their house with maybe a backpack or somethin', and they had this look in their eyes like they knew they weren't really goin' anywhere. They were goin' out to disappear. Like a dog does.

David said nothing. He glanced at the house.

Where we went to get the horses. The world already moved on. There wadn't enough good left to keep things going.

He closed his eyes tight. When he opened them O H was staring at him. He took hold of David's hands.

I wish I could give you something like you gave me.

David shook his head and pulled away. Don't. I didn't give you anything. Look where all my kindness got you.

O H's face drifted aside. You don't know what you're sayin'. What if this was the best we was ever gonna have? Huh? And you gave it to us. He pushed their hands down. He gripped them tighter. I want you to be strong enough to keep doin' everything you can. Give it all you got until you're dust. God can't damn a good man's effort. He can't help but bless it. O H let go. Tell everyone I love 'em, man.

O H. Please.

Already gone. He started walking through the ashes. David stood there and watched his gray footfalls and he watched him pass back onto the reddish dirt now thinly grown over with weeds. He watched as O H reached the road and on until he was small and only movement among the treeline. Everything was still. He made it to the porch and took the rifle and held it staring at the yard. The grass was pressed flat where they had gathered around the body. The rough circle grew for him, larger and magnified until he saw nothing else and then he wasn't seeing that, he was seeing in a reel O H walking away and Melanie's legs and her shoe and the sun behind them and Anna stiff in bed and he thought all the dead of his life might parade before him and continue to until he joined them. His mind seemed to move off from his head, pushing through the air and the dirt and tunneling deep underground.

His hand ached. He'd been gripping the rifle and had to pry his fingers from the stock. He stepped back from the porch railing to go inside and when he began to reach toward the door he stopped. His head craned up as though he'd see through the wood into Samuel's room, see them seated there on the bed, Helene reading or smoothing his hair, trying to feed him or get him to drink. Stepping inside he called up to her and waited for her to come out. She braced her hands on the banister and stared down at him.

I'm gonna ride into town for that lotion.

She didn't move.

I won't be long.

Her head sank slightly. Okay.

He saddled his horse and rode for town, rifle in hand. The sky was still palled. Riding he felt the same focus to his vision but nothing rose to haunt him. The trees along the roadside were thick with buds and the grass was rich. Coming into town he saw that all the doors and windows of all the houses were shut, the blinds drawn. The street was empty, sand striping along the faded centerline, down the gutters. He could feel eyes on him. A stillness hove through the town, as if everyone were holding their breaths, hiding from a plague.

He tied the horse to his mother's mailbox and walked to the door. The blinds rattled in the front window and the door opened and she stood with her hands on her hips.

Get in here.

He ducked inside. Hey, ma.

She shut the door after him. Is everybody alright? I called a half-dozen times.

We're okay. I was hoping to use you as a medicine cabinet. You got anything for poison ivy?

She thought a moment. I'm sure I've got something around here somewhere. She pointed him into the living room and went down the hall. I don't suppose you'd let me feed you before you go. You look peckish.

I need to run it on home. He stood in front of the couch. The television was off and he wondered what it might play, if the murder had reached other towns. If they had their own.

Got you a bottle of calamine lotion. She found him in the living room and held it out to him. About as good as it gets for poison ivy.

Appreciate it. He took the bottle from her and slipped it into his pocket. He peered out the window. Do you need anything?

No, babe. I'm fine.

He made no move to leave, still eying the outside. I saw all this coming.

What?

I had a dream a while ago. And ever since then. I could just tell. Nothing good was coming for us. And Helene's been pushing me to go and I knew she was right, I think. I knew it. But I kept us here.

Davey. You couldn't know this was gonna happen.

Not this. But something. He turned and they went to the door. I better be off.

You give my love to the family.

I will. He nodded and stood there on the doorstep for a moment before walking to the fence and leading his horse into the street. It was empty as before and there was a slight wind that he could hear through the trees and the fence rows. The sun was an hour from setting but he could see all the houses were lit up, the occasional silhouette behind the blinds. A figure stood on a porch at the edge of town, smoking. David raised his hand to it and the cherry of the cigarette brightened. He found himself wishing the horse was quieter.

The road ahead and behind was clear and as he reached Danvers' house the moon crested the woods. He put the horse up and walked home. The front door unlocked as he came into the yard but he stood there, looking at the square of ash, at the rope they'd strung between the homes, until Helene opened the door. He climbed the porch steps.

Got some calamine.

She let him in and they went upstairs together. Samuel was sitting on the bed, reading from a science book. David stood by and took out the bottle of lotion. How're you doin'?

Samuel's face was vacant, and then he gazed up at David. I'm okay.

How's the itching?

Pretty bad.

Well come out here to the bathroom and we'll get this lotion on you.

Samuel slid to the floor. He took the bottle from David and slipped past Helene. I can do it. He shut the bathroom door. David looked at Helene and she put a hand to her temple and smoothed her hair.

20

That night he slept for a few hours before a dream woke and left him. His stomach felt full of bile. Helene sighed and rolled over and he waited for her to settle before getting out of bed to dress in the hallway. There was a stab when Macha didn't come to him, still. He turned on the porch light and frozen in it was a coyote, mid-step in the yard. Dark back to it, ruddy legs and flank. It hadn't moved and he hadn't, and he saw the rifle in the corner and picked it up by the shoulder strap and bolted through the door. The coyote jumped and was gone around the side of the house. David tugged his boots on and ran. There was a smell in the air of wet dog and game. The sky had gone cloudy again and but for a little moonlight everything was black and felt enclosed. He paused to listen for the coyote and heard it straight on and he ran ahead, boosting off a post to hop the fence. He slid the rifle onto his shoulder and held it steady with his arm, imagining the shape of the land from his years in it. After several minutes he stopped, listened, let his breath break and panted. Something shuffled, a few blades of grass rubbed, and he sprinted after the sound. A patch of white leapt ahead of him, disappeared, leapt again further on. The moon was beginning to break through or his eyes were getting better and the dark took shape, the grass at his feet, a fallen tree to his left, the white flash of underbelly ahead of him. It disappeared and then he was running on air and fell rolling down the bank of the creek. When he hit bottom something cracked him on the side of his head and pierced his vision.

He stood, stumbled, pants soaking up to his knees, and

climbed out of the creekbed. He closed his eyes and lay with his chest propped on the edge of the bank and set the rifle against his shoulder. Training the rifle on the first rustle in the grass he shot and fire leapt from the barrel, staining purple in his eyes. The report echoed and thinned in the dark. He stared up at the sky with the phantom of the muzzleflare blotting out the moon. His shoulder ached and he felt at his head. His fingers were wet but he was unsure if it was blood. For a moment he thought he might wake up. He struggled upright and continued on. The purple was clearing from his eyes but the grass was empty and it was too dark to track by sight. Turning to get his bearings he could find nothing, no landmarks. He kept going forward, searching for any light, any sign. Nothing and nothing where the mine would be and then a small square of orange, a lamp, almost half a mile away. There was no other landmark on his way until he came to the fence and realized where he was. The light was coming from inside one of the abandoned houses near the edge of Skillman's land. He checked the breech on the rifle, ejected the cartridge and let it fall to the ground and levered in another before climbing over the fence. No one had passed since he caught sight of the window. He approached from the corner of the house and crept to the light. The lamp lit a tree outside the window and it seemed like daylight to him. There was an old pallet and blanket in the middle of the room, the lamp set at a desk in front of the window, and an endtable with a paperback wedged under one of the legs. There was a wide discoloration in the floor and a matching waterstain in the ceiling, the plaster cracking and ready to drop. He stayed at the window a while waiting on someone to come in but no one did, and he stepped back to the corner of the house and rounded it, climbing over the tipping balustrade to the porch. There was no other light in the house and the door was boltless. He pushed it open gently and stepped in, slipped the rifle into his hand with the stock pinned between his forearm and side. The first three steps on the stairs were broken and the banister was gone, the walls on all sides stove in, struts pulled out and empty boxes for outlets and switches lying on the floor.

The house groaned overhead and his finger slipped from triggerguard to trigger, breath easing out through his teeth. There was a scuttling, a thumping, and then the sound stopped. He relaxed. He stalked to the rear of the house first and took the lamp and went from room to room. In each there were lines of black where thieves had ripped through the walls to take the copper. The whole place smelled, partly of mold and partly of a hot sweat. In one room was a soiled mattress with a faded brown stain that could have been blood. He felt suddenly as though he must be somewhere else. A needle cracked under his boot. This was not his town, his world. He walked back to the room that had held the lamp, replaced it, and rifled through the sleeping bag. The front door creaked as David touched the barrel of a pistol. He froze. Footsteps through the hall. David rose and lifted his gun and a man stepped into the doorway. He was lank and unshaven and was tying a length of balingwire around his pants.

What the fuck?

You. It was the addict that had broken into the shack. David put the rifle to his shoulder and sighted the man. The addict raised his hands, dropping his pants to his crotch. The light dimmed.

Don't shoot me. I'll clear out of here. I didn't know this was your place.

It ain't my place. What's the pistol for?

What pistol?

The one in your bed.

The addict's throat bobbed deep. I got to protect myself.

How've you never been shot?

I was. I got a hole in my leg you can hide a quarter in.

You're about to get one in your head to stow a baseball.

How long you been here?

Here?

In this house.

Three or four days. The addict's pants fell further and he reached a hand to pull them up. His skin was mapped with blue veins and the hair so dark it seemed just a hole. David's eyes were starting to haze.

You been in town longer?

I got out of jail a few weeks ago. I'm from Baltimore. They don't let me back there.

The lamp was dimming, the room closing toward darkness. He set his finger beside the trigger. What caliber is the gun?

I don't know. I'm not good with guns.

You steal it?

I found it.

If I reach in there and pull out anything bigger than a twenty-two I'm killing you dead. Come ahead a step.

The addict inched forward. He looked to his side.

Don't do that. David let the rifle sit on his hip and he trained it on the man's midsection. He padded through the bag with his left hand until he found the gun and the lamp flickered and the man jumped in the last frame of light and then the lamp was out. The addict's legs flashed in the air as the rifle lit the room again and everything was black. He dashed forward, smacking into the wall and running toward the door. Light slipped through the doorframe and it swiveled and widened and slammed shut. Clopping footsteps on the porch, grass, gravel. David threw the door open and ran outside. Gravel was scattering to the left and he tore after it until his ankle popped and he fell, skinning his palms and his forearm. He tried to stand and to limp on but the man was long ahead and could have hidden anywhere. He sat down in the road and for a while was still and then he beat the ground with his fists until they were numb and he'd flung strings of blood over himself. A horse was coming down the road and he stood and wiped the grime from his hands. Clothes covered in dirt, hands shredded. A deputy was riding the horse and he touched his hat and stopped beside him.

Mornin', gent.

David looked up at him. It was the deputy he'd given coffee to.

The deputy let him call home as soon as they got to the office in town. David told Helene what happened and that he'd be there shortly. He told the deputy the story twice, and the deputy called in the sheriff. He was bandaging David's hands and David waved him off when he began to pick through his hair for the gash in his head. The sheriff stepped into the doorway and appraised him.

Looks like you was in a scrap, Dave.

I wish I was. This is all self-inflicted.

I didn't think you were that kind of guy.

Yeah, well. He stared away dumbly. He told the sheriff about the coyote and the addict. The sheriff put up his hand.

What was his name, Leonard?

Murphy.

Right. Not from around here. Did you get the gun?

No, I wanted to wait on you.

We better hope that little bitch didn't go back for it. Did you see what the caliber was on it, Dave? She was shot with a forty-five.

No. I didn't see it. I don't know if it was that big.

Well. Leonard'll take you home. I'll let you know if I find something.

David stood. Let me go out there with you.

The sheriff rose up. You're about to fall over, Dave. We'll handle this.

Sheriff.

He left the room. Leonard almost patted David on the back and they went out into the hall and into the light. The clouds had broken and it was bright and warm. David felt hungover. The deputy helped him onto the horse and led it down the road, to the house. Riding he drifted into a daze and he thought of Melanie and O H and Delia and he thought maybe he had hit the man, maybe he'd run off on the adrenaline and drugs and now was dead and stiffening in the weeds. When they cleared the bend in the road Helene came out of the door and she jogged into the yard to help David down.

Thank you, sir. Helene took David by the arm and he shrugged her off and limped to the porch steps and fell to sit, letting the rifle drop into the grass. She looked from him to the deputy and the deputy turned and rode out. He was watching her come toward him across the grass, barefoot, hair sleepy. She smacked him like a dog.

You woke Sam. He was up crying the whole night thinking you ran off and got shot. Her eyes were bloodshot and underscored with lines. He said he heard you scream.

David stared at the ground.

What's happened to you?

I don't know.

She sat down on the steps, room enough between them for another person. She leaned away from him. I know it's hard. I know what it does to you.

He said nothing. She made a coughing sound and wiped at her eye.

But why can't you just stay with us? Why is that so hard for you to be around?

He shook his head. His mouth was gummy, hot. It kills me seeing you two. You don't eat anymore and Sam's a wreck. He held his hands out. Moving them the knuckles felt filled with rubber. I failed. I messed up.

You didn't fail. It's an everyday thing, David. You have to keep working, every day.

His eyes were stinging. Am I doing anything? Am I helping anyone?

How can you say that? Of course you are. You help more here than anywhere else, David. You always will. You know that? She reached over to him. Listen. You've done more for us than you ever did in the war. It may not seem like it. I know you don't think so. You're doing more for us and for the world right here.

He leaned his head against the railing. In the field ahead the weeds were growing high and he felt a meanness against himself for it.

You've got to be at peace at some point. You have to be able to rest.

He looked up at the sky. His head hurt and his eyes ached from the light.

21

They moved about the house as though they had just woken up. He had undressed and showered and Helene cleaned the cuts and abrasions and rebandaged them. She made breakfast and he limped down to the basement for a jar of preserves and the air was cool and he felt alright. He came up the stairs with the preserves and Helene made toast and eggs and asked him to try to bring Samuel down. The house quieted as he climbed the stairs and when he got to Samuel's room it was perfectly still. He was pretending to sleep. David knocked on the doorframe and entered.

Hey bud.

Mm?

How you doin'?

Okay.

David straightened. Mom's making breakfast.

What happened?

Oh, I was chasin' a coyote. I fell, like in the cartoons. He smiled.

What cartoons?

His smile dropped. Nevermind.

Samuel looked away. Did you get him?

I don't think so. We don't know if it's him yet or not.

Samuel turned back over.

Come on and eat, bud.

I'm not hungry.

David's face contorted. Alright. I'll bring some up to you. He went to the door. On the bedside table were the envelope and letter from Red, gone cottony at the folds. David stepped out and he stood in front of the stairs for a moment before going down. Helene handed him a plate as he stepped into the kitchen.

He'll come around.

Yeah.

She went up to give a plate to Samuel and came back down. She had combed her hair at some point and it gleamed and he felt far away, watching the kitchen table through a telescope.

You mind if I get out there today?

Where?

Just the fields. I need to weed.

She stood up with their plates.

I won't ever be out of sight of the house. It really needs done.

Can't you leave it be just for today? She put the dishes in the sink and leaned against the counter, hand set on it and elbow out. Are you suffocating that badly?

I'm just trying to feed us.

She closed her eyes, nodded.

I can't get behind. It's just me out there now.

She looked out the window. He imagined what she saw, wondered if she saw it differently. Why don't I go out and weed and you stay in?

What?

You need to spend some time with Sam. And sleep.

I'll work until dinner and we can take a hell of a nap, how's that?

She smiled thinly. He went out the backdoor and shut it behind him. He got the hoe from the shed and walked out into the field. He raked at the dirt around the shoots of beans, spinning the blade to cup the weeds and throw them aside. His hands were stiff and the knuckles moved slowly. It wasn't long before he'd peeled off his shirt and wrapped it around his waist. The road was empty and stayed empty. Helene came out briefly to watch him work. When he came in for a drink of water she was carrying a laundry basket up from the basement. She said nothing but jutted her hip out to bump against him at the counter and she went out to hang the wash on the line. He smiled and it fell as he passed through the house. In the field he picked up the hoe to begin again and he stopped and turned south. His hands were throbbing and his back was knotted. Months ago the land was red and there was no hope of growing anything at all and yet he wished for that, for the storms, for the dust in his mouth. That he could spit out. The storms were implacable as God and he could do nothing against them but keep on and sweat. Melanie and the purple and thick dark red he could trace back, line the actions up. He had ordered them just so, had put her there and Samuel there, had taken in O H and not told them to move on, had not left with Red, had not died bringing him home and had not died in the war.

He got to his feet and left the hoe where it lay in the field. The phone was ringing and he could hear it through the screen door, rattling off the walls. He wrung his hands of dirt and walked to the house and the door clapped shut behind him and the phone was still ringing. He picked it up. It was the deputy that had found him in the road. David's spine straightened as if pulled.

Was it Deputy Leonard, or is that your first name?

It's my first name. I wanted to let you know we put as best a bolo on your man as we could, let the adjacent counties know we were lookin' for him. Soon as we did Gosper County called us back, said they saw him. You must of spooked him good because he had to've run all the way there. He looted a place outside Claremont and ran out while the owners were coming home from church.

David looked out the window, at the field.

You there, Mr. Parrish?

Yeah. I heard you.

I thought you'd want to know. Gosper don't have much of a sheriff's department. He was quiet a moment. They said he had a gun.

David nodded to no one. He glanced up at the stairs, empty. Where was this house? Leonard told him and he went over the directions in his head and hung up. He went upstairs and pulled the attic steps down, climbed them and opened the box marked 'Army.' He took out his combat knife and slipped it between his pants and belt and shoved the box back to the wall. When he stood he could hear someone moving below. He peered down the steps. Samuel was looking up at him.

What's going on?

A deputy just called.

Samuel's face tilted.

He said someone broke into a house a couple towns away and they saw him leave. It was the guy who tried to get in at O H's. I saw him last night.

Are you going after him?

Come with me while I fix some food.

At the corner of Samuel's lips there was a faint upturn. They went downstairs together and he pulled leftovers out of the refrigerator, Samuel watching from the kitchen table. A floorboard creaked and Helene stood in the doorway. He hadn't moved the knife from his belt.

David.

He turned around, Samuel's plate in his hand.

Why do you have that knife?

His palms were sweating. He put the plate down in front of Samuel and wiped his hands on his jeans. They saw that druggie outside Claremont.

For a moment her face was still and then her eyes became bright and dried almost as quick. She breathed through the trap of her mouth and stood there, the doorway hiding her from Samuel. She was still, and the glare she shot petrifying.

He said they don't have much in the way of police over

there.

Jesus.

I can't let him go. He moved toward her. She stiffened.

You were supposed to stay with us.

I'm not leaving you. Gosper County's not fifteen miles from here. I went further to get horses.

But you are. She smiled. You can't do it. You can't just stay. She was looking away. I should probably give you credit for staying this long.

He tried to pull her deeper into the hallway. I can't let Sam down.

Oh, oh David. You are. Her voice was going soft, dark.

He can't grow up seein' guys like him run free.

You're going to get killed. Then he'll grow up without you.

I have to go. No one else is going after him.

She breathed, wiped at her eyes with her fingertips. Don't come back here.

Helene.

No. Don't come home. I won't deal with this again, and I won't have him turn into you, fatherless and mad at the world.

He said nothing.

He'll be as bad as you, thinking you have to go to war and kill people to prove yourself. Thinking you have to set everything right. I won't let him. That broke you.

Helene. Don't.

Try me. Walk out again.

His eyes narrowed. She said nothing but in her face he saw the threat.

You're not the one making sacrifices. We are.

He wanted to shift the moment somehow, bring it to something he understood. Instead he walked back to the kitchen and put his hand on Samuel's head and kissed his hair like he was little. The lunch he'd made lay cold and untouched and David told him to eat. She still stood there in the hall with her head down and when he was almost past she gripped his arm and leaned to his ear.

It would be better if you had never come back at all.

She let go and he moved as quickly as he could down the hall, grabbing the rifle by the door and walking out into the yard and he left that and in the roadside ditch around the bend he let himself fall and let her words gut him. He marveled at how they circled, at how clear they were and how perfectly they had cleaved him so that he split above the part that was open-mouthed and sputtering in the dust and whispered into his own ear that if it were so he was now free to work, free to wreak the justice demanded. The rifle had fallen beside him and he reslung it over his shoulder and stood. He climbed out of the ditch and started on without looking back, because he had to do it without looking back.

Down the road Danvers had seen him coming and was at the door shaking his head. You got that glint in your eye, boy.

I'm going after that druggie. The guy that broke in at O H's. We think he killed Mel.

Who's we? Come on in here.

Me and the sheriffs. He followed Danvers in. The kitchen was dark.

Am I supposed to just drop everything and watch over your place?

He raised an eyebrow. You got something going on?

Nope. Danvers went behind the table and leaned a hand on it. So where is this guy?

Somewhere in Gosper County.

I see you don't have any food with you.

I'll be alright.

Let me get you something. He opened the refrigerator and rummaged through it. He brought out two greasy hamburger patties on a plate and set them on the counter. And I've even got buns. He found them in a cabinet and got out a paper sack. He bagged the hamburgers and handed them over. Now if you'll just give me one minute. I've got one of your snares somewhere in the broom closet.

What are you gettin' that for?

I already baited you. Danvers stared at him for a moment and flicked his hand toward the door. Go on, now. Go get him. I'll look after the family.

David nodded thanks and went to the mudroom and out the door. Danvers stood watching him as he walked to get his horse and he was still there as he started toward the road.

Gosper County lay to the east. He'd only been there once before. Riding past the house he hurried the horse on and let it drift away and he realized he was taking the same route as Red, as O H.

In his head the place had been dust. He'd imagined desert when Leonard had called him but the land was the same as his. The fields low but the grass green. The roads were together save for drifting islands of blacktop on the old state route and bare dirt where there had been gravel. Grasshoppers fled his shadow, flew forward only to take flight again. He saw no one and few houses. A pair of dogs ran down an overgrown drive after him and he shooed them off. He thought of Macha, and of home, and it seemed more distant than it really was. He turned the horse north at a crossroads and within twenty minutes he reached Claremont. Everywhere houses were leveled and debris lay in the road, long sections of fractured wall molded by rain and heat and floor joists open on foundations, boards flung into backyards and into fences and trees. There hadn't been a tornado in the area in a few years. Further in he found an old gas station and as he passed, a man exited a sidedoor bewildered, his hair strung straight out and beard long and greasy, his shirt stained yellow. The room behind him was crusted with what looked like feces. The man was bubbling his lips until David tried to hail him and the man flung himself back against the wall of the station and scrambled along it. He twisted at the corner to run down the street, past old brick and wood storefronts.

Hey! David followed him, pressing the horse. The man kept running until his bare foot caught on something and he tumbled. David halted the horse and stepped down and stood over him.

I just wanted to ask you a question.

The man spat and it dropped across his cheek.

Do you speak English?

Fuck you. Fuck you. He spat again. David nudged his head with the toe of a boot.

Are you on drugs?

No.

David looked along the street. You know where I can get some? See any people high around here?

Don't see no people.

How do you eat?

Don't eat.

You sure shit a lot for someone who dudn't eat.

Don't shit. The man started smacking his own arm.

Who does, then?

The fairies. The man started to roll over.

Where are these fairies?

In the trees. Idiot.

David let him get to his feet. The man faced him and made the sign of the cross backward and shuffled away. When he was far enough the man spun about and ran west down the street. David watched him go and walked to his horse. It had drifted toward a small bridge at the edge of town. It crossed a wooded creek and he let it go to drink and he sat on the bridge railing and studied the intersection. The wires on the poles had been cut, the glass insulators left littering the ground. An immensity came over him, the size of the world and the strangeness of it now, wires cut, the country wild. During the war he could send a letter home and get one back in two weeks. A helicopter flew to the mountain with the mail, with water, with food and ammunition and now a letter might never get anywhere. Now there was no flying. Fifteen miles from his home the world seemed in ruins.

The bay came back from the creekside and grazed by the bridge. In the far distance he heard the rumble of a train. He watched birds flit overhead, perching on a young oak beside the creek. Sparrows. One flew off and he followed it overhead and it disappeared into the woods along the creek. There was a wood box a few hundred yards away, tucked up in the fork of a tree. He called for the horse and led it around to a field beyond the bridge and they walked deep until he let the reins drop and went into the woods.

The treehouse was old, the paint long worn away and the wood beginning to rot. A single slanted sheet of roofing topped it. Broken two-by-fours were nailed to the trunk of the hickory it stood in and a soiled doll lay facedown in the dirt by the ladder. He took the first step in his hands and tested it before easing his way up. Clearing the steps he saw into the little room of the treehouse and under a table was a hunched child. He gripped the doorframe and stood off the ladder. He expected the child to unfold and to turn and eye him but it did not. It didn't move when he stepped across the tiny room nor when he lifted the table away and he saw it was a wretchedly thin girl holding a little boy. Skin dessicated, dirt-streaked. The toddler was naked and his forehead humongous, malformed. David needed to sit. He had to sit. He put the table aside and stumbled back and nearly tilted through the doorway. He caught the wall and a retch slipped through his teeth. He scaled down the ladder and dropped the last steps to the ground and ran. The boy was floating behind his eyes, the swollen head. He broke through the treeline in front of the horse and it cried at him and he fell back. He didn't get up. It was a long while he sat there peeling memory from the present. He saw a boy totter down a dirt road. He wore a ragged shirt that hung to his knees and behind him he trailed water that flowed down his legs. He was thin and seemed untroubled, only walking on toward David. Before he reached him the boy sat down. Down the road a whole village poisoned. People had tumbled from their doors and fallen in the road, vomit soaking into the dirt. He had been following stories. They didn't know his name but he matched the description, and David had known. They called him a santo. The boy sat down in front of him again and again. Maybe three years old. Light skin, unblemished. He found Red on the other side of the village, watching him from the mouth of a tunnel. Standing there he was unsure who had gone mad.

The sun was passing behind the trees when his horse nudged him. He got up into the saddle and rode the way he'd come, turning north where the light had been and riding on through the fading day. Something was wrong. The knuckles behind his forehead had gone through, had blown the wiring in his eyes. Everything was faded blue the way it was after a day in the sun. Instead of pressure there was a skating levity, a feeling that he was not touching the horse, the horse not touching the ground, his fingertips not meeting his brow. The horse took him to an intersection in the middle of an open field. He pressed the bay left and they went on another mile in the dusk passing a house and a church. There were distant trees that the last light threaded through, pink and yellow from clouds yet to pass. He rode on a few miles and came to Clintonville, the city flat and quiet. Signs stood for restaurants long closed. There were two horses tied up in front of the only open bar and he got down to tie his own, the reins flopping about in his hands until he dropped them over the rail and went inside. There were three customers, one of them asleep at a table in the back and the others at the bar. He stood just inside the door and the bartender swiveled his head to look at him, bent over in conversation with an old man. David waited a moment longer before he came toward them and rested an elbow on the counter. The bartender sniffed and straightened.

She's by the church on Wing Road.

What?

Macy.

I don't know who Macy is.

The bartender's eyebrows lifted. Oh. I figured you were huntin' some strange.

What in the hell are you talking about?

He waved his hand over the bar like he would wipe something away. My mistake. What can I get you?

I'll take a bourbon.

I got some moonshine, no bourbon.

David shrugged. Why not.

The bartender turned for a bottle of clear liquor and he poured a shot. He slid it toward David and put the bottle back. David took the glass up and smelled it and had a sip. It burned. He set the glass back and scanned the bar again. The door at his back made him itch.

I came in on Wing. This Macy runnin' a whorehouse?

The first man down the bar reached for his beer. Methhouse is more like it.

David lifted his chin. He drank half of the glass and held his breath until his throat unclenched. She's a druggie?

Whores herself out for it. Used to be a hot piece.

The bartender was watching them both and nodding sadly. David tilted his glass and set it back. You guys know anything about a fellow named Murphy?

Can't say I do.

The bartender rested against the shelf behind him. Murphy who?

One that broke into a house north of Claremont.

What are you after him for?

David eyed the door.

Are you from around here?

Yeah.

Where exactly?

Don't you worry about it.

The bartender lifted a hand. I'm not tryin' to pry.

David finished the shot, slapped it down and stood away from the bar. The customer closest spun on his stool to face him.

Are you workin' hard to be an asshole or is it coming naturally?

He settled and glanced at the man. I think it's been a secret talent all my life. He turned to the door and stopped with his hand on it. This Macy. She have kids?

The bartender took his glass and put it below the counter. Believe so. Probably sold 'em by now.

Thanks.

It ain't my business, but watch your ass if you're headed out there. She keeps company with a couple rough boys.

Rough how?

Tied a customer to a chair once. Started a little campfire out in a field and sat him over it.

You're kidding me. David wrinkled his face.

Nope. Didn't even set him on fire directly. I guess they let him go once the fire burnt through the ropes. He's the one that told the police, before he died.

He shook his head. Thanks. He went out. It looked as though no one had come by, the air itself unmoved. The city was dark but for a few unshot streetlights. Riding the way he'd come he passed a stripmall and a few empty restaurants and houses. Beyond them he was in the country. He got down from the bay and walked it along a creek half a mile from the church and tied it to a tree. The water smelled of moss and he could smell the grass and the weeds in the cool air. Back on the road he checked the chamber on the rifle and held it in his hand by the stock. The church was dark and rounding it, the house was as well. He went up the front steps and drew the knife and blasted at the door with the handle. There was no answer. He'd put dents in the wood. There were no sounds in response and he tucked the knife away. He kicked the door and it broke off its hinges with him following like he'd ride it into the room. It was pitch dark inside, humps of furniture standing in what was the living room. He could barely see the staircase and to the left the black of a hallway. The door rattled on the floor when he stepped off of it and walked deeper in, hands seeking. In the middle of the room the hair stood on his neck and he looked up to the stairs. There had been a sound.

Who's there?

David eased the rifle out from his side and raised it. It was a man's voice.

I got a gun trained right on you.

David guided the rifle back to his shoulder and aimed for the voice. Same here.

Bullshit.

Shoot, then.

There was no answer for a moment. We don't got any drugs.

I'm not looking for drugs. Is this where Macy lives?

Yeah.

She know a guy named Murphy?

Who?

David waited. There was a sound from the back of the house. He slid farther from the open doorway and the little light it cast. There was a sound of metal on wood and he guessed the man had set his gun on the banister. Whispers. A shadow came through the door and rushed toward him and David toppled over. His shoulder struck a doorway and his knee slipped across tile and he punched into the trunk of whoever was atop him. Struggling to stand up he found the person's head and he took it two-handed and hauled it toward the wall beside them and it bounced off with a cry. He stood and gave a look toward the stairs and he saw another shadow. The attacker cut an elbow at his shin and David reached down and grabbed the arm, thin, and pulled the man into what he guessed was the kitchen. He drew the knife and hauled the man up with it to his throat and the man shouted. They backed together to a countertop and then a match popped in front of them. David winced and saw a man holding a shotgun and a woman behind him holding the match. The man in his arms was wiry and stank and David turned the blade slightly to let the man with the gun see it. The match went out. Swirls of blue in the black.

Light another.

His attacker squirmed. Don't kill me.

Light another match.

The world came back and the woman stretched out her hand, match held in her fingertips. Her arm was bruised and pitted.

I'm just here for Murphy.

The man with the gun shook his head. I don't know any Murphy.

The match was burning quick. David shifted the druggie in his arm. He killed a girl.

We don't know anything about it.

I don't want to hurt any of you.

The man he held jerked his head. You got a knife to my fucking throat!

David tightened his hold. Just tell me where this guy is.

The woman slung the match out and lit another. He doesn't stick around anywhere. He comes by to score and leaves after a day or so.

When was he here last?

This afternoon.

Where did he go?

The man with the gun smacked her hand and the match went out. David's vision starred and he slashed with the knife and one of them groaned. He was hit again and he tried to keep hold of the man under his arm while scrabbling away but the man slipped free and kicked him. A drawer fell open and metal clattered. David looked for a window, for any light. Someone was at his left and he thrust and the blade sunk deep into meat. He was grabbed and thrown into a wall and he charged back and hit someone with the knifehandle and glimpsed the night sky through a transom and barreled out the door. He slipped against the wall of the house and kicked the first shape to cross the doorway and ran for the road. No one following, no gunfire. He found the creek and his bay and he patted it with shaking hands. He'd begun to haul himself up onto the horse when he realized there was nowhere to go, and he dropped back. He took the saddle down from the horse and untied it and he set the saddle against the tree and leaned against it. The grass was cool but the ground warm. He let himself sink. The branches of the tree covered in leaves, the sky half obscured. It felt like rain, like high pressure, a night-long storm with hours of thunder and purple light.

No sleep had come but he woke into daylight, tense and bound by his own muscle. His ribs were sore, eye swollen. The world through it a slit. He stood slowly and tried to stretch, halted from the pain, then reached to saddle the horse. Walking it to the road he saw the blood on his pantleg from the knife and he felt the blade sink into the leg again. His throat narrowed but he kept walking, mounting up on the road and going on to the house. He left the horse across the road and went to the open doorway with the knife out. Light footsteps coming quick as he went through the doorway and the woman stood in the middle of the living room. Her eyes were all white. She was very thin and her face drawn but he could see from her eyes and hair she had been beautiful.

You almost killed my cousin.

A moment for the present to slide back into place. I expect he deserved it.

She started backing, hands out for something to grab.

You broke into our house!

This ain't your house.

Her mouth trembled. She was nearly in the kitchen. David stepped over an upturned chair. His rifle was standing in the corner of the room by the kitchen doorway.

You Macy? Where's the other one?

He took him into town for help. He was bleedin' bad.

David nodded. The anger returned and he felt better. I met your kids.

She stiffened. You what?

I imagine they're yours. You oughta be strung up.

What are you talking about?

He reached for his rifle and slung it onto his shoulder. You are among the lowest things I've seen on this earth. And I been places. I've seen some things. He kept coming, his pace slow. Between Macy's feet a narrow stream of blood had collected from a slant in the floor. She stepped in it and glanced down and shivered, stepped over it to the counter. She stared at David but palmed around for anything to wield. David stood in the doorway. She was whimpering.

Just leave. Just leave, please.

David's head loosened, panned to the table where they'd set her cousin. The blood was dry there and a bead of it was hanging from the edge like cooled wax. Tell me where to find Murphy.

Okay. Okay.

He killed a little girl.

He's up in Clintonville.

I was just in Clintonville. They didn't know anything about him.

He doesn't talk to anyone. There's an old restaurant at the edge of town. They used to cook everything up there. People still go there to hide out.

He turned.

They'll shoot you. They'll see you comin' a mile away.

I don't mind that. Fact I prefer it. He left and walked across the field.

22

Riding into Clintonville in daylight the city seemed even emptier. The day warmed quickly and everywhere he looked the pavement sprawled and the sun thickened the air into pools of quicksilver. The sky was paling and he waited for the wind while circling the parking lots and restaurants at the outskirts of town. He found nothing and the wind never came. He rode on into town and checked the ends of the main streets and then the sidestreets and going back and forth people began to watch him. They all seemed leaner, hungrier than he was used to. Outside the bar he saw the customer who'd spoken to him the day before, smoking. He gestured with the cigarette up at David and David stopped his horse.

You find that Murphy guy?

No.

Who did you find?

David grimaced. Nobody.

The man pulled on his cigarette and looked off. Somebody found you, seems like.

He'd covered the perimeter of the city by the middle of the afternoon and saw nothing. Most of the restaurants were shuttered. When he circled back to go out of town a man rode up with a badge glinting on his chest. Nearing him the officer lifted his hand.

Howdy.

David nodded to him.

You lose your wallet?

He stopped his horse across from the officer's. Is everybody in this town a smartass?

The officer ignored him. You been in a fight?

Not in your jurisdiction.

Well, that's good. Hate to have to take a report. He glanced around himself. Couple folks called in said you were patrolling harder than I was. Is there something I can help you with?

I doubt it.

Try me.

Can I find drugs in this town?

The officer laughed. Where you keep your balls? In them saddlebags?

I look like a user to you?

No. Which begs the question.

I'm looking for someone.

Why don't you come with me. Go into the station, get outta this heat for a minute.

I'd rather just keep looking. He saw the officer eye him, and David didn't move.

Don't make me insist.

They both sat on their horses. David watched the officer's face tighten and then droop and his hand slipped toward his gunbelt. David began to smile. I was just leaving.

The officer rocked to the side slightly. Go ahead.

David started his horse. After a minute he looked back and the officer was still there on his mount, watching him leave. Once he was out of the city he wandered the sideroads and old farmers' paths heading roughly westward until he was through Gosper County and on his way home. The southwestern wind finally picked up dry and hot. The horizon blurred. He went north of Dixon to avoid passing the house and as he turned to head into town the first wave of a duster came over the fields. He rode through it. It faded outside Dixon and a few people were walking in the falling haze. They watched him like they had in Clintonville. Fogel came up from out of the grocery and tried to slow his horse but

David stared him down and went on. It had been winter when Red and he came back to town but they had come in as tired and bloody. It had been dry that winter and the snow that fell collected in the pockets of dead grass at the side of the road. A state behind them Red had found a last cigarette in his jacket pocket and they shared it on the shoulder of a highway, the land barren and forgotten as far as they could see.

Before he got to the edge of town his courage waned. He turned the horse down a sidestreet, toward the granary, to ride on a little longer before going toward the house. Past the silos he heard someone call from the train station. Skillman was standing on the platform and David wheeled toward him.

How're you doin', Dave? You alright?

David squinted. Yeah. He pointed at Skillman's bare head. Happened to your hat?

It was the damnedest thing. Blew clean off a few days ago, lost it down a mineshaft. Unlucky I guess.

You don't have any spares or somethin'?

Skillman shook his head. How're you all doing? I don't think I've seen you since before, well.

We're gettin' by.

You sure you're okay? You look like you got kicked by a mule.

I'm fine.

Skillman nodded, solemn. Well. I'll let you get movin'.

David held the reins up and backed the horse a step. Where are you off to?

My side project.

Ah.

Skillman smiled and reached to doff his hat for nothing. I'll see you around. Take care.

David turned the horse and they rode north, past the post office. Miller was coming opposite on horseback and his glare fired from under the brim of the Stetson.

Heading for the barn he stopped the horse at the door,

and pulled it on to the gate and the pasture. Some distance out he turned east. The house came into view and he sat the horse and waited for something to move, a curtain in the windows, a door. All he saw was the slow wheeling of the shadows along the yard. He circled the horse back in a long loop, bringing him closer, and then away again.

He found an old hoe in a corner of the equipment barn at Danvers' and started into the fields. He weeded for hours, until the sun was nearly down, and took the bay back out of its stall to check the cattle. He found a yearling heifer with its head caught in the eastern fence, most of the herd already gone away from it. Dropping from the saddle he went for his gloves and stopped, walked up to the heifer barehanded and circled its neck with one arm. He gripped the top strand of barbwire and flexed it up and twisted with his hips to heave the calf out but it kicked and began to bawl and the wire slipped from his hand and sprang down, bursting the heifer's eye. He cursed and regripped, letting go of the wire and grabbing under its legs. He hauled up and the calf sprang free and they flew back together, the calf's head striking him breathless. It rolled up from beside him and ran, loping. He stood slowly, stumbling to the horse and gripping the saddle before getting up and riding to the far ends of the property. He roamed near the house until there was no light and then he let the horse find its way back. At the barn doors he realized he had nowhere to go. When he came back with Red he'd come home to an empty house, the two of them drinking in the living room, building towers of beer cans, passing a bottle of bourbon back and forth. Macha watching them. And even when Red started disappearing he still had the house, still had the familiar walls. And then he'd brought her back.

Weights seemed attached to his legs as he crossed the drive. He knocked on Danvers' door before going on in. He stood in the mudroom doorway a moment, looking at the counter and the kitchen table. No note in the open, nothing from Helene. Danvers was in the living room reading with a single light on and when he glanced up he shut his book, then he started and stood, peering at him.

What in the hell happened to you?

I need to use your phone.

Well, I. Go ahead.

David called the sheriff's department. He told the deputy that answered about the children and hung up before the deputy could ask his name. After he set the phone on the cradle he relaxed against the kitchen counter and his eyelids sunk.

You gonna tell me what happened?

Got in a fight.

With a gang, what?

A couple people.

Danvers took a step toward him. Have any luck?

I don't think you'd call it luck. I got a lead.

Good.

She say anything to you?

No. Not a word.

She call?

I just said she hasn't spoke to me. Come on in here and siddown. I'll get you a blanket or something.

No, I'm gonna go to the barn.

What for? You gonna sleep in the hay?

David shrugged.

Are you stupid? No, I know the answer to that one. Are you trying to punish yourself or what?

I don't know.

If you think you did something wrong you gotta apologize. Sleepin' out in the barn ain't gonna make her do anything but pity you.

He raised his eyebrows. I dunno. Maybe I need the air.

Danvers lifted a hand to wave him away. Suit yourself. There's some supper in the fridge if you want it.

Thanks. David turned and headed out the door. In the barn he climbed up into the hayloft and it was warm and dark. He cut the twine on a haybale to bring more down for the animals and he sat for a moment, the bale falling apart, and he leaned back. A firefly had come into the loft and it clung blinking to a rafter. He closed his eyes. His head was excavated, hollowed out, the images there standing lonely. Wood creaked from the southwest corner of the barn, crickets sang. Hunger like a solid knot in him, a knurl, coal black hair. He could smell himself and he rubbed at the bristles on his cheek. He was beginning to sleep and a dream slid through his thoughts, spliced with them. Samuel in a hole, wounded. The smell of copper and gunsmoke. He shook his head because it made no sense, and then he was asleep.

Light was shining through a split in the wall. Stretching he lifted a curl of dust and it spun through the beam. The floor whirled sideways when he stood and he caught himself and waited for the blood to rise to his head. He climbed down and left the barn and went into Danvers' house. Danvers was seated at the kitchen table with the little plastic radio going, nothing but static.

You look even worse today.

I feel it.

Eat somethin'.

David opened the refrigerator and pulled out a dish of meatloaf. He stopped. Time is it?

Ten o'clock. Glenn Fogel called after you. Said he saw you ridin' through town yesterday.

He nodded and brought the meatloaf to the table. Danvers leaned over and pulled a fork out for him and handed it over.

I don't suppose you'll heat that up.

No. David started to cut into it. The telephone rang and the sound shot through him and spidered up his back. The ring died slow in the quiet. You not gonna answer it?

Danvers shrugged. Probably for you.

David stood and reached for the phone. It didn't ring again. He sat.

You know Helene brought that down.

He breathed in and stabbed the fork into the meatloaf, let it stand.

Why don't you stick around for the day?

They said this guy moves around a lot.

Danvers' face pinched. You're givin' me gray hairs.

You're bald.

You're givin' someone gray hairs.

Probably myself. I haven't looked in the mirror lately.

Maybe you should.

The roads of Gosper County became familiar to him. He wandered Clintonville on foot and on horseback, rode the edges of town and circled like a raptor. A tent city lay on the dried-up fairgrounds, the people mostly from Claremont. He spent the night across the street from the stripmall to case the few restaurants there. He camped on the porch of an abandoned house watching the wide broken expanse of the parking lot. All night there was nothing. A policeman walked by once, and later a raccoon. A man and woman argued down the street. Just before sunup he went for his horse outside of town and he started circling again.

He ate rarely, drank from creeks. At night he would leave his horse and stage wherever he could to watch the outskirts of town and each night he saw nothing. The light still played blue to him, as if the world had gone bloodless. He had waking dreams where his body seized around itself and he spun on the ground. Saliva flooded his mouth like he was preparing to vomit. He'd sit away from the horse as he did after the treehouse and unwind himself, pry himself open like a trap. Things he'd done and seen, during the war and after. Memories he had to wear smooth before he could put them away. He'd reached into wounds to pinch arteries closed, felt the quiver of muscle from inside. Diaphragm ballooning against viscera, Lieutenant Collins holding the man's hand and teaching him how to breathe. He'd piled organs onto open chests and stuffed a field of gauze into a stabwound and watched the men flown off in helicopters and timed like an explosion their deaths, his arms finished in blood so uniform and bright. And when he'd find he was back at the roadside or in the field he was emptied and hungry and somehow nostalgic. He wanted to miss his wife, to be doing the simple thing, the heroic thing, to be ordered. He wanted to be there to wish he were home.

For a month he roamed Gosper County and every few days he returned to Danvers' to work the fields and watch over the house. Toward the end the weeds were drying out and the dusters burying them. The beans raced the ground. Twice there were heavy storms that caught him afield and he worried the bay would choke. He'd pass his shirt from his face to the horse's muzzle and sparks jumped from his hands.

People began to recognize him in Clintonville and the police and few deputies in the county stopped him from time to time but they never did anything. He spoke with the family Murphy had robbed and he walked the back streets and rode the countryside. Every shack, every shed. All the houses that had been abandoned were stripped of copper and in several he found sign of addicts. Near the county line he rode past a man walking the other way and saw it was a miner. The man kept his eyes down and his gait quickened. Hours later Danvers was waiting on him with a letter in his hand, passing it over the moment David came in the door.

The lady gave me your mail. I guess word got around.

David shook his head and looked at the envelope. It was from Red.

Dave,

Your boy wrote me, wanting me to come up, so I figured I'd write you, too. He told me about everything that happened. I wish I could help you out but you know I can't do anything. You know the trail's cold. All I'd be if you did find him is someone to hold him up while you knock his teeth out.

I can't imagine what this is doing to you. Seeing something like that, you know people say you get desensitized but I don't think I ever did. I guess they get less important, like years as you get older, but they don't ever hurt any less. I still think about those times, the bad ones before you came and got me. While you were there, too. I wish I'd left with the rest of the boys but there's no chang-ing that now. You probably realize I'm just clearing my throat. It's years and years late but man I'm sorry for ever dragging you back down there. I really am. If I could regret someone saving my life I would, but that'd be cursing a hell of a gift. You're the best man I ever knew, and I know you're gonna get through this.

Keep your head down,
Red

He read the letter again. There was another page and he saw Samuel's name at the top. He flipped the page over, tapped it against his hand.

Well. He say anything important?

David looked out the window. It was July and the beans weren't far above his ankles, struggling. He passed Danvers and left the letters on the kitchen table. He showered and shaved off the few weeks of beard and he stood in front of the mirror to examine his face. There was still a cut on his cheek and the little roundness there had been to his jaw was gone. His arms were brown from being outside so long as the sun was up and at his chest was a V of red skin. He'd been the same color in the mountains.

He walked to the house, bowlegged, Samuel's letter stuffed into his back pocket. His palms were damp. He tilted his hat up and swallowed when he rounded the bend. Nothing was in disrepair, nothing overgrown. He cut through the yard and stood before the porch steps, then climbed them and knocked on the door. Samuel opened it and David pulled him in for a hug, staring down at him and then looking up to see the hall, the kitchen. Samuel fought his way out of it.

I came out to see you Tuesday.

David grimaced. He had no idea what day it was. I was out.

You weren't working.

I was out looking.

They quieted. David sensed a growth in Samuel, something from their distance.

How's school?

It's going okay. Those kids have been coming out here.

What kids?

Brandon and Tyler.

David shrugged.

Moore.

Ah. The weird ones.

Yeah. Mom makes me go out and run around with them.

Probably good for you. David smiled. He brightened further and pulled the letter from his back pocket. Red wrote you.

Samuel took it and scanned the front.

Don't you want to read it?

I will. He looked into the house and David followed his eyes. Samuel turned back to him. You look tired.

I'm alright.

Do you want to come in? Mom's not here.

Sure.

He stepped back for David to enter and shut the door. David stood by, waiting on Samuel. Nothing was changed, no pictures, no furniture. The bedroom door was shut and he thought to just stand in the room and to touch the bed, the sheets. Samuel went into the kitchen and opened up the refrigerator. He pulled out a bottle of milk and a package wrapped in butcher paper and got a loaf of bread from the cupboard and started making sandwiches. David stood up to the counter and watched.

How many do you want?

One's fine.

I eat two.

Two then. He cracked a thin smile. How's your mom?

She's okay. She's at the grocery a lot. You knew she got a job there a couple weeks ago, right?

No.

She brings them a big basket of stuff from the garden every day or so. He finished a sandwich, put it on a plate and pushed it toward David. He poured them both glasses of milk.

Is that all the food you've got?

No. Mom doesn't like me using the stove when she's not home.

I'm here.

Samuel shrugged. He kept on making sandwiches. She

looks kind of like you.

Tired?

Yeah. His eyes on his work, spreading condiments. Mom told me about you and Red. About you going to save him.

David's throat clenched.

I was writing him a letter and she told me. She said she didn't want me to think he was so perfect.

Nobody is.

She said he almost killed someone when he was here. When I was a baby.

David nodded. He had reason. It was a bad guy. He hurt a friend of ours.

She said he did it a lot. Fought people. She said some guys followed him back to the house once, and they had a gun.

That's true. He was quiet for a moment. The war was hard on him. It was hard on both of us. You come back and still see problems and you think you ought to fix 'em.

Samuel finished making the sandwiches and set one on top of the first on David's plate.

Mom tell you anything else?

No. Just that I shouldn't think fighting's a good thing.

It's not. David set two fingers on the plate of sandwiches. He moved them away. It's just a necessary thing.

Yeah.

David eyed him. Don't say 'yeah.' You don't know. And you shouldn't.

Samuel was quiet. He bit into his sandwich and chewed like he was eating cloth. He swallowed. I do know. I know what happens. I heard you and Mom. If you have to leave to fight it's okay. I know she says it's not but it is to me. You can't let people get away with doing bad things. You can't let this guy go.

I won't. But she's right, though. It's not worth losing you both, going after him.

Aren't you too late?

She's that mad, huh? David set his sandwich down.

No. I don't know. I mean you already started. He looked off. Will the police get him?

They might. David waited on him to respond.

Okay.

I know it's hard. I lost a friend too.

He nodded.

I feel like your mom's gonna walk in any second and ground me.

She won't.

Well. You want to come to Phil's for a bit?

I'd better stay here.

He thinned his lips. Alright. Samuel had stood to clear the counter and didn't look back at him. He felt low.

23

He could not bring himself to go to the grocery, so he went to the bar and bought a bottle of unbranded whiskey and took it into the hayloft. He opened the loft door and sat watching the sky and draining the bottle. Below him Samuel's bay rustled, chewed at a beam and stopped. Swish of a tail. He and Red had gone riding far into the pasture that summer, and they let the horses go and David watched him lie in the tall grass, the grasshoppers bounding away. He lifted a rifle to the sky and fired. At the clouds, he'd said, to make them rain. The horses spooked and their hides shivered in the light. He fired again, adjusting his aim. Eventually they heard the breath of dust from the bullet landing beside his head. He'd smiled and stood and they left. That night he broke into a house and came out the front door with a man, knife to his throat. The man had beaten a woman and thrown her out of the house hours before, locked the door with her child inside. Red snuck in the basement and came out with him in a minute. David was on the street with the police, spotlight trained on Red catching him in the doorway like an animal. He threw the man aside and ran and was gone in the morning.

It was after noon when David woke, and he spent most of the remainder of the day in the loft, waiting for a glimpse of Samuel or Helene on the road. That night he drank again and finished the bottle. He held it in his hands, rolling it between them, tossing it back and forth, wanting to pitch it at a wall. He was still drunk in the morning. A duster had passed in the night and coated him in a skin of red clay. He found the bottle empty and unbroken beside him.

He rode out into the fields with his sweat reeking sweet from the whiskey. After a while the horse began to shiver. David sat up and saw a coyote in one of the old snares, belly-up. Flies cavorted around its open mouth and eyes. When he dropped from the horse the coyote kicked a leg and the bay bucked sideways. David had put the knife in his belt and he took it out and with his free hand wrenched up on the snare. The flies clouded and with them a putrid green smell. He spat into the grass beside his boot and wound the snare tighter until he had the coyote's head between his knees and he pressed down on its neck with his forearm. It hadn't moved since the first kick and he let it drop. He searched around for something to hang the body from. Bushes, fallen fenceposts. He glanced up at the horse and then uprooted the snare and stake and cinched the wire around the coyote's hindlegs and pounded the stake back into the hole with the butt of the knife. Pulling the legs taut and sitting lightly over the swelling belly he cut around the hindpaws and dragged the tip of the blade along the back of both legs up the hip and joined the cuts at the tail. He turned away and snuffed in a breath, wiped under his nose with the side of his hand. The skin was pliant and warm when he dug his fingers in and began peeling at the legs, sliding them up toward the body. He cut a slit along the tail and worked at pulling the wire of bone free. Standing up he lifted the back of the coyote and cut at the white tissue connecting skin to muscle and began hauling on the torso and it came away until the hide was half inside-out. The skin flayed with a sound and it grew thicker until it crawled up David's arms. He stopped when it was skinned to the forelegs and he cut the legs like chaps and went on skinning. When he had it to the snout he stepped away and it was like a beast being born of itself, twinning, shining and placental and the blood where he had cut too deep still ran a vivid red along the darker meat and when he cut the cartilage free of the snout there was a shudder from the corpse like the last give of a muscle, of

194

loins. David fell away and in his hands was the hide and he stood up to whirl it into the grass. He stabbed the thigh of the carcass and stopped, stared around himself.

He went back to Danvers'. His vision had gone bleary and he saw the kitchen through wax paper and stopped to drink glass after glass of water. The phone rang. The phone kept ringing and he stood and groped through the air for it and answered.

Where you been, Dave?

It was the sheriff. David leaned against the wall, bringing the phone with him. His head drummed and he could feel the blood flow through it, feel the delay from bottom to top. Out.

Out where? Gosper County?

Yeah.

Well you missed all the action somehow. Apparently your man was shot last night outside Clintonville.

He closed his eyes. You're kiddin' me.

No. Old farmer caught him sneaking into his barn, crept up with a shotgun and blew his shoulder clean off.

How'd you find this out?

We hear about double-homicides, even these days. Word gets around.

So Murphy shot back?

Popped him in the side. They said he must've had a heart attack, because he didn't bleed enough for the shot to have killed him. Had to take the wife to the hospital here just to get her calmed down.

Goddammit.

They recovered the gun. It ain't the one that shot Miss Reckard.

David held the phone away and stared wildly at the room as if he could lay the blame somewhere in it. Are they sure it's him?

It's him. He's got a record over there.

He could'a just been using a different gun.

He could have, yeah.

There's no way it was someone else.

No.

What about Spangler? Did we ever think about him?

For what?

Killing her.

The sheriff cut himself off at first. We questioned him. He's got an alibi and you've known him long enough you ought to know better than that.

How good's the alibi?

His wife and him were out for a ride, Dave. He covered her eyes when he saw the girl.

David gripped the phone. The sheriff stayed on the line. Do you know what all's going on over there, around Clintonville?

Yeah, I do.

I saw some kids dead in a treehouse, Sheriff. Their momma just left 'em. I mean I can't say that for sure but I can put it together.

I know.

Is that how it is everywhere else?

A lot of places. Some places it ain't so bad. Clintonville isn't that far from civilization.

I don't remember any civilization being like that.

There's never all that far to fall, Dave. You should know that. He breathed deep. Be careful goin' over there. I don't mind you doin' it and not because it's not my county, but I do mind if you wind up hurt.

They hung up. He sat on the floor, the phone still in his hand. His brain was made of shaved ice. It grated, broke up. When he stood he nearly fell over and his arms swung about. He bounced off the wall. He drank two more glasses of water and went into the bathroom to shower. He tried to think of nothing. He shut off the shower and reached for the towel, let it fall on top of him. Water dripped from his chin.

You alright in there boy?

Yeah.

What's the matter?

They found him. The druggie. Some old man killed him.

That's good, ain't it?

It wadn't him. He wadn't the guy.

He dried off and dressed, shaved, and stared at the sockets of his eyes like his eyes weren't there. He left the bathroom. His hat was on the table. He got it and put it on and Danvers came from out of his bedroom and stood in the doorway.

Where are you goin'?

Clintonville.

What for?

To make sure.

Danvers sighed. What exactly were you supposed to get out of this, Dave?

What do you mean? I was supposed to get the fucker, see if it was the right gun, and kill him.

And what would that have solved?

The hell are you getting at, Phil?

I'm just trying to see in that head of yours. You've been off your rocker for about a month now. Danvers went over to the coffee pot and turned it on. Helene called here the other day, when you was out. She said she'd seen you out in the fields just sittin' there on your horse, watching the house.

I go to see everything's alright.

Well. If you want to be sane about it you walk up onto the porch and you knock on the door. Say, 'Hey, you all doin' alright?' You're worrying me, son.

He closed his eyes for a moment and shook his head. She's dead. That's all I got, Phil. She's dead and she was Sam's best friend. O H was a good guy. One of the best I ever met.

I know.

What am I doing if I don't put that right? Who am I? I

can't look at myself knowing I didn't do a thing.

What I'm trying to tell you is what you're doing ain't right. You're acting crazy. Do you get me? I mean crazy.

David's eyes went away, over Danvers' head. Maybe that's the problem. That's the problem with everything. You think I'm being crazy. He shook himself and started for the door. He got his horse from the barn and rode. The sun was high and brilliant and the sky the dry white color it took on after the dusters. He felt the light might pierce him and the heat seemed focused upon him by a lens. Beams of sunlight scattered, he'd look up and the light would dial about his eyes. He was sweating, breath fuming with alcohol. The road was straight for miles and he dropped his head, closed his eyes. Every so often he woke up and found himself farther down the path though the terrain was nearly identical, the short corn and white sky, telephone poles ground clean and smooth. Weeds. He passed a sign for Clintonville, full of holes. Home of state wrestling champion: name shot away. Behind him the sky thickened.

In town he rode the horse around to the rear of the restaurant and kicked in the backdoor. He had the rifle in his hands. The door rebounded off the wall and a bucket skidded across the filthy tile floor, cutting a track in aged grease. A fried smell seemed to cover him like a net, and a smell behind it, acrid. The restaurant was dark, the only light coming in from behind him. From the ceiling hung racks for skillets and a hood extinguishing system that had been ripped apart. Glassware filled the countertops. A mouse ran from one end of the room to the other, scrambling over an empty roll of kitchen foil. He let his eyes adjust and stepped away from the door. Outside the wind shifted and he thought he could hear the sand grinding against the side of the building. The way to the seating area was open and he found rows of tables and booths covered in refuse. Rays of weak light slipped through cracks in the plywood over the windows. The wind strengthened and he felt closed in, the walls like a faltering shield. He slipped the rifle onto his shoulder and began tossing the contents of the benches, pulling them out onto the stained carpet, stomping them smooth. He found a burnt spoon, several pipes. Bullets for a twenty-two but no gun. He kicked a table and it rocked, fell back. At the last booth he stopped himself from yanking a blanket from a dead man, eyelids cracked open and beneath them a wrinkled yellow surface. The body was dry. Nothing to the arms but bone and tendon, the hair coarse and standing straight off the scalp. He covered the body and turned away.

The door sucked closed when he tried to crack it and he could barely slip through. The bay had gone to the side of the restaurant and he hunched his shoulders against the wind and sand and felt it lashing at him. He led the bay to the street and rode. It was coming on evening and the duster was still strong, the sky a heavy orange. The town was quiet. Riding down a sidestreet he saw a woman and a young girl look out a picture window at him. The lawn in front was overgrown. He took the horse south out of town. He thought about the body in the restaurant and about the children and he churned the thoughts until they were built up in him like ink, something impenetrable. His brain preserved in it like formaldehyde. Adding droplets of other memories to the suspension. The duster was getting stronger and even caught in a lash he could see more coming, heavier, hitting him in darkening waves until it was black behind him and ahead almost maroon. He drove the horse into a ditch and he tried to haul its head down to his level as he sat but it would not bend. The dust built up at his collar, in his hair. It thickened on his hands, in his sweat. Once a shell had struck a tree and pinned him to the earth. Waiting to be dug out he was taken by the weight, comforted. Like a heavy blanket or parent's arm in sleep. A wave of dust rolled over onto his back and he was in the draw. They'd fled with the remaining Republicans and the few loyal villagers and they were mostly dead. A hill burned open at their backs and the draw lay between them and the Jimenez. They fought for a day and into the night and Red and he watched sleeplessly, and watched as the clouds broke and a low wet moon emptied milk into the draw and it covered the soldiers advancing. In the morning their bodies were strewn across the sand. Women among them, long black hair. With the full daylight they spent their last rounds on both sides and, taken by some spirit, they rose and left their cover, rushing to meet each other. Fighting with knives and clubs, rocks pulled from the riverbed. He was thrown and pushed deep into the sand and it sucked him down until he could feel the stiff crack of a windpipe against his knuckles. Coming free of the earth he was heavy with it and the rain and Red was cutting the femur from a soldier. Sweeping the field there was no one else standing and so he fell to the man at his feet choking on the cartilage of his own throat and David cut his trouser leg open and he stabbed the knife into the man's hip and pulled the blade to the sand. Blood poured down the fissure. David cut through the meat to the socket tendons at the hip and knee and he lifted the femur and turned the bone in his hand and lifted the lateralis from where it hung over the head and cut it off. The man's leg lay hollow and the flayed muscles were draped across his uniform. He had stopped breathing only when David had gripped the bone in his hand.

The duster abated. The church was a few hundred yards away. Time reversed, the sky brightening and the sun rising over the west. The light angled through the front windows of the church and he could see a shadow behind the stained glass at the side of the building. The bay was shivering beside him and David climbed out of the ditch for the rifle and began leading the horse. The shadow in the window froze, twisted, and raced out of sight. A man started running across the field at the back of the church. David blew out the muzzle and chamber and lifted the rifle. He lined the shot, paced it just ahead of the man, exhaled, and fired. The shot echoed off the trees and he slid the rifle into the scabbard and rode forward. He slowed the horse beside the body and slipped off. The man was facedown, wide bloodstain and rip in the back of his shirt. David stooped and flipped him over onto his back. The bullet had hit him near his heart. The corner of a paper wrapper stuck out of his pocket and David pulled it out, felt the powder inside. He tore it open and let it drop. There was a clean and empty feeling behind his forehead, staring at the man, the body. The horse had gone a few yards back to the road and David led it to the church steps. He went inside.

The sanctuary was long, a single column of pews on either side. The cross was toppled behind the pulpit. David came forward, walking down the aisle. He turned to make sure the door closed and through the shrinking gap the land had a poisonous sheen to it, the dust like flecks of gold. There was the same ammonia smell from the restaurant. Nothing in the pews, no blankets, no clothes, no refuse. When he opened the sacristy door Macy lay sprawled across a heavy leather chair in front of a desk, her eyelids fluttering. Her head raised partway toward the door and David swooped to the side. The air was musty, salty.

Who is it?

He said nothing. Her head relaxed. She raised her hand and made a slow waving motion. She wore a thin white dress stained and wrinkled. On the preacher's desk was a stack of papers, in and out boxes, a spoon. He wondered if people still came here, or if the church was recently abandoned. He went on around her and stood behind the desk.

Where are your kids?

Who?

Your kids.

Hm.

You had a water baby.

I did.

He watched her. Her eyes were closed and she was smiling softly. She kicked up her feet and he saw the bruises between her toes. He wanted to burn the church down. He sat in the preacher's chair and watched her, watched the room. She made little movements back and forth and then seemed to settle. The front door opened and shut. Someone walked toward the pulpit and then a ragged young man stood in the doorway.

Oh, shit. Sorry.

David waved him off. Don't worry about it.

The young man started away and leaned back into the room. Are you gonna be much longer?

Not long. David shook his head slightly. The young man went out. He heard him walk away and the front door opened. There was a book of matches by the spoon, set into a small candle holder. He searched through a cabinet off to the side of the room and found a box of candles. He put one on the desk and lit it and waited.

You hear Murphy died?

Yeah. I never liked him.

Me neither. Where was it he was stayin' at?

The old Top Hat Buffet. Hey. Macy sat up and looped her head around to try to see him. He stepped to the side and took the needle from the floor at her feet. He heated the syringe and sucked up the little pool of wax at the head of the candle and he strode over to her and tilted her chin to the right. Not so soon, baby. He covered her eyes and she tried to stand up. He stuck the needle in her chest and pushed the plunger. Her eyes went wide and the muscles in her neck rigid like she was about to choke and her hands grasped at his and then she started convulsing, shuddering. He pulled out the syringe and dropped it. He walked out and paced down the aisle and out the front door. The young customer was petting his horse. Sand drifted from its mane and blew off, the duster fading.

She just OD'd on me. He held his palms up.

No shit?

I guess. I don't know what to do.

Well fuck.

I wouldn't go in there. If someone found you they might think you did it. He pulled the reins from the railing and got on the bay. He leaned slightly forward to put his hand on the riflebutt. The customer spun around where he stood, looking back and forth from the road to the doorway. He rubbed under the bay's chin and looked at David.

This your horse?

Yeah. He tapped on the woodgrain, felt the smooth side of the stock.

The customer dropped his hand. I had a horse once.

David stilled his hand on the rifle. What happened?

Couldn't afford to keep her no more.

That's a shame.

It is.

David looked at the young man and then south. He turned for the road, touched his hatbrim and was off. Near the county limits it was fully dark. His hangover had passed. The night cooled and with it he realized he had been calm. He thought long about it, riding through the dark bands of woods and over the creek, through fields of corn muted with dust. There was no grinding, no grit, no fist.

24

In the morning he woke in the loft and the daylight and everything was clear. When he tried to trace the feeling back he couldn't. It was new. Not long after he ate breakfast with Danvers they heard a knock at the door and Samuel was there. David had to stop himself from picking him up and swinging him.

Hey bud. How long do I get you?

All day.

David smiled. You want to come riding with me? Stay out late?

Alright.

Let me pack us some food.

They walked to the barn with a bag of sandwiches. Samuel saddled his horse and mounted up and David led his bay out to the gate. They rode toward the sun, now over the woods. There was no wind, only the sound of the horses stepping and the creak of the saddles. David watched Samuel from the corner of his eye. His head and upturned fist dipped with the horse's gait, little plumes of dust from its hooves. The land sloped gently and when they reached the crest they saw the cattle along the creek to the south and they turned to ride by. The grass had grown tall deeper into the pasture and as they rode birds flew from the cover and Samuel watched them rise. David made a circle in the air for him to check the cattle and he watched Samuel take a circuit and come around.

I didn't see anything.

David nodded and they went on. He was smiling to himself. They crossed the creek and followed it west. When the cornfield came into view David guided them southward, looking over the fence at the stalks, light green, near dry. After a while the fence jointed east and they swerved with it. Several minutes along David saw there was a sharp bow in the fence, the wire and the posts jerked outward and sagging at the center where a twisted flag of cowhide and bones were tangled.

What is it?

I dunno. They rode on and when they reached the damaged fence David dropped from the horse. He gripped the hide, holding his breath. The head was tilted over the fence and when he flipped it back he saw it was the calf he'd freed, eyesocket empty. He pulled it loose of the wires and flung it over onto the other side. In the grass below were pieces of bone and fur and the grass all around was matted where scavengers had fed. He glanced at Samuel. He'd stepped up beside him and David pointed back. Grab me that bag there.

Samuel jogged to get it and brought it to him. He went over to the nearest post and set it up and stomped at the dirt around the base to hold it fast. From that angle it seemed as though the fence were blown out in an explosion. The staples in the post had been torn loose and he pulled a remaining one and let it drop to the grass. He took a spool of wire and a fence tool from the bag and gave the spool to Samuel. Go on to the next post and hold the whole thing up against the far side. Up top.

Okay. He started walking and David held the tip of the strand and went to the other post. He pulled out a staple from the bag and set it against the post and threaded the wire through. Down the fence Samuel set the spool by the post and David gave a thumbs up. He used the tool to hammer in the staple until it was halfway embedded and he looped the wire around and pounded the staple flush. He walked the fence to Samuel and stapled the other post. He cut the slack with the tool and they traded posts and repeated the process. When they finished they walked to the middle and David pulled on the top strand of wire and let go. He put the wire and tool away.

That'll do for now. He started for his horse and Samuel followed. The sun was high and the land around them bright and warm. They went deeper into the property and began to hear the hum of the high-tension towers.

How's your mom?

She's okay.

Just okay?

Yeah.

They rode beside a tower. Samuel looked up when the wires ran overhead and David stopped the horses. There was a ring of green around it, brush and weeds. Rust lined the bolts and bottom rods.

How far do these go?

Clear across the county. Seven or eight miles down there's a power station, outside Banning.

They sat in the grass and dust by the nearest leg of the tower. There was a small tree growing beside it and they were partly shaded by a branch. David put the bag between them and they ate the sandwiches and passed a jug of water back and forth. When they finished they sat against their saddles. David crossed his hands over his stomach.

Your godfather and I used to ride out here, the summer before you were born. It was dry then too. We took the cattle out past the property, out that way, before the mine bought everyone out. He gestured south. Phil came with us a couple times. 'Course, back then we had a lot more cattle.

There was a faint smile on Samuel's face and David matched it.

We'd set and eat just like this. He stared at the sky. A breeze came and went. They were quiet until Samuel shifted onto a knee.

What was it like fighting?

David rose up on his elbows. Where'd that come from?

He shrugged. What was it like?

Hard to say. I mean it's hard to tell you. He paused. You know what it's like being caught in the dusters? That first one we had?

Yeah.

It's like that almost all the time. You didn't sleep. There wasn't a lot of water or food.

I mean what was it like to actually fight?

David's face hardened. You mean to kill someone.

Samuel said nothing.

He rubbed at his jaw. He was quiet until he dropped his hand. It takes something away that you can't get back. It takes away this freedom you had. There's always something you feel, like you have to worry about carrying it. Like you've got one less hand because you have to carry this guilt.

How many people did you kill?

I don't know. I lost track. Sometimes you think maybe they got away or you didn't hit 'em at all. You end up not wanting to know. You oughta live with that number in your head forever. But you don't. He cleared this throat.

I heard the guy you were chasing wasn't it. He wasn't who killed Mel.

Yeah.

I want to find him.

You don't know who it is, though.

I saw his shadow. He was just standing there. It looked like he waved to me. Samuel gripped a fist and relaxed it. I couldn't see. He stared at the ground.

David had leaned forward. He wanted to push the idea away, to let the dead and himself be. To keep it from Samuel. You don't remember anything else?

No. It was all dark. Then I ran and hid.

What were you doing?

He was quiet, pulling at blades of grass. Just exploring.

David watched him. He breathed out slowly and stood.

You okay?

Samuel said nothing.

David made a weak gesture toward the horses. Let's keep ridin'. We're about halfway done.

Okay. They resaddled and rode eastward. The land smoothed out and the creek ran far ahead. They passed an old row of fallen fenceposts, the wire removed, rings of rust in the gray wood. They were quiet for a long time. Samuel was sitting straight and high but his head was bowed and the hand that held the reins clutched them as if they were a rosary.

You alright?

Samuel turned to David. Yeah. His hand slacked.

It was mid-afternoon when they reached the eastern edge of the pasture. They followed the fence until they reached the creek and they rode west to find a crossing. Samuel went through first and David watched the horse on the slope and saw the favor of the right hind. He rode after and they stopped to rest on the far bank. The horses grazed and drank. Not long after, David and Samuel saddled up to ride on. The sun was sinking over their shoulders. The house came up on the horizon and grew out of it with their approach and Samuel stopped and they both sat looking at it. He thought of Helene inside, in what room.

Can we stay out tonight?

If we get permission.

Samuel nodded. David breathed in and tilted his head to the house.

Why don't you go ask?

He got down from the horse and led it to the fence. He draped the reins on the wire and climbed over. David watched him go and watched the door open. A sliver of Helene there through the threshold before it closed. He let go of the reins and put his hands on his legs, stretched, searched the pasture for something to hold his eye. The paint on the shed was worn away at the edges, eroded, and the wood itself smoothed from the dust. After a few minutes the door opened and Samuel came out dragging sleeping bags and a knapsack. David put the bay forward to the fence and got down. He watched Samuel cross the yard and saw Helene in the kitchen window. Samuel held the bags out and David lifted them over the wire.

Mom said Deputy Miller was just here.

What for?

He's been coming around. Samuel hopped down from the fence and got on his horse. He wants to talk to me.

David's jaw jutted and he kept himself from grinding his teeth. Next time he comes around you call me.

Samuel nodded. They rode southwest, side by side. The light was warm and still yellow. Can we make a fire?

David nodded with the pace of the horse. If we're careful. And find some wood.

They led the horses at an angle until they crossed their own tracks. The sun set and they rode on with the stars appearing overhead and the constellations were fully cast when they reached the thicket where they'd first seen a coyote. They dismounted and dragged piles of brush through the dust and Samuel began scalping grass for fuel. David drew an old fencepost to the brush and pulled a box of matches from the knapsack.

We gotta be careful, now. It's dry enough out here the whole field could catch fire.

Yeah.

Just watch for sparks. He struck a match and with the light found the grass and stuck it in. He blew softly over the smoldering blades, watching the smoke rise above them, adding larger pieces of kindling. The first flames caught and popped and David told Samuel to get the bags. Samuel snapped the first out and sand showered from it and rattled against the grass and ground. He spread them near the fire and brought their saddles to the heads of the bags and they leaned up against them watching the flames rise and spread across the post. The pot was set beside the fire on another post to heat the beans. Neither of them ate. They slid lower against their saddles until they were both watching the fire from between their boots. The flames were even and quiet and put off little smoke without the grass. The stars wavered through the heat and David watched Samuel reach his hand out as if to grip something there. His hand dropped and he breathed in deeply.

What happened to Mel's parents?

Went home, I think. I know O H was goin' home.

Just O H?

Well, I think Delia left before he did.

How would you find him now, the killer?

I don't know if anyone can, just by looking.

What are the sheriffs doing?

Not much.

Do they know anything about him?

No. All we know is that it was a big gun. Big caliber.

His eyes were nearly closed. David could see him reliving it, the shots. I feel bad.

I know. I do too.

I ran away.

There wasn't anything you could do, son. He rolled over and crouched beside his bag. Samuel shut his eyes and the tears rolled from their corners.

I didn't even try. I didn't do anything. His mouth bunched up and shook and he put his hands over his face and turned. When David reached out for him he shrank away. David encircled him and pulled him close. He hoped the day and the fire and the stars were enough. He hoped as if he had created them and he realized this and he was humbled and if not for Samuel in his arms he would have fallen prostrate for anything to give to his son that was truly his to give, for something to protect him.

25

David rose with the sky already bright and the sun nearly over the trees. The fire was out and he stood and heeled the ashes with his boot to check for coals. The post had been eaten in a rough oval. He rubbed at his face and smelled the smoke on his hands and saw Samuel asleep in his bag. David crouched and put a hand on his shoulder and he sat up. Samuel stretched and rubbed his eyes and they rolled up the bags. Before they got on their horses Samuel emptied the jug of water over the ashes and they sizzled and spiraled into the air. They rode toward the pasture gates and by midmorning they were in sight. David stepped down from his horse at the barn doors and stopped when Danvers stepped outside and yelled.

I thought it was you just came through.

David shook his head, handing the reins to Samuel. Huh uh.

Somebody was pokin' around in the barn and started ridin' up to the house.

David's brow creased and he thought for a moment. Keep an eye on him. He pointed at Samuel and started to run toward the house. A deputy was at the door and David slowed. Miller! He walked into the yard and Miller pivoted to face him. He was smiling and he took a step down from the porch. Helene was in the window.

You've got about five seconds to get off my property. David stopped at the foot of the steps and it was all he could do to keep from flying the space between them.

I'm just doin' my job here, Dave. I heard Sam was there

when the Reckard girl got killed.

Who'd you hear that from?

It's a rumor goin' around.

The door opened and Helene stood in it. Miller turned partway to glance back.

It's a lie.

If Sam was there I gotta talk to him.

And you decided to come up to the house after seein' my horse was out of the barn?

Miller said nothing. He leaned back slightly and he raised his chin. His eyes shifted to the road behind David. Danvers and Samuel were coming into the yard. David put his hand out to keep them away.

You're not gonna talk to him.

Hey, Sam. I got a question or two for you.

David sidestepped in front of him. Don't say another word.

David, stop. Helene moved to the porch railing. Just come inside, we'll shut the door and he can talk all he wants. She fixed her eyes on David to keep him still and he was until he saw Miller begin to smile.

You were there when that girl got killed, weren't you, kid? He stood on the last porch step and was looking just over David's shoulder. 'Bout how fast were you goin' the other direction, huh?

Helene hung her head and Miller's smile bloomed. He started walking and shouldered into David. Danvers and Samuel were in the corner of his eye as David pulled his fist back and then they were a whirl when he let go. The next thing he saw was Miller spin and land on the bottom step. He wasn't moving. David felt blood run down his fingers. His middle knuckle was cut and the tendon was open to the air. He was still, the blood dripping by his boot. Helene waved Danvers and Samuel on and when they stepped onto the porch David started forward. He scanned around himself at the empty yard and rolled Miller onto his back to pull the pistol from the holster and he stuffed it in the rim of his jeans. Blood was still flowing from his mouth and it ran down his neck onto the porch steps where it pooled in the flaking blue paint. His eyes opened as David stepped over him and went inside, passing Helene on the phone. Danvers was sitting at the kitchen table and he tipped his head when David walked in. He put his hand under the tap and he let the cold water run and flush the blood from the wound and from his fingers. Helene was standing beside him.

I called the sheriff.

David frowned. He looked at Samuel and their eyes met, both vacant. Helene took David's hand and shut off the tap. She had a bottle of peroxide and she poured some over the cut and it bubbled and hissed.

Tell me what I need to do.

Huh?

Tell me what I need to do. They're coming to arrest you.

He was quiet. He turned the water on again and washed out the peroxide. Weeding is the main thing. The grain bins need hosed out. Sam's horse needs checked on.

Helene took his hand and began to wrap it with a cloth. What else?

Hell. That damn fence. He glanced at Danvers and Samuel. Just gonna have to keep an eye on it. He leaned against the counter and shook his head.

We could have just gone inside and ignored him.

David nodded. I ain't arguin'.

Why'd you do it? She opened a drawer and brought out a roll of tape.

He came out here behind my back and he made sure of it. He paused. You didn't see his face. He knew what he was doin'.

You like being his pawn, then? She wrapped the tape over the cloth twice and pressed it tight. Now he can come right back out here and ask what he pleases.

He was quiet for a moment. He'll be askin' with fewer teeth than he expected.

Danvers laughed and stopped at Helene's glare. He rubbed a hand across his chin. You know I'll help you out.

I appreciate it. David held his hand up and clenched it. The middle finger was still. He grimaced and went to the front door. The porch steps were empty, Helene's reflection floating in front of him.

You took his gun?

Yeah. He can have it back.

Helene shook her head and walked down the hall toward him. I thought this might be a nice morning. I'd surprise you with some breakfast, we'd talk things over. With each step closer the heat rose as if she were a flame, her eyes darkening as they burned. What kind of example have you set for Sam? Did you think about him at all? Of what might happen? She was staring at him inches away and he could see all the weaving and threading in her irises. The heat passed like a shadow.

That boy is the only reason I get up in the morning. You don't ever have to doubt he's what I'm thinking of. He breathed. I didn't want him to get dragged through everything by that son of a bitch, have him relive it all. He does that enough on his own.

She stared up at the ceiling, eyes wide to dry them out. You can't do this again.

I won't.

I mean it. This is the third time you'll leave us. There's got to be a line where you stop and just live with yourself.

I know. I'm there. He reached for her hands.

She pulled out of his grasp and went to the kitchen and he followed her. Danvers started to stand.

Am I in your seat?

Nope. He reached out to stay him. I'd be much obliged if

you'd stick around here while I'm gone.

Sure, Dave. I'd be happy to.

Thanks. You remember those letters, Sam? In the attic?

Yeah.

You can read 'em if you want. Get Mom to pull the stairs down for you.

I can do it.

Alright. David leaned against the wall by the doorframe and watched Helene open a jar of green beans and pour it into a pot on the range. She put porkchops in the oven. After a while Danvers put his elbows on the table and glanced from Samuel to David and back.

So. Hot, huh?

David put his hand to his eyes and smiled. Helene stood to check the food and she began setting the table. There was a knock at the door before they finished eating and David put down his plate and answered it. The sheriff stood there and he removed his hat. Two deputies waited in the yard, one of them Leonard.

You ready, Dave?

David stepped out onto the porch and shut the door. If I could have a moment to say bye.

Sure, sure. The sheriff gestured at the door.

Oh. I got his gun. David spun and put his hands up. The sheriff took the pistol from his jeans.

That's a little insulting, wouldn't you say?

I dunno. I was insulted he came sneakin' up while I was gone.

The sheriff sighed. Go on in, say goodbye.

David ducked his head as he opened the door. He left it wide for the sheriff to see in and went to the kitchen. I gotta go. Helene and Samuel stood and they came up to him and he held them. He pulled Samuel close and gripped his shoulder. I'll be back soon.

Take it easy, boy. Danvers raised his hand from the table.

Bound to. He looked at Helene. Sheriff seems pretty casual about everything. I don't see any deputy at the backdoor. He must know better.

She nodded. Yeah.

He took another step back. Love you.

We love you too. Helene's bottom lip lifted.

He took them in his arms and turned and left, shutting the door behind him. The sheriff was talking with Leonard in the yard and he met them. The sheriff tilted his head.

All set?

Yeah.

Let's go then.

No handcuffs?

The sheriff raised an eyebrow. You think you'll need 'em?

No.

Then no. He pointed to the road. Go on.

They walked down the road to Danvers' and the sheriff let him saddle his bay and they rode on together into town. He kept his head up and the few people out on the streets watched them pass and he paid them no attention. On the western end of Dixon the deputies relaxed and the sheriff rode up to pace with David. It was hot and the sun was powerful on him without the wind and by the time they reached Banning he was soaked through with sweat and his horse had started panting. The deputies rode forward and sat high again until they arrived at the courthouse. They led him through the halls and there was a smell like an old dampness in the air. They passed through a heavy metal door with a fallout shelter sign on it and the deputy on his right pointed him down the narrow hallway. At the end of it he could make out the cells. When they reached the jail Leonard flipped a switch and two shaded bulbs popped on in the middle of the room. He extended an arm and David went forward.

First on your left.

David hesitated and stepped in and Leonard slid the bars

closed. He locked the cell and flashed a crooked grin.

It's funny you punched him.

Why's that?

He and Skillman've been pushing this nonsense through with the county commissioners. Trying to get you evicted, let Skillman take your property so they can expand the mine. Lucky for you everyone thinks you're a nice guy. Only beat up drug dealers and the like. Leonard leaned back and glanced out the door. They're thinking about doing away with the commissioners anyway. Not much for them to do anymore. He shrugged. Well, I ought to get.

David nodded and Leonard went out. He sat down on the bench and the sheriff came in immediately and stood in front of the cell. He cracked a knuckle and David saw he had no wedding band.

If you got convicted, Dave, you'd be put away for a year. You aware of that?

David was still. No, I wasn't.

When your wife called I just sat in the office twiddlin' my thumbs. I doubt that woman ever spoke a word of a lie in her life, has she?

David shook his head. Not that I ever heard.

Well, I sat there for what must have been a half hour, knowin' she was telling it just how it happened. You're got, by law. And I'm supposed to be a servant of the law, what law it is, these days. He leaned to see down the hall. If it'd been me I would of drew my gun. But I'm not supposed to think that way— if I was in your shoes, I'd do this or that. That ain't even for the judge to decide. He shifted. He started to speak and stopped. I guess I feel like this isn't a time for the straight word of law anymore. It just doesn't work nowadays. His eyes had wandered and he looked at David again. Am I borin' you yet?

No.

If I was we'd just call it part of your term. He smiled and

David tried to laugh. What it boils down to is that I think we all ought to be with our families as much as we can. Spending time where it's important. I guess I've been keepin' on as sheriff to make sure that happened, try to ease us all out.

Out of what?

This world. He breathed sharply through his nose and hiked his belt. We'll send a deputy your way soon as we're able, get your horse home.

When's my court date?

I'm not takin' this to court. The charges'll be dropped or get lost somewhere. He had been avoiding David's eyes and still was but his lips thinned and nostrils flared. I'd appreciate it if from now on you didn't hide anything from me.

David said nothing.

Well. The sheriff pulled on his belt again and left. David wanted to lie down but he was restless. He washed his face in the sink. His hand began to throb.

Samuel visited that Sunday. A deputy led David out into a sitting room where he waited. There was a small table in the middle of the room and two folding chairs. The deputy shut the door. Samuel got up from his chair and they hugged and David held him by the shoulders at arm's length.

I'm about tired of not seeing you, boy. He took Samuel's chin in his hand and examined him. You don't look any different. How long've I been in here?

Samuel pulled away. Just five days.

Seems longer. They both sat. How's Mom?

Okay. She's been working in the garden a lot.

Why didn't she come out?

I think she's still mad.

He smiled. Uncle Phil staying with you?

Yeah. We go out riding sometimes. We fixed the fence.

David put his hand on the table. You're lying.

We did. Samuel smiled. And I've been weeding.

I think you're kiddin' me. Let's see those hands.

Samuel put his hands palm up on the table. David leaned in and stared at them. They were red and worked dry in places. There was a blister on the side of his thumb and David smiled.

Well I'll be. He put their hands together, Samuel's smaller, smoother but growing. He sighed. You doin' alright?

Yeah. I'm fine.

You like being man of the house?

Samuel rolled his eyes. He sat back and drummed his fingers on the table once. It seems lonely.

What does?

Being the man.

I guess it can be. But it makes you strong. If it's just you then you can't quit.

Samuel nodded. They were quiet again and David wondered how much time they had left. Samuel lifted his head slightly. I read your letters.

Yeah?

You're missing some. There's a gap in the dates.

There weren't any. It got too bad.

Oh.

The door unlocked and opened. The deputy stood there and he tilted his head back. They both stood. Samuel came around the table and David hugged him. They went out the door together and hugged again in the hall.

Take care of your ma and Phil. Tell them I love 'em. I love you.

I love you too. I'll come back.

You better.

Weeks passed. David saw Samuel twice more before his release. He was tan and his hands were callused. He told David about the work he was doing, about cleaning the grain bins. He and Danvers rode out to check the fences. Helene and David's mother came with him and she brought lunch for the four of them. Leonard was on shift and let them sit on a bench in the empty parking lot behind the courthouse. They talked quietly. Before Leonard led him inside Helene told his mother and Samuel to go on to the front. She took his hand and traced over the gouge in his knuckle, mostly healed.

Come back, when you're out.

Yeah?

Yeah. She pursed her lips. We need you.

I dunno, Sam said he's doing alright.

I don't mean just to work. She slapped his hand lightly, then held it between both of hers. But that, too. I keep thinking of seeing you, when he was handing you the sleeping bags. Watching him in the field without you. It's lonely for the both of us.

David nodded.

Are you okay?

Yeah.

Really?

I am.

She smiled slightly and dropped his hand. I'll see you soon, then.

He watched her go, watched her look back before she rounded the corner of the building. Leonard opened the door for him and followed him inside.

Most of the time he was one of the few inmates but there were nights that a drunk or addict was booked. The drunk would be released in the morning and the druggies were taken away. His last night a Mexican was brought into the cell across from him. He was young and scrawny and his hands were blueblack with ink. The deputy left the jail and the Mexican sat on the bench and stared at David. Even after the lights were off he could feel the man's eyes. He was too young to have fought but a cousin or brother may have. David remembered little Spanish and what he did was useless. How to say 'freeze,' how to say 'on the ground.' 'Chingate, pendejo.' A storm rolled in he guessed around three in the morning and thunder began to reach through the bunkerlike walls of the jail. David strained to hear, slowed his breathing. There was the altered hush of rain, a different silence. When the storm eased David could hear shuffling from the cell across from him, murmurs, and when the lights came on again in the morning it was as if the Mexican had never moved. He sat on the cot, hands on his knees, looking across the cell.

Hours later the sheriff came and walked David out and they stood on the sidewalk in front of the building. The few trees around the courthouse had dropped smaller branches and leaves were scattered, but nothing else. David was wearing the clothes he came in with and he noticed the blood on his pants leg and the heavy wrinkles after he was given berth by the few people out walking. The sheriff lit a cigarette.

I hope we never do this again.

Same here.

Sam's comin' out with your horse. Oughta be here in a bit.

Alright.

You damn near busted Miller's jaw. The sheriff took a long drag and blew the smoke out of his nose. If you have trouble with him again you pay attention to your woman. Go inside and lock the damn door.

He was going after Sam.

I get that. But that don't give you the right to break someone's face. Let alone a deputy.

David looked at the ground. Thank you for this.

The sheriff put up his hand. It was my choice. Don't make me regret it.

He nodded and stopped. I wanted to ask you. What was that Mexican doing in there?

Drug running. He was carryin' a backpack full of meth on

foot. The sheriff skewed his jaw. Pays good, I guess. You'd be hard pressed to catch me afoot through here these days, no food.

David nodded. Is the demand really that high? Are that many people using?

High and getting higher. Drugs're a good way to make this place tolerable.

I can imagine.

There's no stopping it, not really. You just got to fight it where you see it. He pivoted at the waist. Speaking of. Gosper's half cleaned up now. I guess you put the fear of God into them Clintonville dopeheads.

I doubt that.

You didn't have any luck findin' the gun?

If I had any I would've told you.

Mm. He snorted a breath. What'd your boy tell you he saw?

Just that it was a man, waved at him, apparently. I don't know if that means he's local or a sick son of a bitch.

Neither's a good answer. The sheriff nodded to himself. They were quiet. He began to back away. I gotta get back inside. Throw out a certain stack of papers, lose 'em someplace. Maybe in a fire.

David smiled. They waved after walking apart a ways and David started toward Dixon. Samuel met him at the edge of town and they rode out. Samuel took lead and after a while evened with him. They put the horses up at Danvers' and walked home. They climbed the porch steps and Samuel took out the key to open the door and when it was wide he called in.

Dad's home. He stepped aside for David to enter.

26

That winter the dusters fell to nothing more than a coating over each snow. It was very cold and the harvest had been poor as David knew it would be. He installed the wood cookstove from the shack in the kitchen and mounted the pipe through the back wall. There was no money for coal or shale oil and the mine was still behind, prices high. They burned wood and corncobs and cow chips to heat the house and sold a dozen head of cattle to the butcher along with any coyote hides David skinned. They had already sold the draft and one of the mules.

When the cold weather broke it began to rain. The last of the dust in the fields was overtaken by the local brown soil and the grass and corn grew. It had been just over a year since the murder and there had been nothing, no sign, just Samuel moving daily further away.

Helene asked them to build a chicken coop one morning in June. There was a little wood left over from building the shack and the rest they scrounged from the barn and when they had the frame together Helene called them in for lunch. She had already made up the plates with chicken and vegetables, a cucumber sliced and placed in the middle of the table. Samuel and he washed side by side at the sink and when they sat she reached for a slice and salted it.

Haircuts today.

David cut into his chicken. You want this coop done or do you want us lookin' pretty?

You'll make time for both.

Samuel was picking at the vegetables and David pointed

with his fork. Eat up, boy. Get some meat on them bones.

I'm not hungry.

Sam.

They fought by their eyes a moment and Samuel forked a piece of chicken and ate. David glanced at Helene and then the ceiling and breathed slowly. It was getting hot. When they finished David brought a chair from the table into the backyard and faced it toward the pasture. Helene came out with a pair of scissors and Samuel followed her. He sat and David went back to hammering at the coop, putting up sheets of plywood. From the corner he watched her cutting the hair at Samuel's forehead. The line of Samuel's cheekbone showed, catching the light, the youth already dropped from it. He thought of him in the woods, running, falling. The more hair she cut the more he seemed to age and when she was nearly finished he seemed so old, and the land could have easily been fallow, weeds growing tall and the cattle wild. For a moment he knew Samuel's heart and knew its trajectory, like a star loose from constellation. He'd stopped hammering and Samuel stood from the chair. Helene was looking at him and she beckoned him over. He passed the hammer to Samuel and sat, pointing at a sheet of plywood and one of the last gaps in the wall. She pulled his shirt up and draped it over his shoulders.

You were a little spacey for a second there.

Just getting a breather.

She rested her hands on him. The blade of the scissors cool over his collarbone. She angled his head and began to cut across his crown. He closed his eyes and his thoughts slowed and stopped as her hands ran over him. Hair tumbled down his chest. She guided his head to one side or the other and leaned over and crossed her arms around his neck and kissed him, covering him in her shadow. When she straightened the sun was bright and hot. He stood up. Samuel had finished putting up the walls and was coming around the back, spinning the hammer in his palm.

Will that keep them for the winter?

Probably not. I'll hunt up more supplies in a bit. This'll work for summer, though.

Helene pulled the shirt from his shoulders and dusted him off with it, smacking his back. Okay then. Do me?

He grinned and she hit him again. He grabbed the shirt from her. How about after I get the rest of your coop together?

She rolled her eyes.

He let Samuel go for the rest of the day and got his horse. He rode through the countryside, out to Storm Creek and back, searching through all the abandoned buildings. He broke to muck the stalls and check the animals' water and he went back to the house. Samuel was coming down the stairs as David walked in and he rubbed over Samuel's close-cropped hair.

Hey bud.

Samuel ducked and batted David's hand away. He trudged on into the kitchen and David sighed and pulled off his boots. He went into the bathroom to wash and when he came out to the bedroom Helene had a blouse over her head. She pulled it off and smiled at him standing there and picked a tanktop from the bed and put it on.

It's too hot.

He sidled up to her and put a hand up the back of her shirt. Yeah.

You didn't find anything?

I did. I'll go around with the cart tomorrow.

You want to cut my hair after dinner?

I'll make a mess of it.

It wouldn't be any worse than cutting it myself. She pushed his hand away and he followed her to the kitchen. He looked out the window at Samuel, standing at the edge of the yard. Helene pulled leftovers from the refrigerator. The land was flat and golden for a time and in the distance they could see where it dropped and just before the horizon the shadow where the creek ran. Samuel had set his forearms on the fencepost and his head rested on them. He looked at some point between them both, face tilted slightly, and he breathed in. David waited for him to speak. The backdoor opened.

Time for dinner.

Samuel nodded into his arms. He dropped them from the post and David followed him to the house. The woodgrain was etched into his forearms. They went in and Helene served them. David watched Samuel eat and their eyes met briefly and Samuel stared at his plate. Helene let him go without finishing and they watched him walk upstairs. David grimaced and carried the chair back outside. The door shut a moment after he was in the yard and she stood beside him.

He's in his room.

Hm.

She passed the scissors to him and sat. He lifted the hair from the side of her head and held it between his fingers like he imagined he ought to. How much?

Here. She pulled the hair to her face and held it pinched a few inches from the end. He took the lock from her and cut. He drew her hair back again and his fingers traced along her jaw. There were crescents of dark brown around the chair and when he stepped away to see better they were lit up by the sun. When he set his hands on the slope of her neck he could feel her pulse, slow and heavy. He cupped her chin in his hand and lifted her head and she opened her eyes and smiled at him. Her arms wrapped around him and he bent and lifted her from the chair and walked with her stumbling to hide behind the shed.

When they finished they stooped for their clothes and dressed, smiling. Helene held the door for him as he carried in the chair and he set it at the table. She fell into his back and they stood in the kitchen, catching their breath. Samuel came pounding downstairs and he was out the door before they could see. David looked back at Helene before running down the hall to see Samuel standing in the yard. He joined him outside and Samuel pointed at a massive yellow cloud, squatting in the northwest. It seemed blown out, as if a bomb had been dropped inside it, ridged and complex like a hive.

I haven't seen a storm like this in forever.

Samuel nodded and went on to the road. A wind hit the trees and they could see it coming for them across the field and David shivered when it blew past. A clutch of swallows slipped overhead and were gone around the house. The phone rang. Helene answered it and he listened to her, knew it was his mother. She came to stand beside him at the front door and they watched Samuel from there, the porch roof cutting off their view of the storm.

She was checking on us.

It's looking pretty mean. He stepped forward and opened the screen door. Why don't you come inside, Sam?

Samuel grinned and didn't move. David went to stand beside him and already the storm filled the northern sky and the bottom of the cloud had gone broad and dark, the air below it a bright sick green. The first tremors of thunder hit them and the wind intensified and they both craned their heads up to see lightning from the innards of the anvil flash and moil. The underside of the cloud rolled. Lightning struck behind the trees across the field and there was a seizurous boom and David reached for Samuel. From Dixon they heard the high wail of the tornado siren.

Let's get inside.

Samuel shrugged him off.

Come on. He started back for the porch. The thunder was still going from nearly dead above them. Sam! Get your ass up here.

Samuel turned and made for the porch. He stood on the steps and David moved to the door. Another bolt of lightning wired down and brightened, disappeared and flickered back.

The sky and ground darkened and in the cloud were seams and wrinkles of cobalt that glowed as if the whole thunderhead were alight. The air shook. David took Samuel by the collar and guided him indoors. From inside they could only see the green air bright as neon. The wind bent the trees and the house creaked. Samuel went to look out the window in their bedroom and David followed, Helene behind him, and they watched a black cloud the shape of a slug twist down from the sky and a plume of dust rose to meet it.

Alright. Down we go. David pulled Samuel away and ushered him down the hall, Helene closing the window. He led Samuel to the basement and waited at the door for Helene. The phone rang and she came around into the doorway and they both went down. The phone stopped and David smiled at them in the dim light. The house seemed to lean and he left the stairs and stood by them. Dust sifted down from overhead. After a little while the air got quiet and the phone rang again and he started up the steps.

David. Let it ring.

He climbed the stairs and answered it. It was Danvers. After he hung up he looked out the windows and opened the basement door. I think you can come up. It doesn't look so bad now.

The phone rang again and he answered it while watching Samuel go out the backdoor. His mother told him a tree had come down at her neighbor's and hit his roof. He hung up and stood with Helene in the kitchen. Samuel was at the fence.

Ma said a tree dropped, hit the Stephens' place.

Did anyone get hurt?

Nah. Shook up the old fart livin' there. He began to smile. I'm gonna make you and Sam a little mad.

How?

I told her we'd help him fix it.

She sighed and her lips started to curve. The air above

the fields was wrapped in rain and the cloud was amorphous, a dark slab groaning southeast. Samuel's hair was flat on his head, his clothes dark.

The next morning the air was dry and the ground had soaked up all the water. There was little sign of the storm at the house, only leaves and small branches in the yard. He told Samuel to pull the traps for the year and left to see how bad the damage was in town. Most of the morning he was caught helping clear limbs from the streets and when he made it to his mother's to check in it was nearly noon. She led him over to Stephens' and they talked for a little while. The tree had missed the house but a limb had struck the porch roof and it buckled all the way to one of the eaves. He told Stephens what they'd need and made a list to order from the lumber supply. The old man had set a ladder out and David scaled it and stood by the edge and heard an engine. It came closer and he stepped toward the sound, toward the square, and saw Danvers' truck pull into town. It slowed at the intersection and David saw Helene, Samuel in the passenger seat, and the truck went on.

He climbed down the ladder, still watching the intersection as if the truck would roll through again, repeating. A few people came out of their houses at the sound. He told Stephens that he'd place the order and pick it up the next day, and he left. The horse would never catch up to them and it would be blown out by the time he was halfway to Banning. He'd promised to keep enough diesel in the truck for emergencies but it had been almost a month since he'd started it up to keep it able. There was nothing he could see from his vantage but he stretched the memory of Samuel taut. He tried to think of any darkness through the window, any blood. The sinking redoubled when he thought they were leaving, and he searched the memory over for luggage, for bags.

Danvers was standing in the road and he took a hand from his cane and raised it high. David slowed and gave a faltering wave back and when they closed the distance Danvers yelled to him, and he stopped.

Everything's fine.

What?

I said everything's fine. He shook his head and started walking to meet David. Helene came through here with Sam a minute ago sayin' something about a coyote biting him.

Where?

His ear, from what it looked like.

Was he out in the woods?

I imagine. I heard a few pops out that way but didn't think it was the aught-six.

David stopped, put a hand on his hip and leaned for breath. He wadn't shot was he?

No.

It must've been the Moore kids. David looked back down the road. He lifted his hat. Has the gray come in yet?

It'll look good on ya.

Mhm. Well. He sighed. I guess I'll head home then. Take a nap or somethin'. Maybe run circles in the yard.

Have at it. Danvers went with him a pace and then drifted toward his house. David walked to the backyard, staring at the chicken coop. He worked on it a while with the few remaining scraps of lumber and went inside.

When they got home Samuel went straight upstairs. David leaned out from the living room doorway, Helene taking off her shoes.

What happened?

Ask him. He came home with blood all down his shirt and I threw him in the truck. I thought he'd been shot.

David looked toward the stairs. He touched Helene's arm as he passed toward them and stopped. Are you okay?

Yeah. She smiled.

I thought maybe you'd pulled a me. Run off.

It'd serve you right.

He lingered a moment and started up the stairs. Samuel's door was closed. Hey bud. There was no answer. David tried the door and it opened, Samuel sitting up against the head of his bed. Two red lines started at the middle of his neck and descended below the collar of his shirt. His left ear was bandaged.

Hey.

David pulled the chair to the side of the bed and sat. You wanna tell me what happened?

Samuel shrugged. We were out pulling traps like you said. I went one way and they went to the woods. I was only gone for a little while and I heard a shot, so I went to find them. When I got there Brandon was shooting at this coyote. He was really old looking. He'd shot the top part of his mouth off and he was bleeding all over.

What was the other one doing?

Laughing.

David frowned. What did you do?

I punched Brandon. Then I took his gun away and the coyote jumped on me. I shot it. I was so angry.

Well. David thought. I don't blame you for bein' angry, but you shouldn't have beat the kid up. That ain't how you do things.

What should I have done?

I'd settle for telling him to stop.

You think he would have?

You don't know. That could have been all it would take.

You punched that deputy.

I got thrown in jail. Want me to call the sheriff?

Samuel cut his eyes to the floor. That's what Mom said. She said it wasn't my place to punish him.

Your momma's right.

Samuel stared at the foot of his bed, then faced him again. It shouldn't matter who did it. It should just matter that he got stopped.

Sam.

What would you do if you saw the guy who killed Mel? If you knew who he was?

David tried not to think about it, to say the quick lie. I'd get the sheriff.

I'd kill him.

The words seemed to roll on in the room, to repeat. David could say nothing.

Someone has to do it.

He stood up. He glanced out the window and to the door, turning. Are you hungry?

No.

He went around the chair to the door. He wasn't sure if he was shaking or not.

———————

Sleepless. All night his chest could barely rise for breath. The sun wasn't up and it wouldn't be for another hour. He slipped out of bed and stood in the hall, leaning toward the stairs and away, thinking. The bedroom door creaked when he opened it again. Helene let out a waking breath and she sat up on her elbows.

What's the matter?

I'm worried about Sam.

She motioned for him in the dark, patting the bed. He sat down on his side and after a moment she rose behind him.

What about him?

He's still talking about catching the guy. Mel's killer. I can't blame him, but.

He wants to run away.

Did he say that to you?

No. She shook her head. I can see it in his eyes. It's a familiar look.

David said nothing.

Didn't you want to run away at his age?

Yeah. And eventually I skipped town and joined the Army.

You're going to have to trust him. I've learned with you Parrish men.

You kicked me out.

Sam's not as far gone as you.

He rested his chin in his hand. She made no move to touch him. You were just gonna let him go, let him do this, when he does?

You can't hold him here, or tell him he can't go. He'll be sure to leave if you do. She turned in the bed. You've got those hides. Let him go to the butcher by himself. That's a decent journey, right?

Yeah.

If we let him go now, then he sees he can. He sees a little freedom.

You don't think it'll make him want it?

I think he'll know it's there if he needs it. He'll know we trust him.

David paused again. Do you trust me?

I do. But I know better than to have expectations.

He studied the floor and stood. Alright. I'll send him off.

Now?

Yeah. It's a haul. He left the room. Samuel's door opened before David was halfway up the stairs and he came out.

What's going on? Samuel pushed his hand against a yawn.

I was wonderin' if you'd like to deliver those hides to the butcher. By yourself.

Samuel glanced at the floor and looked at David. Alright.

It's a long ride.

I know. I'll get ready.

They were waiting with a small knapsack of food when Samuel came down. Daylight was just beginning to show through the windows. Samuel stopped at the second to last step.

I'm not going to war or anything.

David held a breath. He stepped forward and opened the door. I'll help you load up. He went out onto the porch and watched Helene hug him and pat his shoulder on the way out. They went down the road together in silence. David brought the last few hides down from the rafters while Samuel readied his bay. He got the shotgun from Danvers' mudroom and put it in the saddle scabbard. They walked the horse outside and David smiled tight as Samuel mounted up. He lifted the shotgun to him.

There aren't any shells in it. It's just for show.

Samuel nodded.

I gotta run into town. Mind the company?

No.

He walked beside him, glancing up at him in the saddle every so often. When they reached the square he took hold of the reins. Be careful.

I will.

Don't rush it. That leg's been bothering him lately. And call once you get to the butcher's. David stepped away. Samuel started on and David waited on him to look back but he didn't. When he was out of sight David turned and went south to the train station. His order was late coming in from Banning so David went home. He thought of going out to cut hay but instead stayed with Helene and helped in the garden. They put a roof on the chicken coop. They ate leftovers for lunch and went to sit in the living room together, Helene with a book.

When's the last time we had a moment like this to ourselves?

She smiled. About thirteen years ago.

Are we old yet?

Getting there.

He touched her hair. Sam oughta be there in a couple hours.

Yeah.

He patted his leg and looked out the window. When he reached for the radio Helene took his hand and held it.

David. Relax.

They sat there a few minutes longer before David got up to go outside. He stood at the fence facing west, trying to envision where Samuel might be, where in the road. When he imagined the land it was still red from the dusters and Samuel was riding over drifts, scanning the horizon. The trees were bare. He couldn't picture it green. The phone rang and he left the fence and went inside but Helene had already answered it. He stood in the doorway waiting and when she hung up she shrugged.

Was it Sam?

Yeah. He's gonna be late getting home. He said the horse is limping pretty badly. He wants to walk it as far as he can.

David looked over his shoulder. I should have made him ride mine.

She came toward him. It'll be fine. Gives us a little more time to ourselves. She kissed him and pushed him back into the living room, onto the couch. She hiked her dress.

He waited up that night in the living room, eventually falling asleep. When the porch steps creaked he rose to let Samuel in. He ground sleep from his eye and smiled.

How was the ride?

There's an aurora. Come outside.

David followed Samuel onto the porch. When they walked into the grass they looked up and David nearly gasped. The sky was red. The light came across in broad furls like a wind-blown sheet or whirling snow or dust across a road. He could see the shape of the world by it, the vault. The grass and the corn and trees were all reddened.

How long's it been doing this?

Since sunset.

He put his hands on his hips. They walked out to the road and heard a humming from the powerlines. Their shadows on the road were the color of wine, the gravel pink. After a minute the powerlines began to crackle and he thought before the lights of town snapped out that he could see sparks running along the wires. He looked at Samuel.

That's bad news.

Mhm.

They stood there in the road, watching the light. When Samuel yawned they went in. Samuel pulled the hide money from his pocket and David peeled a few bills off and gave them back. He reached around Samuel for a drawer in the hall table and he took out his combat knife. He watched Samuel as he handed it forward, holding the blade in the sheath.

What for?

David shrugged slightly. It's time you had a knife.

Samuel smiled briefly.

It's sharp. Don't fool with it.

Okay.

I'll try not to wake you too early tomorrow.

Samuel smiled and went upstairs. David stood there looking after him. He thought of waking Helene to show her the aurora but when he went into the bedroom he stripped and got into bed beside her.

There was nothing when he tried the switch in the bathroom a few hours later. He flicked it twice and gave up and he opened the door slightly to let in a little light and searched for the rim of the toilet. He finished and flushed and the water gurgled away but did not refill. Half asleep he thought little of it until he tried to wash his hands. He left the bathroom and shut the door and stood against it looking at the white slope of Helene still covered by the sheets. In the kitchen he found a book of matches and went into the basement. He popped a match. and held it up to reset the breaker. There was nothing when he tried the light. He shook the match out and blue flecks peppered the dark of his eyes as he walked up the steps. He sat at the kitchen table and poured himself the remainder of a pot of coffee and drank it cold looking at the empty chair across from him. The phone was dead. He walked out the backdoor headed for Danvers'. The barn light was off when he went into the yard and he rapped on the side door and turned the knob. The door was unlocked and he let himself in and tried the lightswitch. Danvers cursed in his bedroom.

Don't bother with the light. It ain't workin'. David stood in the mudroom for a moment and came into the kitchen, hand on the wall. The knock of the cane on the hardwood floor came toward him.

What's that?

I said the lights're out.

I figured that much. Danvers grumbled. I can't see a damn thing.

Just wave that stick of yours around. David felt in his pocket for the book of matches and lit one. Danvers winced at the light, leaning over his cane.

Was there a storm?

An aurora.

A what now?

It had to of been a strong one. The sky was all red last night and now we got no power.

Well shit the bed.

David pinched the match. Do you have a lamp or something?

I might have a antique one down in the cellar. Don't have any oil for it.

That idn't any help. He could hear Danvers moving to the kitchen table. He pulled a chair out and sat on it and David could almost see him.

What're you gonna do?

Ride out to the power company, I suppose. The phone's

dead too.

Danvers exhaled.

It could be a raccoon got in the transformer, the aurora's just a coincidence.

You know better. Even if it was just a raccoon, you'd probably have to climb up there and fix it yourself.

Yeah. David was quiet for a moment. One less bill, I guess. It's kinda funny, really.

If you say so.

Maybe funny ain't the right word.

It ain't a funny idea for me. You know what goes with electricity? Indoor plumbing. I don't want to get up in the middle of the night in my underoos and walk to the outhouse. I'm an old man.

David laughed. Out the window he could see the lawn and the gravel drive. I'd better get back.

Danvers began to rise and David put his hand out for no one to see.

Siddown. You'll fall and bust your head open. He left. Walking east he could see the horizon whitening in a band and the clouds above it seemed nearly like daylight. He went into their bedroom when he got back and sat on the side of the bed and put his hand on Helene's thigh.

Hey. He shook her slightly. Hey.

She rolled over. What's the matter?

Power's out.

She sat up and rubbed her eyes. Was there a storm?

No.

Didn't we pay the bill?

Yeah. There was an aurora. It blew something.

She sat there beside him for a moment and she let her head down and threw it back. Her hair slapped against her nightshirt. She rubbed her hands over her face. Oh. She laughed briefly.

That's what I did too.

She held her hands up. What else are you gonna do?

Nothing. Keep on.

Yeah. She took hold of his hand and gripped it. There was enough light through the window now that they could see each other clearly. She was smiling at him and she shook her head.

I know.

It just doesn't quit.

I know. But this isn't anything. He squeezed her hand. The corn out there's growing good. This—

Hush. You don't need to solve it for me. She lay down and pulled on his hand. She brought him down and kissed him and began to kick out from under the sheets. He slipped away and stood.

David. You had better get back here.

He shut the bedroom door. He smiled and climbed over her into bed.

They woke up sometime later and went into the kitchen. Helene opened the refrigerator and David saw her feeling around at things. She frowned at him.

I don't know what to do about some of this.

David shook his head. I guess we're gonna eat well for the next day or so. We'll have to do a lot of canning.

A lot more, you mean.

He nodded. What did people used to do? Salt things?

Yeah. Keep things in the pantry, use ice blocks and saw-dust.

He raised an eyebrow. Well. He sat at the table. Samuel appeared in the kitchen with circles under his eyes. He stood in the doorway for a moment.

My clock broke.

There's no power. I think we're fried. I'm gonna ride into town and see about things after breakfast.

Helene served them and sat down and they ate. When they finished David rode into town. People were milling about, coming into town on foot or horseback or coming out of their homes, and they hailed David from the sidewalk and they all exchanged the same news. He rode up to the town office and there was a sign on the door that said they were checking the local power stations. He peered in through the glass door and saw nothing inside and he rode down the street to the railroad station. The clerk said all the trains were delayed. A crew had come through afoot and told him their train was dead on the rails. David thanked the clerk and headed out of town. Someone called to him. He stopped his horse and saw Skillman coming up the street riding a blue dun. David let his bay take a few steps forward. As Skillman got closer he touched the brim of the gray Stetson on his head and David pointed.

Find your hat?

Came about a week ago. I feel like I've been walking around naked for the past however long.

I bet. And you got a horse.

Yeah. He stopped the dun and they both looked off away from each other.

How do you stand?

Skillman grinned. Couple miles up shit creek. We got a lot of coal-driven equipment, but all our conveyors and such were hooked up to generators.

Generators? Those aren't working?

Fried. We cracked the casing on every machine we got. Everything's burned out. I'll probably have to lay everyone off until I can figure out what to do.

Well. Sorry to hear that.

I imagine you made out okay.

We're alright. Lot of work ahead if we don't get power again ever.

They were both quiet, nodding. Skillman put out his hand. Good talkin' to you, Dave.

Same. David took his hand without pause. Good luck

with everything. He turned his horse and Skillman doffed his hat and rode away. David rode slowly and went out of town, a little pleased. On the way he watched the sky, the cattle he passed near the fence. He couldn't help but smile looking at the corn. He put his horse up and walked home.

27

They dug a deep cesspit and built an outhouse over it. They built one for Danvers the next day and they dug new wells and David rode out to Banning and ordered hand pumps. It was mid-June before they finished everything and they returned to town to work on Stephens' house. At night they brought home the blades on the small reaper and David and Samuel sat out in the yard sharpening them and the sickles. They sat together in the dusk with the smaller blades in their laps or leaning over toward the ground to lift the larger ones up. They talked about the corn already tall and the cattle, about old hunts and trapping. About Red. Stories from David's youth of things Samuel would never see, snowmobiles and movie theaters and concerts. When the light was too weak they came inside, hands streaked gray.

One morning David woke Samuel early and they brought in the water from the well and ate breakfast alone. The sun hadn't yet risen but the moon was still up and nearly full. They walked to the barn together listening to the corn rustle in the dark. David picked up the lamp from inside the barn door and lit it and they readied their horses and took them out. David went to the equipment barn for the cart while Samuel grabbed the toolbelts from the table and he put the hammers in the loops and poured the pouches full of nails. They rode into town, a line of clouds coming in from the west and the growing light gray. They stopped at the granary office for the price of corn and they rode to the train station. He signed the ticket for the pallet of shingles that had arrived and they rode up to Stephens' house and unloaded the pallet. Samuel cut the lining on it and they began pulling the sheets apart. David steadied the ladder at the edge of the roof and Samuel stepped in the front porch to see if Stephens was awake. When he came back out they hauled the roofing up the ladder and stacked the sheets to one side. David handed up their toolbelts and climbed the ladder and they stood together on the incline.

Just a few minutes. We want to be civil.

Samuel smiled at him. We're gonna wake everyone up, aren't we?

David shrugged. I never did anything productive with a day that I didn't get up before eight o' clock. He hooked his thumbs on his toolbelt and they watched the line of clouds come on. He pulled the hammer from his belt and looked at Samuel and they started.

David's mother came by with lunch and a pitcher of lemonade around noon. They were nearly done. Samuel ate on the roof and David sat on the porch with his mother and Stephens. The sun was breaking through the clouds on occasion and it was warm. Skillman rode up on horseback and he stopped and waved high to Samuel. He said hello from the side of the street and David waved and Skillman made a show of doffing his hat at everyone on the porch and rode off. There was a thud overhead. Something rolled along and the lemonade glass fell from the roof and broke on the brick walkway below. The sun was shining at that moment and he could see lemonade dripping from the eave as he stood and went into the yard.

Sam? He came out onto the grass and saw Samuel grab the rails of the ladder and climb down, dropping his toolbelt to the ground. David stepped toward him. What are you doing?

Samuel climbed up onto his horse and his face was hard and as ashen as the clouds. He pivoted the horse and rode it out past the fence before David could step in his way and David watched him put the horse into a gallop and he was gone. Hoofbeats echoed back, then faded and he turned toward the roof. His mother came to stand in the yard beside him.

What was that all about?

David said nothing. He glanced at the roof again and walked out into the street. Skillman was distant, headed to the mine. He jogged the block to the square and stood in it looking down the road out of town. The sunlight vanished. He felt cold. His legs were held fast and his arms were hard and pulled to the ground by his fists and he could not move them until Samuel came into sight and he and his horse passed David by and the galloping stopped to make the turn south and then David registered the slobber at the horse's mouth and the rifle clutched in Samuel's hand. He spun so fast he nearly fell to the ground and he ran back to the yard. His mother had been beside him all the while, yelling distant and tinny into his ear. He leapt onto his bay from the porch railing and rode after Samuel. The land dipped past the square and rose by the granary and he could see Samuel already riding up level with him before he could push his horse to gallop. The horse cried sharp as he clutched at its mane and he twisted sideways and low on it with his shoulder back. The shops passed and the silos of the granary passed and the creek passed and the road flattened and narrowed and in the distance he could see Samuel and the broken gait of his horse. The houses at the edge of the mine had been torn down. The horse tilted with each fall of its lame leg. David moved his horse out to flank as he neared and Samuel looked back and jammed his heels into the horse's side but gained no ground. He matched Samuel's horse and he reached out for his collar and missed and he reached again and missed and saw the horse half-mad and walleyed, slavering onto its neck and he was the same, Samuel was the same. He shouted and swatted the horse's rump and it skidded and began to rear up. He slowed his horse and sawed it around. Samuel was holding tight and leaning forward in the saddle and he held the gun up for balance and David leaned out as he rode back by and snatched the rifle out of his hand and rode on toward the mine. He did not look at Samuel as he passed. He slowed on the mining grounds and rode over the path toward Skillman's cabin at the far end of the mine. It was quiet and the air very still without any men or equipment going. The dun was tied up outside the cabin and it nickered and tossed its head. David climbed the steps to the cabin door and opened it, swinging the rifle to his waist. Skillman was sitting at his desk with a tall sheaf of papers on either side of him. David kicked the door shut and felt for the lock above the handle and twisted it home. He took three paces toward the center of the room. Skillman put his hands flat on the desk but was still otherwise. There was a clock ticking between the roar of blood in David's head.

My son is on his way here to kill you.

Skillman shifted in his chair. He wet his lips and turned his head slightly. What are you waiting for, exactly?

For you to explain yourself.

Why?

David said nothing.

He put his hands back down on the desk and looked to the side for a moment. David's eyes followed his and Skillman smiled. He drummed the fingers of one hand and then the other on the desk. He began to speak when Samuel battered on the door. David raised the rifle and shot Skillman in the head. He levered out the cartridge and stopped to watch him slide in the chair and to watch the blood flow down his lips from the hole where his philtrum used to be. David's mouth seemed full of metal from the gunsmoke. His ears were ringing. He held onto the rifle by the stock and stood straight, watching Skillman's body settle, the blood dribbling onto the chest of his dress shirt and rolling over the bulge of his waist into his lap. The wall behind him was coated with matter. Samuel was pounding at the door and the wood was splintering. When David turned his knife was stuck through beside the doorknob. David unlocked the door and opened it and Samuel was nearly pulled into the room by his grip on the knife. David grabbed the handle and held the door fast by his heel and pulled the knife free. Samuel was staring into the cabin and David pushed him back and shut the door and Samuel fell. He was still staring at the door. David went around the side of the cabin and led his horse to the front and climbed on. Samuel had gotten up onto the steps and David grabbed his arm and pulled him down, already riding away. He stopped long enough to let Samuel boost up and Samuel put his arms around David's waist. At the road he reined the horse for town and Samuel's hands tightened.

Dad. Go the other way.

I'm not hiding this. He put the bay forward and they kept the same course.

Are you sure you killed him?

Yeah.

He killed Mel.

I know.

Samuel shifted behind him and David thought he felt Samuel's cheek on his back. Did he say anything?

No. Samuel's horse was ahead of them, grazing in a ditch. He pointed for Samuel to get it and he slid off. Just give me the reins.

Samuel went over to the horse. He gave the reins over and David wrapped them around the saddlehorn. He helped Samuel back up. They passed a house just outside of town with the whole family standing in the yard watching them ride by.

They're going to go see.

He sat straighter in the saddle and he looked briefly at the gun in his lap. The clouds were getting thicker and he thought it might storm by evening. Helene was coming down the street, riding the mule, and they met in front of the granary and stopped their animals. Her hair was blown back, her eyes dark. She began to speak and David started the horse forward again.

Let's just get home.

They rode on together. The town was quiet and he saw people looking out at them from storefront windows and front porches. He heard the mule clopping behind him and they rode east at the square. People were still watching and before they made it out of town one of the granary workers approached from his yard.

Hey, Parrish.

David's hand went to the rifle in his lap and the worker backed off. They rode on past. When they were out of town Helene brought the mule forward to pace with them. She stared at him and he waited on her to speak but Samuel did first.

We could find Red. We could go live with him. We have his address. Samuel shifted to the side for David to hear better. I can't harvest on my own.

They were nearing Danvers' yard. The barn showed through the gaps in the trees. They cut across the drive and David handed back the reins to Samuel's horse.

Go put him up. Quick.

Samuel pushed off the horse and took his into the barn. The side door opened and he glanced at Danvers coming down the steps. He looked at Helene.

I shot Skillman.

She rocked slightly. No. You can't do this to us.

There wasn't any other way.

You can't do this. You didn't.

It'll be okay. Sam's got Phil and he can call on Fogel to help him. It's gonna be a good harvest. There'll be plenty of money.

Oh, god. David. She breathed and covered the side of her

face with her hand. You're picking his life for him. He won't have any say.

They won't put me away forever. He almost smiled. Danvers was looking at him and David gestured toward the barn for him to get Samuel. Helene covered her face. He dropped from the side of the horse and he helped her down. I'm sorry, baby.

Don't. Oh, god. Don't. She pushed him away. Her cheeks were mottled and wet. She pointed at him and looked like she might reach out to hit him. He doesn't want this life. You're going to leave me again and pick his life and he'll hate you for it.

David shut his mouth. He stared at the barn. Danvers came out bringing Samuel to them and he gestured vainly with a hand and rested it on his hip.

What can I do?

David breathed deep and looked at the swath of pasture beyond the gate. Help me hitch the mule. He turned to Helene. Take Sam and go pack.

David. She began to protest and he held up his hand.

I won't be but a minute. Get started. He stepped away, watching them both. They went to the road. Danvers hung his head and shook it.

Jesus Christ, son.

David took hold of the reins on Helene's mule and they started for the equipment barn.

Sam told me. I saw him run by before and then Helene came through. I sort of figured it had to be somethin' bad.

They hitched the mule in silence and when they finished David helped Danvers onto the cart and led the mule out. He walked the horse beside the mule and he glanced down the road toward town. The ground passed underfoot. He made his way back through all the forked paths of his life and he saw the right he'd done. He was unsure of everything but those moments. Because there was no relief, no joy to them.

They rounded the bend and the porch already held a stack of blankets and boxes. They brought the cart into the yard and he stopped the mule by the porch steps. They stopped at the sound of someone running and his mother rounded into the yard.

Oh, David. She met them at the steps and she hugged him. You're tryin' to kill me.

How'd you get here so fast?

I started walkin' soon as I saw you all leave town.

He held her tight. I'm sorry. Would you help us pack?

She stepped back. Lord. She stared at him and went inside. David climbed the porch steps and began to load the boxes on the cart. Danvers stood by the door and held it open for Samuel, coming down the steps. He carried a small box and he put it on the cart and turned to David.

I'm done.

That's all you're takin'?

Yeah. I already packed some clothes.

David frowned. Go on and help your ma.

Samuel walked back inside. David loaded the rest of the things gathered on the porch and paced to the kitchen. Jars clattered together in the basement and he climbed down the steps.

Babe?

I'm just getting some food.

He stood beside her at the shelves as she took down the jars of vegetables and fruit. We gotta get goin'.

Alright. She didn't move. Would you get the picture albums?

Yeah. He went up the steps and got the albums from the living room. He saw his mother through the open door to the bedroom and she came out with an old purse of Helene's and she lifted it.

This has all the jewelry and money. What else is there?

He shook his head and held the albums against his hip. I

don't know. If you could help Helene, she's gettin' some food together.

Alright. She handed the purse to him and he took it and the albums to the cart. He passed Danvers, still holding the door.

You about done?

David dropped everything in the cart and pushed some boxes forward. Should be.

I wouldn't wait any longer.

I know. He faced the house.

Get a good look when you're ridin' out. They're comin' right now.

He exhaled, leapt the porch steps and ran inside. He called for everyone to stop and Samuel came first and David put a hand on his shoulder and let him walk out the door. David went to the kitchen and met his mother and Helene at the basement steps. He took an armful of jars from them.

We gotta go.

I know. Helene pressed her lips tight.

He let them pass and followed Helene out into the hall. He listened to their steps and he gazed at the walls half-bare now and the table empty. They walked out onto the porch and he breathed deeply and he looked at Danvers. Okay.

Danvers let the door shut. He came down the porch steps and they all stood in the yard for a moment before David's mother hugged Samuel and she went along the line to embrace them and started to weep. David held her and finally he stood back. She pulled him down and kissed his cheek.

Oh. Her chin quaked and she turned away and found Danvers and he put his arm around her for a moment before setting her hand over his on his cane and covering it with the other. He stared at David with his chin tilted up.

Dave. He stopped. Boy, I wish you built a bigger goddamn cart. He laughed and pulled a handkerchief from his pocket to dab at his eye.

Me too. David motioned for Helene and she climbed onto the seat of the cart. Danvers pointed to her with a crooked finger.

You keep these two in line, now. You're the only one in the family has any sense.

They tried to smile. Samuel got into the cart and David stepped up onto his horse. He looked at his mother and Danvers and at the house. The sky above it was still heavy gray and he wished for just a patch of blue. Then he took the horse toward the road and he heard the wheels of the cart beside him. They stopped once they were on the gravel and David lifted his hand. Samuel called out over the goodbyes and all the voices were crushed by the boom of the shotgun.

It seemed a long while before David tilted to the side on the horse. His hat fell to the road. He gripped the saddlehorn, leaning as if he would be sick. Blood ran from the side of his head and swept by his eye and dropped onto the brim of his hat. He breathed for the first time since the shot and he felt across his head and back grains of fire crawling through him and he heard Helene yelling. His eyes were wide and his heart jolted and he spun back to see Jacob Miller afoot with the shotgun leveled. David's right arm was still up to wave and he touched the back of his head with it and his hair was sticky and there was a small rise where the shot hit him. His hand came away bright red.

Keep that hand up, Parrish! Off the horse. Miller smiled and it split into a gapped grin as he came nearer. He waved the shotgun to the side. Get down.

David twisted in the saddle to see Helene. She and Samuel had their hands up. David turned away long enough to step down from the horse, eyes locked on the rifle in the scabbard over the saddle. He backed from the bay and stepped on his hat, bent to pick it up and swayed. His shoulder was stiffening and he felt the blood weighing down the back of his shirt.

The hell are you doin'? Get over here. Hands up.

A chill hit him and he started sweating. He raised his arms and closed his eyes to the pain. Miller stood ten feet behind the cart and David walked toward him.

Stay right there. Miller pointed at the ground with the gun. He looked toward the cart. Get off that rig. I saw the rifle, Dave. Don't even look back.

Helene and Samuel climbed off the cart and stood ahead of him in the road. David didn't move. Blood dripped back down his arm and he was getting cold. The shot in his shoulder ached through the bone. He felt as though he were underwater and everything in his periphery was black.

Come ahead, by your little killer, here. Miller jutted his chin to Samuel. Down on the ground. Facedown. He took his hand from the gun long enough to point. David came forward and tried to meet Samuel's eyes and sank to the ground. He dropped to his hands and pain throbbed all through him. Blood on the road already in drops and small splatters. He was missing part of a finger. He leaned down onto his elbows and Miller kicked him across the face before pushing him down with his bootheel. He had the shotgun on Samuel and he tipped it.

You too, boy.

David saw Samuel kneel and then his vision was jerked aside as Miller wrenched David's hands behind his back. The barrel of the shotgun hung from the crook of Miller's arm while he reached for something on his belt and David reared up. His hands went free and he heard the shotgun cock and the weight came off him as Samuel crashed into Miller. The gun clattered to the road and David got to his feet and staggered toward the ditch where they'd fallen and Samuel lifted his shirt and pulled the knife and drove it into Miller's ribs. David fell on the grass and he heard the crunch of gravel as Helene stood over him. He was so dizzy with his head back. A line of stars fell across his eyes dragging night behind them and voices came soft and then were gone.

White ceiling, cool and quiet. From the open window it seemed the middle of the day, and he thought he could hear the corn in the breeze until his eyes cleared and he realized he was in the hospital. He reached for his stomach, felt the old scar there. He was stiff and bandaged tightly around his shoulder and upper chest and he thought he woke because of the trouble breathing. His right arm ached and when he lifted his hand to feel behind him he saw the bandages over the stub of his right ring finger, over his forearm. He must have made a sound because the sheriff stepped into the open door and David's breath seized and he shut his eyes and turned away.

Hey.

David looked. The sheriff was at the foot of the hospital bed, holding onto his hat. He held a hand out for David to be still.

It's alright.

Where's Sam?

The sheriff thumbed over his shoulder. Why don't I get your wife. She just went for somethin' to eat with your ma.

Wait. David stared at him. He couldn't form the words for a question.

The sheriff began to pay the brim of his hat around in his hands. You remember when I told you about my philosophy? He stopped his hands a moment and started again. If the law ain't servin' the best interests of its people, I figure it ain't worth following. He paused. Your boy killed Skillman.

No.

I didn't hear that.

I killed him.

I didn't hear that either. The sheriff shook his head. And anyway it's too late.

David's lips parted, dry. What. The word barely came out.

It's been a whole day since everything.

He looked away again.

It ain't my place to tell you all this, Dave. I came here to make sure you're okay and to tell you not to breathe a word of anything to anyone. I put the murders on Sam, since he could get away.

He gripped the bedside and stretched his head back. He was breathing fast and he felt so tightly bound he might crack open.

You need to calm down.

Go to hell. He tried anyway. There were lights in his eyes.

You'd have been put away a long time. You might have even gotten the death penalty.

It wadn't your choice.

You're right. It was his choice. And he chose it.

He's thirteen.

I got a feeling that's a lot older than it used to be.

He swallowed. He tried to see how it had been. The sheriff coming and Samuel in the road or the house waiting for him. Waiting to shoot him, maybe.

Why don't I get Helene. The sheriff started to the door.

What about Miller?

I fired him a couple weeks ago. You must not've seen he didn't have a badge on what with the shotgun and all. I imagine whoever saw you ridin' saw him next. I don't doubt he was comin' out just for the excuse to blow your head off.

Sheriff.

He looked at David. I know it ain't how we're supposed to operate. But I just don't see any good coming out of putting you away. I may not be doing what's right. Figure I'll answer for that eventually. But this makes me feel a little better about failin' you all before. He paused. I'll go get your wife. The sheriff put on his hat and left the room.

David kept his eyes shut until she walked in. She sat in the chair next to the bed and the life flew out of him. She was pale as if she had been the one shot. He put his hand out for her to take and she did.

———————

Home, the next day. He woke before first light and thought of Samuel. Riding down a dirt road in the dark with trees surrounding him and the birds singing louder than they ever did in the daytime. The sun coming up on his left, stopping for breakfast, watering the horse. Afield later, riding under silent powerlines. David wondered if he envied him or if he only wished to be with him. He lay unmoving, facedown in bed and thought of getting up to water the plants or to weed. He could feel the dew wetting through his boots and the grease and bloodstained gloves, the feel of the handle against his palm. In the dark he could make out his bandaged hand.

You okay?

He lifted his head. He could see Helene's eyes and her hair framing her face. Yeah. Did I wake you?

I don't think so. Can I get you something? She rolled onto her side. Her voice was thick with sleep.

No.

She draped her arm over him. They both lay awake for a while.

Could we go after him?

When you've healed.

He closed his eyes. When they woke again the sun shone through the window. They hadn't moved. The light swept across the room by hours and they said nothing.

Danvers came late in the morning to check on them. David and he stood along the fence in the backyard facing the pasture, Helene behind them, tending the garden. The day was hot but a breeze was coming from the west and there were rainclouds gathering over the town.

How're the wounds?

David dropped his arm from over the fence and flexed his hand. You want to see about the funniest thing in the world, come watch me wash my face. I forgot I was out a finger. He sighed and the long breath made him dizzy. David stared out over the pasture, watching the cattle group together for the storm. He looked toward the woods in the east and back.

So just about everyone you expected to stick around has up and left you someways.

David smirked. Yeah, and you're still here.

Ain't that a bitch.

The cattle moved in. Danvers pointed out a flicker of lightning beyond town, soundless. David heaved up and let out a long shuddering breath and Danvers put a light hand on his shoulder.

He's a good kid, Dave. He's smart and he don't take shit from anyone. You couldn'a done better than that.

I feel like I failed him.

You tried. He don't blame you. God knows we don't.

The breeze went cool and constant and the grass flattened and the leaves in the tree beside them turned silver. You were the last one to see him.

Yeah.

Was he okay?

Danvers glanced toward the sky for a moment. I'd say he was ready. He rode your horse off lookin' like you did back before you got old. He looked good.

Did he say anything to you?

Just goodbye.

David nodded. The storm was growing up over the town and was going dark on its underbelly. He's gonna be alone when it hits him.

When what hits him?

That he's killed someone.

They said nothing, then Danvers turned and tugged him around and they watched Helene leave the coop with a small basket of eggs. She came over to them and they saw the corn swaying and the trees in the side yard and Helene's dress beating around her knees. She stood in front of them and spoke against the wind to bring them inside. The clouds overtook the sun as they crossed the grass and went in. Danvers sat at the table and David got a sheet of paper and a pen from the cupboard and sat beside him and Helene watched while he wrote. When he finished Helene took the letter and folded it into thirds and put it in an envelope. She slid it on the table to him and he sat looking at it. He had felt warm while writing and he hadn't wanted to quit but it was good to hold something his son might see and touch. He held the letter like he might impart something into the paper and setting it back on the table the first drops of rain began to rap at the side of the house.

ACKNOWLEDGMENTS

I would like to thank Leonid Leonov for his constant hand in this book. Leah Angstman and my other editors for their keen eyes. Chris Abani for his guidance, Susan Straight, Andrew Winer, and the rest of the faculty at UC Riverside. Kent Dixon and Rick Incorvati for their continued advice and friendship. The folks at the Pine Crest Bed and Breakfast in Valparaiso, Nebraska, for their hospitality and kindness. Thank you to all the friends and acquaintances along the way that fed, sheltered, and encouraged me before and after I wrote this book. And thank you to my mother and father, my sister, my grandmother, and to my uncle Ron, without whom I wouldn't have had a damn thing to write about.